THE HOUSE BOOK

SUSAN GREENWOOD

To my poor, neglected husband.

PROLOGUE
17th July 1669, West Sussex

anging on the door wakens her from a deep sleep. "Mistress needs you, come quickly." Still groggy and barefoot, she shivers a little in the chill night air, reaches for her shawl and opens the door. "Come," the master says. He takes her arm and leads her to the back stairs; it's the wrong way and she hesitates. There's movement behind her, but before she can see, a hand clamps down firmly over her mouth, forcing her head back as her feet are swept from underneath her. "Get her out quick," she hears him say.

The shawl falls from her shoulders as she bucks and squirms and claws at the forearm tight across her throat. Down the stairs, out through the kitchen door and into the yard they go. She still can't see her attackers. The master grabs a handful of her hair, winds it round his fist and brings his face so close that she can smell the spirit on his breath and feel the spray on her face as he spits out the words, "There'll be no more mischief in this house, mark my words. This is where it ends." He turns to the men holding her, "Put her in," and takes the reins whilst the others haul her into the back of the cart. Landing heavily on damp sacks, she is winded and they gag her before she has the chance to scream. Two men hold her down as the cart makes slow progress across the farmyard and past the cottages, only picking up pace as it enters the lane.

Gradually, her eyes become accustomed to the dark and she can see the men's faces. She does not know them. The one tying her feet together is young, probably no more than eighteen, and is thick set with long, greasy hair. He smiles slyly, showing a row of rotten teeth, as he runs his hands up her legs. "She's pretty, though, in't she, Pa? It'd be a shame if we can't take advantage, like…"

The older man, a fatter, greasier version of the boy, is straddling her, holding her hands above her head. "Just come over here, son, and tie her hands, will you? She's bucking like a bleeding mule". She can feel him getting hard and he starts to grind himself against her. The boy now has her hands. The father pulls up her nightdress and moans as he fondles her breasts then quickly clutches her buttocks and pushes himself against her one more time before rolling off and roughly covering her up again.

He laughs and wipes the saliva from his mouth with the back of his hand. "Aye, it's a shame, alright, lad," and he nods towards the back of the man driving, "but he's a pious bastard, this one, and whatever he's going to do with her, I can tell you now there'll be no fun o' that sort." He hands his boy a flask. "Here, have some o' this."

The abuse she can easily bear. It inflames her anger but comes as no shock – the ways of men are no mystery to her – but the madness she saw in the master's eyes terrifies her. She rolls onto her side away from the two men, draws up her knees and tries to quell the rising panic.

***

Three men rise from their campfire by the river as the cart bowls into view. They nod to the master, who brings the horse to a halt and orders father and son to lift their captive from the cart. The older man is quick to size up the situation and he places her gently on the ground. Their eyes meet – hers silently begging for help as she sees the apprehension in his and notes the change in him. He wasn't told about this and he draws his boy away, shaking his head as the master approaches. "If you don't have the stomach for this, Coulson, you can leave us. You've done your bit and been well paid," and the master turns his back on them.

Her scream comes out as a muffled sob; she loses her balance struggling against her bonds and falls sideways amid jeers from the other three men. Her last little bit of hope disappears as she watches Coulson and his son walking away and she finally gives way to tears.

The master hands round a flask and all four men take a long pull, ignoring the sobbing woman on the ground. Pocketing the empty flask, he walks over to the fire, lights a torch and kneels beside her, holding the torch so close to her head that she can smell her hair burning. "You know why you're here." He ignores her shaking head and continues, "You have performed malicious deeds using witchcraft. We will prove what you are," and he nods to the other three. He takes no part in what follows but opens another flask and watches closely.

One man cuts the nightdress from her, then holds the torch whilst the other two roll her over and over in the dirt, rough hands exploring every part of her body looking for a third teat. A scar on her side is suggested as evidence that one has been removed. "Inconclusive." The master remains impassive. "Only one thing will prove it now," and he tosses them a hank of rope. "Get her ready"

Blind panic grips her as they untie her feet and hands to rearrange them in the proscribed manner for ducking – right hand to left foot and left hand to right foot. Head pounding, heart hammering away, energy floods through her body and she kicks and punches, tears away the gag and bites the nearest hand. The blow to her face is hard and swift and the master's boot on her throat puts paid to any fight left in her.

The ground shifts beneath her, faces blur and voices fade as her world slips into blessed black.

***

She comes round to find herself still on solid ground. A horse is prancing on the spot only yards in front of her; its nostrils are huge, flashing bright red in the half-light and its body steams and quivers from being ridden too hard. There is shouting and a new voice that she recognises but can't put a name to until he covers her with his cloak and wipes the hair from her bruised and battered face. She sees the surprise on his face; he was expecting someone else. Walking quickly back to the master, he knocks the flask out of his hand and shakes him by the arm trying to bring back his senses. "Good God, man – what have you done? Has the drink made you lose your mind?"

The master glares at him, wrenches his arm away and points. "That woman is a witch and we'll deal with her."

"You shall not, sir." He reaches into his saddlebag and approaches the other three men. "I don't know where you're from, but this is my parish and my jurisdiction and I do not hold with such barbarity. Be on your way and quick about it."

There is no arguing with the flintlock. The men pick up their belongings, tip their hats to the master, who hasn't yet shifted his gaze from the newcomer, and move off.

The master does not move. He watches silently as the woman's bonds are cut and she is helped unsteadily to her feet, remaining unmoved by the sight of her injuries in the lightening sky. She approaches him alone, holding the cloak close to her body, and speaks with a voice barely louder than a whisper. "If I were who you say I am, I would curse you now. I would swear that neither you, nor any of your blood, will ever live long enough to find peace in that house." She takes a step closer and leans forward, looking up into his eyes and forcing him to look at her. "That is..." and she wipes the blood dripping from a cut lip, "...if I were who you think I am. Think on that."

~ 1 ~

Oakwood Grange, West Sussex,
May 1985

Tom Kelly was in his bedroom, selecting a clean handkerchief from the linen press, when he heard a car pull up on the gravel sweep outside his front gate. He crossed to the window, recognised the flashy car and its equally flashy driver straight away and pursed his lips. The stupid boy had come without an appointment and he'd brought someone with him. Well, he wasn't going to let them in – bloody cheek – why don't people have any manners these days? He stepped away from the window and waited for the sound of the doorbell so that he could ignore it. It didn't come. He went back for another look but there was no sign of them. Looking through the side window, he found them by the five-barred gate to the drive.

The shorter man was waving his arms around, doubtless spouting the usual estate agent's spiel, while the other man was leaning on the gate, one foot on the bottom rail, nodding, smiling and taking it all in.

Tom eased himself onto the window seat, picked up his bird-watching binoculars and peered through the crack between the wall and the curtain. The agent, Ludovic, was over six feet, Tom knew, but the stranger was a fair bit taller and well built with longish, wavy dark hair brushed back from a prominent widow's peak and his face was, he supposed, handsome enough.

He couldn't tell his age, everyone seemed young to him.

The men continued to chat for several minutes more, patently at ease in each other's company, as Tom watched the taller man closely until his arms grew tired. He put down the binoculars and sat, lost in thought, before shifting his gaze to his wife's photo on his bedside table. Another look through the window and his decision was made. He took the stairs as quickly as his knees would allow and headed for the back door, but by the time he reached the drive, he heard the car pulling away.

***

"Well, what do you think?" Ludo's driving style was as flamboyant as his car and his fashion sense, and his inability to watch the road and talk at the same time was making Rob nervous. His right foot twitched for the brake.

"Relax. I know every twist and turn in these roads." Ludo slapped Rob on his thigh, "Now, come on, what do you think?"

"I think," said Rob, hesitating, "that in a world where all your wishes come true, the house is perfect."

"Okay, well that's a good start…and the 'but' is?"

"The 'buts', Ludo, there are several," and Rob indicated on his fingers. "One, we can't afford it. Two, it's too big. Three, it's probably a money pit, and four, it's not really commutable. Oh, and until today, we weren't even house-hunting."

"Rob, Rob, you're speaking with your sensible head on. You're an artist, for goodness' sake, what does your heart say? Anyway, don't answer that until I've had my say.

First off, you don't know the price, and I'm not going to tell you yet, but I know it's negotiable. Also, I think you'll be pleasantly surprised by how much your London place has gone up in the last four years. Secondly, it's not as big as it looks. Believe me, it's three receptions, four beds and three baths by the time you've knocked it about a bit.

What was point three? Ah, yes, the money pit. You will have to spend money on it because it's dated inside, but I'll be surprised if there's anything major. Tom Kelly's a very proper sort who's always looked after the place. Did you notice the roof? Re-slated only two years ago. Believe me, it's far from a wreck. What was point four?"

"The impossible commute."

"Yes, okay, I concede that's not great; 20 minutes to a mainline station and then 40-50 minutes on the train. But, were we not discussing life styles over lunch in the pub?"

"We were," Rob smiled.

"And did you not say how you and your wife were tired of London and wanted to move out; fresh air, kids, animals, garden, the whole bit?"

"I did, but not this far out. Incidentally, we don't have any children. We're still hopeful though."

"Oh, sorry. I mean...I just assumed…" Ludo slapped himself on the forehead. "Foot in mouth. I do it all the time."

"No, really, forget it. We have a niece and nephew and umpteen godchildren between us, so we're not short of kids' company."

"Good. So, I've just thought of something else." Ludo pulled up outside his office, wrenched on the handbrake and turned to face Rob. "You couldn't see it from the gate, but there's an old dairy and milking shed that Tom uses just for storage, I think, but it'd make a great studio. Three or four roof lights *et voila*! No more lobbing out for expensive London premises. Why do you have to work in London, anyway? Believe me, it could work."

Rob laughed. "You've said 'believe me' at least four times, Ludo. Is 'believe me, I'm an estate agent' any better than 'believe me, I'm a lawyer?'"

Ludo straightened his tie and tried to look affronted. "Bloody cheek, I'll have you know I'm known for my fair play and integrity. Ask anyone. Look, I know I'm being pushy but it's not because I need the sale. Heaven knows, I've got more business than I can handle at the moment, and, believe me (he grinned ruefully) that place is a good buy and could be stunning. I've known the house all my life and, unless I was sure it was worth it, I wouldn't be showing it to a mate of Guy's who's doing me a favour."

"I agree, it's a beautiful property and I even believe you when you say it's not a money pit, but it's been on the market for how long?"

"Ages, but there's a good reason for that and I can't go into it now. I've just realised I'm late for my next appointment; they're probably in there, waiting," and he nodded towards his office.

Climbing out of Ludo's car, they shook hands and Rob promised to be down again in about a week or so when he had some preliminary stuff to show him.

Back in his own car, Rob sat for a while and drummed his fingers on the steering wheel. Then he pulled away from the kerb and found himself driving back to Oakwood Grange for another look.

The very idea that he might now be in a position to buy a house in the country made him smile. Five years ago things had been very different. It had taken his first big row with Janie to turn things around….

***

"Why won't you do it?" No sooner had he put the phone down than she was on the attack, hands on hips, brown eyes wide and eyebrows raised, always a bad sign.

"It's wall dressing." If she'd only arrived five minutes later, Rob thought, there would have been no need for all this.

"Does it matter?"

"Yes, it matters."

"Why?"

"Because I didn't spend four years studying graphic design at Art College to produce rubbish for a twenty year old rock star to stick over his fireplace in his stockbroker belt, mock Tudor mansion. That's why."

"Well, pardon me, Pablo." Janie rarely smoked, but she

snatched up one of his cigarettes, lit it and puffed furiously. "Anyway," waving her cigarette at him, "apart from the fact that your canvasses are far from rubbish, you're not exactly overrun with design jobs at the moment." Ignoring his glare, she carried on. "This is paid work, Rob, and if this 'rubbish' is appreciated by someone, it's 'art', isn't it?"

"You can stop right there, Janie, because we are not going to have an argument about 'What is Art.' I'm going to make myself a sandwich, do you want anything?" Janie shook her head and he got up and went to the corner of his flat that served as the kitchen.

As a tactic to silence her, it didn't work. Janie followed him and watched as he placed great slabs of cheese between two thick slices of bread. "I don't think Guy and Tash think that their canvas is rubbish. In fact, didn't you say Tash remodelled the flat around…?" She didn't get any further.

Rob slammed the knife down on the counter, making her jump, and turned to face her, muscles in his jaw tightening. "That was different. It was what Guy wanted, and it was a small price to pay for four years rent-free accommodation. You know that."

"But you also did one for the gallery guy."

"Again, it was a favour. He's a mate of Tash's and I felt I couldn't refuse."

Janie stubbed out her cigarette. "Well, he obviously didn't have the same scruples, paying you peanuts and flogging it for over a thousand."

"Oh right, I see," said Rob, picking up his sandwich and moving back to the sofa, "not only am I too proud to churn out populist rubbish and shit at securing graphic design jobs, but I've also got a lot to learn about business. Well, thanks, Janie, that's cheered me up no end."

Janie ran a hand through her hair. "I'm sorry. I didn't mean it to sound like that. I just…"

But he wasn't listening. "And another thing – career advice from someone who's never even had a job interview in her life and is about to be handed a ready made business, is a bit hard to swallow."

Janie stood there, staring at him and blinking rapidly. "Oh, that's low, Rob – really..." and she tailed off.

"Look." Rob, immediately contrite, patted the sofa next to him. "Come here and let me explain." Janie sat down reluctantly, arms folded. "I have a good life with no real money worries. I love working with Guy, his landscaping business is really taking off, he pays me well and makes sure we always have time off to play rugby." He tried, but failed, to charm her with a dimple-flashing grin before ploughing on. "I know the current design jobs are tiddle-arsed and poorly paid, but I'm not desperate enough to take on stuff like this that I really don't want to do."

They sat in silence for a while, not looking at each other, until Rob brushed a fall of thick fair hair from her face and tilted her chin towards him. "Does it bother you that I'm now more of a labourer than an artist? Is that what all this is about? Or are you worried about what your father thinks?"

Janie pulled her head away from him. "You are such an arse sometimes." She was so cross she had to stand up to put some distance between them. "It's got nothing to do with my father. What it's about, is you; on the one hand, being satisfied with your single bloke's life, and on the other, saying you want us to live together. It's about you being thirty-two and asking yourself where you see yourself in a few years' time; still working for Guy or doing something you trained for. It's about you and me and building something for our future, if we have one."

She turned away from him. Stupidly, she could feel her eyes beginning to well up and she didn't want to play that card.

"Janie, darling." He reached for her hand and pulled her back to the sofa where he rocked her gently and she buried her face in his jumper. He couldn't remember the last time she'd cried. The seconds ticked away. Rob made a decision. "Right, do you know what? I'll take that bloody job if it makes you feel better, but only if he accepts the ludicrously ridiculous price I'm going to quote him." He stroked her hair again and kissed her forehead. "See? I'll make a businessman yet."

Janie hooked her legs over his and, still not looking at him, squeezed him tight.

"I do love you, Janie." There was a muffled response from his jumper. "But this is all new to me. I've never felt this way about anyone before. I'll get there, I promise."

"I know," she wrapped her arms round his neck and kissed him.

The forgotten sandwich was eventually shared, sealing the deal.

"And just so you know," Janie, wiping the crumbs from her jumper, "I did have a job interview once, for a Saturday job at Topshop when I was sixteen."

***

The twenty year old rock star turned out to be one Johnny Williams, a twenty-six year old biochemist from Wales, who had abandoned his PhD at Imperial College when his band's first single raced up the charts. His Cheyne Walk flat was a far cry from stockbroker mock Tudor, and the finished six by three foot abstract sat beautifully over the new Conran sofa. He paid up happily.

Nice though it was to have money in the bank, the real pay-off came two months later when the band's agent rang to say that Johnny wanted Rob to design Taliesin's second album cover and sleeve notes. Rob was on his way, and so pleased that he even forgave Janie for being smug.

~ 2 ~

Wandsworth, London, May 1985

"**H**ello, handsome." Janie reached up to pull him down to her level and kissed him.

Rob hung up his jacket and followed her down the hall to the kitchen. "Whatever it is smells wonderful." Then, noticing the flowers and candles, "Bugger, I've forgotten something, haven't I?"

"No… but we are celebrating." Janie turned to face him and held her arms wide. "You are now looking at the sole owner of Mallory's Literary Agency, or I will be when Papka retires at the end of the month."

"Hey," Rob picked her up and swung her around. "Congratulations. Although, as he's never there now and doesn't know what's going on, I don't suppose much will change."

"True, but the proud Russian in him probably felt it difficult to let go completely."

In fact, at that very moment, Antony Mallory was setting off for a Mediterranean cruise without a care in the world. Eugenie, always Eugenie to him, never Janie, knew far more about the young literary scene than he, she'd become a keen negotiator and had a talent for signing good clients. Proud he may be, but not stupid. His time was over, and he wasn't even sad about it.

"It's funny, I never think of your Dad as Russian. He's so very, very English. I can't imagine him as Anton Malchikov."

"He changed it for business reasons of course, 'Malchikov's

Literary Agency' might not have gone down so well in the '40's. His mother was furious, though."

Rob chuckled.

"What?"

"I was just thinking. Eugenie Malchikova sounds, you know…" he cocked an eyebrow and pursed his lips.

"What, sexier than Janie Mallory? Well, I'm stuck with plain old Janie Whittaker now, although, for a treat on your birthday, I could do the accent if you're good…" She chucked him under the chin, thrust the wine bottle into his chest and went to get the glasses.

Rob poured and made the toast. "To my little business genius, and the continuing success of Mallory's. It's good to know that, if my business falls flat, I can always rely on you to keep me in the manner to which I've become accustomed."

"That's funny. Now you're so busy, I was thinking the same thing."

He quickly showered and changed, and was back in the kitchen, peering over her shoulder as Janie put the finishing touches to their first course, mushrooms in garlic and parsley. "A starter, as well. Did you come home early?"

"Oh – hilarious…" She made a face. "I can't be brilliant at everything. Get me those plates, will you, it's ready now."

They were well into the chicken casserole, and second bottle of wine when Janie said, "So, tell me about your away day down in deepest Sussex. Was it that mate of Guy's you were going to see?"

"Yeah, he's an estate agent in Petworth. God, it's lovely down there. He took me to lunch at a fabulous little pub. It turns out it's not far from where your grandparents used to live."

"No, really? I wonder if it's changed much…"

"I doubt it. Time seems to have stood still down there." Rob got up to clear away the dinner plates. "Anyway, this chap, Ludo…"

"Ludo?" Janie scoffed, "As in 'I play'?"

"No, smart-arse. It's short for Ludovic," and Rob smiled to himself, wondering how best to describe him. "Ludo is your typical 'hunting, shooting and fishing' type of ex-public schoolboy." Janie looked heavenwards. "He's inherited the agency from his father, much like you, and has great plans, just like you, and he has no intention of remaining a provincial outfit. He's going to set up a swanky country house office to rival the big London boys and he needs a whole new image. That's where I come in: new name, new logo, new signage, new brochures and adverts, the lot. And he wants it done quickly. We tossed around a few ideas and I said I'll get the roughs over to him in the next week or two."

"Great, but you haven't got time to do that now, have you? I thought you were under pressure to get the mock-ups for the museum posters done this week?"

"Yeah, well, I think I'm going to hand it over to Gilly after I've fully briefed her. It's time she showed me what she can really do, it'll be a great opportunity for her."

Janie dropped a fancy box of chocolates on the table in front of Rob. "Dessert. I couldn't stretch to three courses. You open them and I'll put the coffee on."

Rob picked up the box, turned it over a few times and put it down again, unopened. "I hadn't appreciated, you know, just how beautiful it is down there, until today."

"Oh, I know, I love it."

He followed her to the counter, wrapped his arms around her and whispered in her ear. "How would you like to live there, then?'

Janie looked at him over her shoulder and laughed. "Yeah, right. How would we manage that then?"

"I have a plan," and he told her.

"You're mad."

"I prefer 'brave and far-sighted'. Promise me you'll come with me next time I go to see Ludo." He waited, more anxious than he imagined he would be.

Janie checked to see how serious he was. In the six years since they met, Rob had demanded so little of her, always allowing her to be the driving force in their relationship, that Janie knew the importance of her response. "Okay."

~ 3 ~
June 1985

Despite her prejudices, Janie couldn't help liking Ludo. He seemed disarmingly honest, which may, or may not, she thought, serve him well in his chosen profession. As they were half an hour early for their appointment at the Grange, they were in the pub and Ludo was giving them some background information.

"Tom's a retired GP, he's been on his own since his wife died a few years ago and I'm afraid he's become more and more crotchety and difficult to deal with as time goes by. He and his wife and my parents were great friends once but he's rather cut himself off now. It's a shame."

"Does he live in that house all by himself, then?" Janie asked.

"He does, and it's far too much for him, although he has someone to come in and clean once a week, I think."

Janie shook her head. "From what you've said, Ludo, I'm not at all sure he really wants to sell. It's been on the market for ages and he's even had offers near the asking price in the past, so…."

"No, he does, believe me," a quick glance at Rob, "but he's funny about people." Ludo scratched his head, wondering how to explain. "He won't just sell it to anyone. It has to be someone he likes, and you'll soon know if he likes you."

Rob and Janie exchanged a little sceptical smile. Ludo continued, "Anyway, he seemed in a remarkably jolly mood when I arranged this appointment so, fingers crossed, he still is."

They spent some time looking at the floorplan and, as Ludo had promised, the house was nowhere near as big as Rob had feared. Janie could feel Rob's excitement. In his head, he was already redesigning the first floor and making plans for the outbuildings, even before he'd seen inside.

Janie wasn't excited; she was confused and conflicted. She was half hoping that they'd both hate the house, avoiding the need for difficult decisions and compromises. But, on the other hand, she was totally unprepared for the huge emotional pull she'd felt driving down through the familiar villages; a trip she'd avoided for the last twenty years.

The worst outcome would be if Rob loved the house – and she didn't.

***

Tom Kelly couldn't rest and he checked his watch, again. He'd opened the gate earlier so that Ludovic could park his ridiculous car in the drive instead of on the road and he'd been round the house airing rooms, turning on table lamps and plumping up cushions. He'd looked in the kitchen to make sure Mrs. Lawson had laid out the tea things and now there was nothing else to do but wait. He tapped his stick absent-mindedly on the floor. Three minutes to go; he hated unpunctuality and willed them not to be late. Ah, no, there it was; the unmistakable thrum of Ludovic's car and he peeped through the side window. They were here. Tom made his way to the hall and waited for the bell. It rang and, after a slow count of five seconds, he opened the door.

Introductions made, Ludo started the tour on the ground floor and, by the time they reached the kitchen, Tom was in there, waiting for the kettle to boil. "Carry on, Ludovic, don't mind me. I'm making some tea, so come back here, why don't you, when you've seen the top floors and we'll have a chat before you do the grounds, eh?"

Ludo seemed a little taken aback. "That's very kind, Dr. Kelly. Thank you, we'll see you shortly then," and he ushered

Janie and Rob back to the hall, his eyes wide with surprise and making a covert thumbs-up sign close to his chest.

Apart from some modernising, there wasn't much to do on the ground floor, but it was true that the first floor needed work. The two front bedrooms were really lovely with tall ceilings and large Georgian windows flooding the rooms with light, but the rest of the floor was a rabbit warren of smaller rooms, most clearly unused for decades and some still displaying evidence of children long since grown up. One huge bathroom with an equally large, cast iron bath served the front of the house, and there was one tiny bathroom at the far end of the landing but, as the agent pointed out, at least there was plumbing at both ends of the house. Other than that, it appeared that Ludo was superfluous, as Rob was enthusing and exclaiming over features in every room they entered. Janie caught him throwing nervous, sideways glances her way. She was very quiet.

Returning to the first floor after checking out the two storage rooms in the attic, they took the back stairs, which led down to the kitchen. Tom was sitting at the head of the scrubbed pine table with the tea tray in front of him. "Just in time, it's brewed nicely, now. Do sit down, all of you," and when everyone was served, "What do you think of the old place, then? Honestly, now."

Rob hesitated and looked at Janie, sitting next to him, but she made no move to speak first. "It's a beautiful house, Dr. Kelly, and I can't think of anyone who wouldn't want to live here, but, because we're leaving London, there are other issues to be taken into account. Janie's work, for instance," and he reached for Janie's hand and gave it a squeeze.

Tom peered over the top of his glasses and smiled. "What is it you do, Mrs. Whittaker?"

Janie returned the smile and cleared her throat. "I, er, I run a literary agency. It's a family firm, based in London.

"Ah, yes. I see that might be a problem, but not insurmountable, perhaps, if you have good staff and good communications. It's all about trying to find a balance between what brings in the money and what makes you happy, isn't it? I can only tell you that this house has been in the hands of one family for a very long time and that my wife and I have been very happy here, and the countryside is spectacular, of course."

Janie spoke, unprompted for the first time. "Yes, it's good to be back. My grandparents used to live not far from here and I visited often as a child."

Tom's eyes lit up and he leaned forward on the table. "Really, my dear? Well, there's nothing I need tell you about the area, then. What was your grandparents' surname?"

"Richardson."

"Richardson, Richardson…no, it doesn't ring a bell. Not one of my patients, anyway."

Ludo had been silently watching this exchange with interest. He could only assume that the old boy had changed his medication. He pushed back his chair and stood up. "Well, thank you for the tea, Dr. Kelly, I think we'll take a walk outside now to see the outbuildings and grounds, if that's all right with you?"

"Yes, yes, dear boy, go ahead. I'll just clear up here and then I think I'll join you. You'll find the keys in the usual place."

Walking down the back lobby and collecting the keys from a large hook on the way, they exited through the garden door. After a quick tour of the grounds around the house, mainly laid to lawn, shrubs and specimen trees, they headed off across the drive and through a gate into a walled garden. "All as expected so far, I imagine, but what do you think of this?" and Ludo flung open the gate and watched the Whittakers' faces light up. It was both rose garden and kitchen garden, as immaculate as it was beautiful. The roses were in full bloom and the scent was overwhelming.

There were footsteps behind them. "I don't do it myself, of course," Tom pointed to the roses, "other than a bit of gentle deadheading now and then. I have a chap who comes in from the village, another old boy, although not as decrepit as me. He looks after it for me and takes the produce I don't need, or gives it to the village shop. I think they do quite well out of me these days, I don't need very much. Anyway, he loves doing it so he doesn't charge very much. It works well."

"Rob fancies himself as a gardener, Dr. Kelly, but I don't think he's ever had to deal with anything on this scale.

Rob jumped in quickly. "Well, I'm not really a gardener, but I did pick up some knowledge when I helped out a mate in London a few years ago; he has a landscape gardening company. Nowadays, I spend my time in a studio doing graphic design, but I could happily spend my free time in here – no problem."

Eventually, Ludo managed to drag them away to inspect the outbuildings, and Tom followed them to the dairy. "You'll be wanting somewhere to work at home then, I suppose, and this would make a suitable studio, don't you agree, Ludovic?"

"I do, yes, Dr. Kelly. Rob and I have already discussed the…"

"Did you study in London, Mr. Whittaker?"

"Yes, Chelsea School of Art."

"Oh, very good, yes, it has an excellent reputation. You're a Londoner then, are you?"

"No. Janie is, but I lived in Brighton until I went to college."

Tom nodded, leaned heavily on his stick, and then quickly changed tack. "I think I'll leave you to it now, my knees are playing up a bit. It's been a pleasure to meet you both and I hope we shall meet again." They all shook hands and Tom added, "Ring me later, Ludovic, would you?" as he limped back to the house.

***

Back in the pub, over pints and ploughmans, "So, Ludo…a difficult, crotchety, old man…"

"What can I say? You two obviously charmed the pants off him, he's not normally like that. In fact, he's never like that."

Rob laughed. "Perhaps you're underestimating the value of

your pre-visit instructions. We were very careful to avoid any mention of alterations, swimming pools or tennis courts."

"And," Janie added, "any discussion about price. We know what you were asking last year and, quite frankly, we couldn't do that."

Rob looked at Janie, Janie looked at Ludo, and Ludo was looking at them both. "Well, first, I need to know if this place works for you. So, why don't you ring me later, when you've had time to talk things over, and let me know if you're interested? Then, I'll call the old boy to discuss his price and get back to you."

"We're interested."

"Janie, we need to discuss this, don't we?" Rob tugged her sleeve to make her look at him. "Don't we?" he repeated.

"Do we? You want it, don't you?"

"Yes, but…"

"No buts, Rob. We're interested, Ludo. Let's crack on, see if we can afford it and we'll take it from there. Okay?"

***

"Are you sure about this? You were so quiet when we were looking around the house, I was sure you weren't keen." Rob was driving cautiously, he wasn't familiar with the narrow lanes and he was concentrating on choosing his words carefully. "Tell me, honestly, you're not going along with this just for me, are you?"

It was a fair question. Janie had bought the Wandsworth house with her own money five years ago, when the original plan had been to find somewhere to rent together. At the time, Rob was struggling. Graphic design jobs were non-existent, the commission for Johnny Williams was taking up all his evenings and he was labouring for Guy during the day just to make ends meet. "So, I'd be what? Your tenant, lodger…?" Janie had played it carefully. "I'm not pushing for a proposal, Rob. I was thinking more …live-in lover," and when that had failed to raise a smile, "There's no need to look so bloody miserable. You won't have to have sex all the time. You can have Sunday off to play rugby." He'd come round. Things were different now, though.

"I'm not, honestly. I love the house, I really do." She tried to make her voice light.

Rob frowned and pulled on to the side of the road. "You're not convincing me. You look as though you're about to burst into tears. This has to be a decision we're both happy with."

"I know, and I am. I'm fine about leaving London and about work, I'm sure I can work that out. I'm just scared we might not get it."

Rob pulled her as close as was possible with the gear lever in the way. "Oh, come here. Look, if we don't get this house, there'll be another one somewhere for us. We've only just made the decision to start searching and it's early days, so let's wait and see what Ludo comes back with, shall we?"

He put the car into gear and drove off, not entirely reassured.

Janie was no longer confused. She couldn't explain it properly to Rob, he didn't have a fanciful bone in his body, but the feeling she had, as she walked along the upstairs corridor, was so strong, she felt a lump in her throat. It was the same feeling that had made visits to her grandparents so special, a sense of belonging and being completely as one with her surroundings.

It felt like coming home.

***

Ludo came back to them with a reduced price that he'd had no difficulty negotiating. Dr. Kelly had reached the point where, according to Ludo, he was 'motivated to sell'.

With the price agreed and pending a second visit, Janie and Rob put their house on the market and found, to their astonishment, that bidding was fierce and offers well over the asking price came flooding in. Buying Oakwood Grange wasn't going to be the stretch they'd first thought.

Their second viewing saw Dr. Kelly in much the same friendly mood as the first visit. Ludo gave it a miss this time; he felt his job was done and he had plenty of decisions of his own to make now that he had Rob's roughs to look over.

Over tea and Mrs. Lawson's walnut cake, it was clear just how pleased Tom was that they were to be the next owners of the Grange. He gave them a potted history of the house, explained all its quirks and showed them a list of tradesmen who'd proved reliable in the past. Janie gently probed to find out where he'd be going when he left the Grange, but he just patted her hand and said, "Don't worry about me, my dear, I'm going somewhere where I shall be well looked after."

They had become so comfortable with each other that they were now on first name terms; at least, Tom was on first name terms with them, but Rob and Janie decided on the halfway house of 'Doctor'.

"So, Rob, tell me. I know Brighton quite well, you were born there, did you say?" Then the conversation moved on to Rob's family and various places along the south coast that they both knew.

He even managed to get Janie to talk about her time at Oxford and her lengthy PhD, not something she usually brought up in conversation. Tom raised his eyebrows at Rob. "Brains and beauty, Rob, you are a lucky man, just think of the advantages your children will have."

Janie stepped in quickly. "Well, one day, perhaps. Meanwhile, we are not without children's company and they will all love this place, that's for sure." Tom caught the look that passed between them. "Actually, do you mind if I pop upstairs for a minute?" she asked, "I just want to measure one or two of the bedrooms."

They watched her go and Tom turned to Rob, "She's a lovely girl," and Rob, surprising himself, replied, "She is, and she'd make a lovely mother, but it hasn't happened yet."

"You're both still young, aren't you? Plenty of time."

"We're not that young. Janie's thirty three and I'm thirty seven."

Tom looked shocked. "Thirty seven – are you now? You look younger."

***

Janie's tape measure didn't leave her handbag. There was a little bubble of joy in her stomach as her fingers trailed across the woodwork, the silky banisters and the oak doors. All felt solid and dependable. She'd noted earlier that someone had opened all the windows to air the little used rooms and the smell of lavender was wafting in from somewhere as she walked along to the back stairs. Funny, that, she hadn't noticed it before.

~ 4 ~

Wandsworth, London, June 1985

It was late, all passion spent, and Janie was tucked neatly under Rob's arm. He kissed her forehead and whispered, "Are you sleepy?"

"Not really, what did you have in mind?"

"Ah, you flatter me. No, I just got to thinking about your mum's side of the family. Being so near to where they used to live today, it made me wonder why you've never really talked much about them. What's the big secret?"

"There's no secret, it's just a bit odd. We lost touch with them when I was a child and somehow I felt responsible, I don't know why." Janie wriggled out from under his arm and turned to face him, head propped on her hand. "I'll tell you about them now, if you like."

Rob nodded. "Go on then."

"Promise you won't fall asleep halfway through?"

"Promise. Just don't stray off the subject."

"Right. You remember I told you that, after the war, Dad's agency was known for having some good poets on his books? Well, would-be poets drifted into his office all the time and one was my Uncle Mark. He was a teacher at the time. Dad said he looked ridiculously young and nervous. Miss Hunter had already given him a hard time, so Dad took pity on him and promised to read his work…

"Excuse me, Miss Hunter?"

"Yes, my Miss Hunter, she started working for Dad when she was fifteen. Anyhow, Dad did get Mark's poetry published and, one day when he visited the office, he brought Fiona, my mother, with him. She was twenty-five, also a teacher, and she and my dad fell hopelessly in love. They were married within the year but, as you would expect from what you know about my Grandmother Malchikov, no one from that side of the family attended the wedding."

"That must have been upsetting for your father."

"He was upset for my mother. Adjusting to her new life was going to be difficult enough without all that, but he soon found out that she could look after herself. Even snotty Mayfair neighbours discovered it was a waste of time trying to put her in her place; she was so popular with tradesmen that they realised it was far better to make friends with her. Dad thought it was all hilarious, he was so proud of her."

"Did Antony's parents ever come round?"

Janie gave a little snort. "Apparently, they did visit when Mum was pregnant with me – funny, that eh? But Dad's mother never apologised for her behaviour and he never forgave her. His father, though, wrote a lovely letter to Mum afterwards and I think they would have become friends." She paused here and Rob knew what was coming next. "And then she died having me."

"Is that when your dad took on Winnie?"

"No. Mum engaged Winnie, as a cleaner, when she was first pregnant. Dad didn't know whether he was coming or going when Mum died and he was left with a newborn baby. He hired a housekeeper and a nanny until he found his feet but he got rid of them as soon as he could and let Winnie take over. It was a very good move."

"What were the Richardson grandparents doing while all this was going on?"

"Oh, they visited regularly in the early years and we'd go down to their cottage in Sussex, too. I used to love the drive..."

"I bet your dad had a Roller..."

"No, he didn't. He had an open top Hispano Suiza. It was

has pride and joy but it only went out on rare occasions, he didn't need a car in town. Anyway, stop interrupting, you're the one making me stray off the point. Do you want to hear about the Richardsons, or not?"

"Yes…"

"Right, when I was a bit older, I used to take the train by myself to visit them in the summer holidays. It was brilliant. When I wasn't with Grandpa learning about the countryside, I'd be in the garden with Grandma; collecting eggs, fruit picking or digging the garden. They had dogs, too, and they were allowed on the sofa when we read together in the evening. Grandma was a teacher as well as Mark and my mum, so there was no shortage of books."

"Runs in the family, then." Rob pulled her close and she lay down next to him again. "It all sounds idyllic, so what happened?"

"I think I was twelve the last time I saw them. I remember Uncle Mark was home and I was thrilled because I didn't get to see him very often. He taught me to fish that holiday. I was meant to visit them again, just before Christmas, but Grandma called it off saying that Grandpa was ill. He died not long after but, for some reason, Grandma didn't tell us until after the funeral. That's weird, isn't it? And then, even weirder, when our letters were returned to us – they weren't on the phone – we discovered that Grandma had moved without telling us. Dad tried to find her, but with no success. Mark, too, had left his teaching job and vanished."

"What, and you never heard from them again?

"Nope. I've often wondered if we should have tried harder but, like Dad said, if they didn't want us to find them, perhaps we should leave it alone. It upset me, though. It still does.

"It's very odd, but you couldn't have been responsible, surely?"

"I can't explain it. I just remember feeling uncomfortable at the end of that holiday. Something had changed."

Rob kissed her and pulled her on top of him. "Well, I can't imagine it had anything to do with you, you were only a little girl."

"True. Not now though…and I'm not tired now, either."

~ 5 ~
Langridge Solicitors' Office,
August 1985

Having read the letter again, Gilbert Langridge was deep in thought, absent-mindedly tapping the end of his pen on the desk as he deliberated about how he should handle this meeting.

His phone buzzed. "Mr. and Mrs. Whittaker are here."

"Good, send them straight in, please, Mrs. Watkins," and he went to greet them at his office door. "Ah, yes, do come in and er…please take a seat over there." Grim smiles were exchanged all round. "I think we'll have some tea, Mrs. Watkins," and he turned to his visitors, "Is that all right – tea? Would you prefer coffee? No? Just tea for three, then, please. Thank you."

Rob and Janie sat facing a huge desk piled high with files to either side, creating something of a tunnel effect to the opposite chair. Langridge sat down, then immediately jumped up and removed half of each pile to the floor. "That's better. Now then, this business is rather unfortunate for you and I'm sure you have many questions, legal and otherwise, so, today, I hope to provide you with the answers and allay any doubts you may be having."

"Well, that's good," said Rob, glancing at Janie, "because we're more than a little concerned about the ramifications of all this."

"I understand. I presume you only know the bare facts of what transpired the other day?" The solicitor steepled his hands and looked at them over his half moon glasses.

"All we know," Rob replied, "is that you found Dr. Kelly dead when you visited the house. It's all very upsetting. Was it a heart attack or was he ill?"

Langridge abandoned his Dickensian pose, straightened his waistcoat and leaned back in his chair with a sigh. "I'm sorry to say that it was neither. He committed suicide. It's not official yet, of course, there'll be a PM, but I thought you should know as soon as possible."

Janie's hands flew to her mouth and Rob muttered, "Oh my God, it was the thought of leaving the house, wasn't it? Did he leave a note?"

"He did leave a note. In fact, he left two; one was beside him where he died and the other was for me, pinned to the front door. Mine read, 'Open immediately' on the envelope, and it told me what I was about to discover. I found him in the walled garden, slumped on the bench with a syringe at his feet. The post mortem will reveal exactly what he used but, being a doctor, he had access to anything he wanted and he knew how to do it properly." Langridge took off his glasses and rubbed his eyes before continuing. "He was a meticulous man, you know, Thomas Kelly, and he made damn sure I was the one who found his body and no one else. He'd arranged my visit a week or so ago and even phoned my secretary the day before to make sure I hadn't forgotten - as if I would." He replaced his glasses.

Janie managed to find her voice. "What did the note say? Can you tell us?"

"Ah, well…the note by the body read, 'So sorry, but I couldn't leave Harry.'"

"Harry?"

"His wife, Harriet, but known to friends as Harry. She died about five years ago, of cancer, and he was a lost and lonely man without her; theirs was a truly happy marriage. Her ashes are scattered in the walled garden."

Janie felt the tears welling. Rob inched his chair a little closer to put a consoling hand on her knee, and she whipped a couple of tissues from the box that Langridge had nudged towards her. "I'm so sorry, but this has really upset me."

"It's bound to, my dear, but you shouldn't be sad. I've known Tom Kelly for many years and he and Harry had a wonderful life together. Her death was a great shock – ovarian cancer, notoriously difficult to diagnose, I'm told – but, being a doctor, Tom felt that, somehow, he should have spotted it and that he'd failed her. He was quite a bit older than she was and they often used to joke that it was a good thing as, chances were, he would go first and she would cope much better on her own than he would. Well, it didn't work out that way. You know the old saying, 'God laughs at our plans.'"

There was a knock at the door and Mrs. Watkins brought in the tea, accompanied by a slight shushing sound of nylon against nylon as she crossed the floor, and Rob had the full benefit of a large expanse of corseted hips straining against her tweed skirt as she bent over to place the tray on Langridge's desk.

"Thank you, Mrs. Watkins, and you can leave us to it now. You go off home and I'll lock up."

"Are you sure, sir?"

"Absolutely. Off you go. Have a good weekend."

Langridge immediately set about pouring the tea, although it was performed more as a ceremony. There was a proper teapot and silver spoons and strainer, no tea bags here, obviously, with delicate china cups and lump sugar with tongs. Relics of a bygone age, Janie thought, when things were done properly, and she felt herself warming to this dapper, little man who, old fashioned he may be, but who, she felt, was totally trustworthy and reliable. Certainly, Tom Kelly had thought so.

"Anyway," he said, as he handed them their cups, "I'm sorry to be so long winded about all of this, but I think it important that you know all the facts before you make any decisions. After Harry died, I think Tom would have done away with himself there and then if it hadn't been for a promise made to her just before she died. I don't know what you know about the Grange, but it was Harry's family home, not Tom's, her family had lived there for generations and she was heart broken that she was the end of the line, as it were. She and Tom had no children, as you probably know. There were, of course, distant cousins several times removed, but Harry always felt that someone coming into such a bequest, with no knowledge or love for the place, would sell it immediately for the best possible price to someone who would knock it about and 'improve' it." He lifted the teapot and offered to pour another cup for them all before carrying on. "So, Tom saw it as his duty to find suitable owners who, he knew, would have been acceptable to Harry."

Janie reached for Rob's hand. "And that would be us?"

"It would appear so," and Langridge nodded and smiled at them, "and you have no idea just what a rigorous selection process you have been through. Tom spent the first two years, after his wife's death, meeting with estate agents, marketing the property in local, and even, national journals, and putting up with people crawling all over his house. He hated it, and found something to dislike in all of them: the man was arrogant, the wife too 'townie', the children too undisciplined, they had a flashy car or…" and he laughed, "I could go on. He used to sit in that chair," and he pointed to Janie, "and tell me all about it. Tom was a most amusing companion in those days, when he believed that the 'right people' were just around the corner."

"And what makes us the 'right people', if we are, that is?" said Janie. "Or did he just give up in the end and take whatever he could get?"

"Oh, my dear, don't think that. No, no – you and Mr. Whittaker are absolutely the 'right people', and I don't want you to think that this was a 'class' thing and that he was looking for some sort of pedigree…"

"Well, obviously not in my case," Rob chipped in.

"…because he was, most definitely, not. His reasons for rejecting people were all excuses, just smoke and mirrors. It was all to do with his gut feeling. Needless to say, his actions made him exceedingly unpopular with the estate agents who could never imagine that they would ever get a sale and, eventually, they all took him off their books."

"Except for Ludo," Rob said.

"Ah, yes, Ludovic. His father and I are great mates from schooldays and, I'm afraid, I rather pulled in a favour and, although his father is no longer in the business, he did ask his son to visit Tom and to look out for anyone who he thought might be suitable. Poor Ludo. I'm afraid, by this time, Tom had become rather irascible and impatient."

Rob laughed. "Yes, he told me the story about the silver ashtray."

"What's this?" Janie turned to her husband, "You didn't tell me."

"Ludo took this couple round the house and, apparently, Dr. Kelly accused the chap of stealing a silver ashtray and ordered him out of the house immediately."

"Really?" Janie couldn't believe it, "he was so charming and polite to us."

Langridge took up the story. "Well, he knew, of course, that the chap hadn't stolen the ashtray, but he'd listened to them talking about how they were going to extend here, knock down there, change the drive, install a swimming pool in the walled garden and he was furious. He couldn't stand it any longer and he thought his little ruse would get rid of them quickly and for good. It worked, but poor Ludo was seriously embarrassed and made up some story about Tom being gaga."

Janie said, "The old devil, I knew I liked him. I'm so sorry we didn't get to know him better; I'm sure he had some stories to tell."

"Yes, that's a shame. However, getting back to the point of all this, and this is the important bit, he was a very happy man since you exchanged contracts. He had no doubt that he'd found the right owners for his beloved house, and he did love it as much as his wife did, he had fulfilled his promise to Harry and he could now join her, which was all he'd really wanted to do for the last five years. So, you see, this is a happy ending and not the sad story it first appears."

Janie smiled at the solicitor, who had visibly relaxed during the telling of his friend's last few years. "Thank you for explaining all that. It does make me feel a little better. What we were worried about, was that he thought this was the only way out; too old to cope with the house but without anywhere suitable to go. With no children, I guess it would have been an old peoples' home and I couldn't see him there. Rob and I had touched on the subject of where he was going to go but he said that it was all taken care of."

"And now you know it was. He had no intention of leaving the place."

Rob shifted a little in his seat. "Mr. Langridge, I don't want to seem insensitive, but where does this leave us vis-a-vis the house purchase?"

"You need not worry; as I said, he was a meticulous man. Before exchange of contracts, he came to see me and said that he feared he was ill and he was concerned that, should he die before completion of the contract, you would be required to wait for probate before the Deed of Transfer could be signed. This, of course, can be long and drawn out and he wished to avoid the possibility of causing you this inconvenience. He asked my advice and I mentioned that we could exchange and complete on the same day, if everyone was willing, but he said he wouldn't ask you to do that. I also suggested that the chances of him dying were very slim (he didn't appear very ill to me and, no doubt, the PM will confirm this) and, therefore, a POA would suffice if he were too ill to sign. But, no, what he wanted was to transfer the legal interest in the property to a trust; Ludo's father and I are the trustees. The trustees can then sign the Deed of Transfer on completion and the sale proceeds as normal. So, in a nutshell, from your point of view, nothing changes."

"I'm amazed," said Rob, "truly amazed that, in his final days, he was at such pains to avoid any hardship to us."

"And that's why he wouldn't entertain the idea of exchange

and completion on the same day, isn't it? Either it wouldn't have given him time to execute his plan or we would have had a nasty surprise waiting for us when we picked up the keys."

"I'm sure you're right. This way it gives you time to hear the full story and come to terms with what has happened. If, however, you feel that you could no longer live there, then Tom left instructions that the contract be cancelled and your deposit returned."

"Good God, he thought of everything," exclaimed Rob, "but we love the place and we have no intention of welshing on the deal. If anything, given what we've just heard, I think we're probably even more determined to have it. Eh, Janie?"

Janie could only nod. Tears were very close.

Langridge waited a moment or two and then said, "I must admit that I'm feeling more than a little emotional about all this, myself. Tom was a dear friend and I shall miss him tremendously, but I'm delighted that he found you two and that he died a happy man. I think he made a wonderful choice. Well, now, it's Friday, very nearly six o'clock and I usually have a small sherry at this time. Will you join me?"

"That would be lovely, thank you," Janie replied, before Rob could decline. He hated sherry.

It was, however, exceedingly good sherry, crisp and very dry, and Langridge led the toast, "To your new home."

Rob and Janie replied, in unison, "To Tom."

***

After the Whittakers had gone, Langridge poured himself another sherry and sat quietly for a moment, a letter open in front of him.

"Well, you got what you wanted, Tom. Let's hope everything works out for them."

He picked up the letter and realised that there were a couple of other things that Tom had requested he discuss with them, but there was time enough for that.

~ 6 ~
September 1985

"Putting you through now, Mr. Whittaker."

Miss Hunter still referred to everyone by their surname when she was on the phone or pursuing office business, and Janie was still 'Miss Mallory', which Miss Hunter thought rather odd, although she understood it was for professional reasons only. No doubt it was important that there should always be a Mallory at the agency. Janie, though, had taken to calling Miss Hunter by her Christian name, Joyce, when they were alone in the office and had suggested, on more than one occasion, that Miss Hunter call her Janie. Joyce Hunter was still trying this out occasionally, although not when Mr. Mallory was around.

"Hi, darling. Everything okay?" Janie put down the contract she was finalising.

"Yeah. It's just that I've had Gilbert Langridge on the phone."

"Oh. Is everything all right?"

"Fine, it's all looking good for completion in a couple of weeks, he thinks. He just wanted to run a couple of things by us, that he'd forgotten to mention, and he thought it best to do it directly rather than going through our solicitor. Are you busy?"

Janie reached for a pad and pen. "No, go on, I'm listening."

"Well, the first thing is about the furniture. All the fixtures and fittings, carpets, rugs and curtains are already included, as we know, and he's happy to arrange for everything else to be sent to the local auction rooms, if that's what we want, or, he says we can keep some, or all, of it. Free of charge."

"Crikey," Janie put down the pen, "can he do that? What about the beneficiaries?"

"According to Langridge, this was all in the letter old Tom left for him. And in his will, there are only four beneficiaries; two of whom are godchildren who each inherit a small legacy plus Tom and Harriet's jewellery and personal effects. Langridge has already spoken to both of them and they are happy with the arrangement."

"And who are the other two beneficiaries?"

"Well, this is a bit of a surprise. Tom had two children from a previous marriage and, after they divorced, his first wife took the kids to Australia and changed her name. Tom never had contact with them again."

"Christ, this story gets sadder and sadder. And, given my family history, it makes you wonder just how many families lose touch with each other."

"I know, I thought that, too. Anyhow, poor Langridge has been landed with the job of trying to find them, he reckons they'll be in their late thirties/early forties by now, and the remaining monies from Tom's estate, minus the two legacies, will be held in chancery for them."

"What do you think, then? Shall we go down this weekend and have a look?"

"Yeah, good plan. I'll phone him and see if he's prepared to do Saturday. There's one more thing though, before you go. Tom wanted his ashes to be scattered in the walled garden. I said 'yes', of course. I knew you would want that, too."

Janie smiled. "Good. Harry'll be pleased.

***

Gilbert Langridge was seated at the kitchen table in the Grange, his papers spread out before him and a freshly brewed pot of tea waiting to be poured. He'd had the foresight to pick up some milk on the way, trusting that there would still be tea and coffee in the larder.

He didn't have to come today. He could have left a key somewhere for them, but this was probably his last chance to sit at this table again, where he and his wife had shared many kitchen suppers, and much laughter, with the Kellys. This old kitchen would inevitably give way to something more modern now, but he hoped it would still be the heart of a happy home.

The Whittakers had started upstairs and he could hear them moving from room to room and the low murmuring of their voices. He didn't think there'd be much to interest them in the bedrooms, but you never knew; each generation had its own ideas about what was merely old-fashioned and what was classic or collectable. He heard them coming down the back stairs.

"I have some tea in the kitchen, if you'd like some, and perhaps we should go over the upstairs inventory now before you do the downstairs." As he suspected, they didn't want any of the bedroom furniture, but Janie was very taken with a table in a back bedroom. "That's called the nursery on here, I think," said Langridge, looking at the inventory, "from Harriet's parents' time," he added. "I think I know the table you mean, seventeenth century, if I'm not mistaken. A good choice, Mrs. Whittaker, you have a good eye."

They all went back upstairs and Langridge put a red sticker on the table. "Yes, a very good choice. It looks as though it's always been here, doesn't it? And, if you like that sort of thing, let me show you something else you might have overlooked…" He was right, and their haul increased by a couple of old footstools, a magnificent mahogany towel rail, lurking behind a bathroom door, and some good quality, Egyptian cotton sheets, neatly stacked in an airing cupboard that they'd missed entirely.

Janie laughed. "Mr. Langridge, you are so much better than we are at all this. I think you should come with us to do the downstairs."

In common with many older houses, the Grange had a Georgian façade, sympathetically built in local stone to match the original, with taller, more elegant rooms and a spacious hall. These rooms were labelled the drawing room and the morning room on Langridge's plan and Rob was keen to keep them just as they were, mainly because they had nothing of their own to put in them.

Janie sat on the window seat in the morning room. "I love this room," and she turned to the solicitor, "I was just thinking, this house must have been quite a bit smaller before this extension was built."

"Oh, no, my dear, it's smaller now than it was originally. Didn't Ludo tell you about the fire?"

Rob stopped examining a painting on the wall. "What fire?"

"Oh, I forget the date, seventeen something, it'll be in the House Book. That's something else I've got to tell you about...I'll come back to that later. The fire destroyed the major rooms, so the seventeenth century part you see now behind the Georgian bit, was really just the informal rooms, domestic offices and minor bedrooms. No – it was probably quite a bit bigger. If you look at the distance from the front of the house to the road, you'll see that it's set back further than you'd expect and, also, if you look out of the upstairs window, you can see a faint ridge in the front garden. That's where Tom reckoned the front of the house used to be, but there's no record anywhere to prove it."

"Goodness, we had no idea," Rob turned to Janie, "Anyway, it's just as well for us, any bigger and we wouldn't have been able to afford it."

"It was also quite a big working farm. I suppose Ludo didn't tell you that, either?" Rob and Janie shook their heads and Langridge continued, "It had several hundred acres, I think, and a few farm cottages, but, of course, like many estates, most of the land has been sold off over the years and most of the buildings have long since been demolished. You still have the dairy though, and the milking parlour. I hear that's going to be your new studio, Mr. Whittaker?"

They moved on to the dining room where everything was to

go apart from a buffet table, some pictures for the frames, and a lovely old mirror. The only other room with anything worth keeping was the kitchen and, much to the solicitor's surprise, they wanted to leave it just as it was, at least for the time being.

There was still an enormous amount of stuff in the outbuildings to inspect and Rob noticed the solicitor looking at his watch. They all agreed that Langridge should go home, Rob reckoned they'd taken up enough of his Saturday, and, when he and Janie had finished, they'd lock up and drop the keys through the office letterbox.

Gilbert Langridge was walking off to his car when Janie ran after him. "Sorry, but you mentioned something about a House Book? You said you'd explain later."

"So I did. It's in the office safe and, on reflection, I think it's better if I show you. Once you're settled in, you should make an appointment and come to see it. It's quite a document – I think you'll find it very interesting."

~ 7 ~
October 1985

Rob shut the gate after the removal lorry and went to find Janie in the kitchen, her arms spread along the range, beaming.

"No regrets, then?" Grinning, he reached into the fridge to find the champagne.

"Are you kidding? I never had any doubts, you know that. Here, we'll have to use these…" She rinsed out a couple of mugs, "…heaven knows which box the glasses are in."

Rob filled them to the brim. "To us, and the Grange."

"We are meant to be here, you know," Janie was eyeballing him over the rim of the mug, "and I know you think I'm being a bit weird, but…don't look at me like that. You can deny it all you like, Rob Whittaker, but I know you think it, too. And Tom Kelly knew it. And, and…" she pointed at him, "I overheard you telling Guy the same thing on the phone the other night."

"I think you'll find what I said was, 'Janie's convinced we were meant to be here.' Anyway, I will admit it feels very … right." He kissed her on the nose.

"Don't patronise." Then in the next breath, "Do you want to come up to my office?"

"Is that code?"

"No. It means 'do you want to come and see my office?'"

"I've seen your office, Janie, and there's nothing in it apart from a table."

She ignored him, took his hand and led him up the back stairs to the room over the kitchen. The rescued, seventeenth century table was up against the back wall with a large cardboard box on the top. Rob laughed. "Marvellous, Janie. If this is to be your desk, why is it facing the wall?"

"It's not. I'm getting a new one. I mean, an old one – you know what I mean. I thought we could take a trip into Petworth and look round the antique shops for one? And it'll go under the window, obviously." Janie put her mug down. "No, this table is for my...wait for it," and she lifted up the cardboard box, "fax machine!"

Rob's eyebrows shot up in surprise. "Well, well. Welcome to the age of technology!"

She continued, still excited, "Joyce suggested we get them. We've got two, of course; one in the office and one here. Don't you think that's brilliant? It means I can probably work from home a couple of days a week."

Rob looked puzzled. "Did you say Joyce, as in Joyce Hunter, suggested you buy them?"

"Yeah. Her friend, Audrey, already uses one in her job and so Joyce read up all about them. She's really keen and I'm discovering things about our Miss Hunter that no one ever knew. Dad certainly didn't make good use of her."

"Right then," said Rob, draining his mug, "I'm going to have to get cracking on my studio as soon as poss. I can't have you swanning around here, enjoying yourself, whilst I'm stuck in London all week."

In fact, Rob had already designed his new studio and instructed some recommended local builders to quote for the job. The dairy, which was at the far end of the building, was to be his office, and the milking parlour, with its large double doors opening into the walled garden, was to be the working part of the studio. It was obvious to Rob, now, that, before the garden was enclosed, it must have been the site of the original farmyard.

The old stalls had been stripped out years before and the

milking parlour was now just one large space. The major part
of the work involved levelling the floor, which was a death trap
with its broken, uneven brickwork and gulleys. Then there was
wood worming and damp proofing to be tackled and installation
of three roof lights on the north side overlooking the paddock.
Luckily, water and electricity were already connected, so the
addition of a washroom, a sink in the studio, storage heaters and
multiple lights and power points was relatively simple. Later, the
builder was to suggest installing a woodburner, he knew where
he could get one cheap, and Rob silently thanked him every day
in the ensuing cold winter months.

Until Tom's things had been removed from the dairy, Rob
had assumed it just an empty space, but he was surprised to find
a massive stone slab, at table height, running the whole width
of the room. The floor in here was fine, so, all he really needed
was a phone connection and some electrics, and he had a ready
made desk. The artist in him was thrilled.

Weeks before they'd moved in, Rob and Janie had spent many
hours redrawing the first floor and had come up with a plan that
they could agree on. The two front bedrooms in the Georgian
extension were to remain as the master and guest bedrooms.
The smaller bedroom, next to the master would be converted
into a dressing room and en suite bathroom. The huge, existing
bathroom, between the guest bedroom and a smaller one, would
remain and serve them both. One large bedroom and bathroom,
plus a new, walk-in airing cupboard, would be created from the
remaining small rooms, and that just left Janie's office. Ludo
was right – four good bedrooms, three bathrooms and an office.
Possibly too big for their needs, but they were planning ahead;
Rob's mother was on her own and already showing worrying
signs of memory loss. And, although Janie couldn't imagine the
day would come when Antony would want to leave London, it
was best to be prepared.

~ 8 ~

Langridge's Office, October 1985

"Right, here you are." Gilbert Langridge placed the archive box on his desk and went back to close the safe, a great walk-in affair from the days when the solicitor's office was a bank. He returned to the desk, removed a book from the box and put it carefully in front of her. "The House Book – and now your House Book."

"Oh my," Janie's eyes grew large, "it's quite beautiful." She took some white cotton gloves out of her bag and held them up. "I've come prepared, can I open it up and have a look?"

Langridge smiled. "Of course, you may, it's yours. At least, it's yours as long as you own the Grange. Although, I think that may be a moot point, and one that's never needed to be tested in court." Janie looked puzzled and the solicitor continued, "You see, Thomas Crayford, who built the house, introduced the House Book as a social record of the life of the house and its inhabitants, and requested that it remain with the deeds of the house, but, of course, all the previous owners have been direct descendants. Now that the house has left the family, it remains to be seen whether future owners will respect his wishes."

"But it's valuable." Janie was horrified. "It needs protecting, and surely something could be done to stop someone pinching it?"

Langridge made a note on a legal pad. "You're right, of course. Now that you've raised the matter, I shall look into it for you.

And, perhaps, with your experience, you can suggest a better way of looking after it?"

"I will." Janie was pulling on her gloves and inspecting the cover. The old leather binding still had traces of the original blue, visible in the spaces under the brass corners and the clasp, but the rest of the binding had faded to a dusty indigo, and the gold leaf on the letters was dull and missing in parts. To Janie, it was perfect just as it was. It was, perhaps, a little smaller than a Victorian family bible and somewhat slimmer. She sprung the clasp and gasped as she opened it to reveal an astonishing, marbled endpaper.

Looking up, she saw Langridge smiling at her. "Beautiful, isn't it?"

"Not only beautiful, but - what's the date of this book, 1641? – it's very early, I think, for this sort of work. I'll do some research, but it wouldn't surprise me if this had been imported from Europe, or China even. Our Mr. Crayford spared no expense, obviously."

Janie looked at the first couple of pages, clearly absorbed, until Langridge suggested she take the book back home with her to read at leisure. "There's no hurry to return it, I can see you'll take excellent care of it. Incidentally, this isn't the book in which you will write your details." He delved into the box and produced a similar, but newer and smaller, book. "That would be this one. Not that the first book is full; I just think that someone decided it was getting too old to use. This one dates from 1849 to the present day and, when you've read the other entries, you'll have a good idea about what you want to write." He was about to put the books back in the box when he held up a large envelope. "I forgot about this. In her last few months, Harry spent a lot of time tracing as many members of her family tree as possible. That's of no interest to you, I know, but first, she copied all the names from both House books." He waved the envelope at her, "It's all in here," and he peered again into the box. "And there are some old household and farm account books here, too, which make fascinating reading for anyone interested in social history." Langridge replaced the lid on the archive box and insisted on taking it out to her car. The age of chivalry may be on the critical list, Janie thought, but at least in this neck of the woods, it stands a chance.

***

Later that evening, once supper had been cleared away, Janie fetched an old damask tablecloth from the airing cupboard and laid it over the kitchen table. She went to pick up the archive box. "Careful, let me do that." Rob took it from her and placed it on the table. "Good God, just how big is this book?'

Janie opened the lid. "There you are, not that big, and, actually, there are two House Books as well as some old accounts books in here. That's what's making it heavy." She sat down, freed the clasp and opened the book at the endpaper, Rob standing behind her and looking over her shoulder. "Isn't it fabulous?"

She turned to the foreword, hesitating and stumbling over the text. Rob interrupted her, "I don't know how you can read that."

"I'm a bit out of practice and, to be honest, I was never very good at reading Early Modern English texts in the first place, but, even if I were, this is difficult."

It was written in secretary hand, common in the seventeenth century, but this was very cursive, the ink had faded somewhat and damp had created some foxing and smudging, which all added to the difficulty.

Rob sat down next to her and Janie began to read out loud again, slowly,

"This House Book was commissioned by me, Thomas Crayford, in the year 1641 to celebrate the completion of my new home 'Oakwood Grange' on the site of the old 'Oakwood Farmhouse'.

It is my fervent wish and request that my family and heirs and any subsequent owners of this property will use this book to record significant events in their lives and the life of this house to thus produce a faithful history for future generations."

Janie turned to the next page.

FAMILY

Thomas Crayford b.1598: Gentleman, Landowner, Royalist and Protestant.

Married to Margaret (1600 – 1638)

Married to Anne (nee Manners) in 1641

Son: Richard Crayford b.1623

Son: Edward Crayford b.1625

DOMESTIC SERVANTS

Cook, Mrs. Lynd

2 Housemaids

2 Kitchenmaids

Various Boys

OUTSIDE SERVANTS

Groom, Edmund Sandford

Gardener, Joshua Tickner

Dairymaid, Jennet Sandford

Stableboys

FARM

Manager, Henry Durling

Farmhands

Milkmaids

LAND

674 acres inc. 196 acres woodland and several farm cottages

The next few entries were written in a different hand and easier to read:

ALICE CRAYFORD

Daughter: to Thomas and Anne, born 3rd September 1643

EDWARD CRAYFORD

Cavalryman & Beloved Son: died aged 19 yrs at the Second Battle of Newbury, fighting for the King. 27th October 1644

RICHARD CRAYFORD

Captain of Cavalry & Beloved Son: died aged 21 yrs at the Battle of Naseby, fighting for the King. 14th June 1645

"So much history, right there, just in the first couple of pages." Janie leant back in her chair and reached for Rob's hand. "And now here we are – part of it."

~ 9 ~
Oakwood Grange, 1658

T he day after her mother died, Alice reached for the book and laid it down on her father's writing table. The binding was dark blue morocco leather, soft as the finest gloves, and still giving off the scent of the bookbinder's studio. The tooling was elaborate and illuminated in gold leaf. Even on this sad day, it delighted her senses and Alice ran her hand over the surface and across the title; 'Oakwood Grange' was written in bold.

She released the brass clasp and revealed the marbled end paper that had so fascinated her as a child and still gave her pause now. Turning to the next page, she started to read every entry, even though, if asked, she could have recited each one with barely a mistake. There was no putting it off any longer.

Alice took some time selecting a quill from the holder, checked the inkpot and settled herself in her father's chair before pulling the book a little closer. Her hands were sweating and her heart racing a little for fear that her poor handwriting was not going to do justice to either her mother or the book. She would have preferred her father to make the entry but, being too overcome, he had entrusted her with this task and so it was to be done.

ANNE CRAYFORD

Most beloved wife to Thomas and mother to Alice, died aged 58 yrs. 20th October 1658

Alice replaced the quill and put the top back on the inkpot. It was better than she had hoped; no blots, smudges or corrections and, although the style was not confident and the spacing somewhat irregular, it was clearly legible. Her mother would have been pleased.

Sitting back in the chair and closing her eyes, she recalled how her mother would struggle to understand how her daughter could be so quick to learn all her lessons, so good at arithmetic and languages, and yet so poor at handwriting. Her father had always countered that the boys were the same. It was surely not the same, Anne had replied, as the boys were poor scholars all round, preferring instead all outdoor pursuits and swordplay.

Alice rubbed her eyes to dispel the unshed tears, checked that the ink was dry before closing the book and replaced it on the shelf.

***

Crossing the dining hall, Alice went in search of her father. The dog was asleep next to his boots by the fire so he hadn't left the house and, with no sign of him in the withdrawing room or the parlour, she went up to her mother's chamber.

Alice cracked the door and peered into the gloom. She could just make out the seated figure of her father, head on hands, leaning on the laying out table. Closing the door softly behind her, she went to stand by him and rested a hand on his shoulder. Bending down slightly she whispered, "I've done it, Papa. The entry is in the book."

He didn't look up but patted her hand and said, "Good girl".

She left as quietly as she had arrived without a glance at the coffin and the wasted shell that had once been her mother.

"Miss Alice, Miss Alice..." Tansy, the youngest housemaid, caught up with her on the landing and bobbed a curtsey, "begging your pardon but Master says I must make up the guest bedrooms and I'm sure I don't know which linen to use."

Alice, only just fifteen and not much older than Tansy, also had no idea. "As long as it's clean, Tansy, and there are no holes or tears then I'm sure it'll be fine." She forced a smile and left her to it, taking the stairs quickly to avoid any more questions she couldn't answer. It was only just beginning to dawn on her that, as the new mistress of the house, all sorts of decisions would be expected of her. Still, she thought, as she made her way to the kitchen, I don't need to worry about food – Cook will have everything under control.

The air was stifling and hazy with flour, smoke billowed from the hearth at the far end of the kitchen and the clattering of utensil against pan was deafening. Cook, at the centre table, was barking orders amid a flurry of flour as she took out her temper on the bread dough. "Miss Alice," she said, as she stopped kneading for a while, "I decided to roast a pig – I hope that's all right – but I don't know how many to expect and I can't ask the master again...I really can't...." and she tailed off, chins quivering.

Alice put an arm around her ample waist. "Mrs. Lynd, I don't know how many to expect either but I'm sure there'll be enough and it'll be wonderful, as always. Please don't fret. Is there anything I can do?"

"I could do with some more cream and butter but Patience is going to go when she's finished chopping the carrots..." Cook turned to glare at the poor girl and raised her voice, "...that is, if she ever finishes," and she turned back to Alice and rolled her eyes, "Who said Patience was a virtue?"

"No," said Alice, "I'll do that. I was going out, anyway. You keep Patience here." She picked up the large jug and bowl and *stopped on her way out to talk to Seth at the spit. He was six years old, one of the farmhand's sons and a favourite of hers with his big brown eyes rimmed with black lashes and his curly dark hair, even curlier now and dripping with sweat. He was sitting on a little three-legged stool with his bare feet perilously close to the drip tray and he wasn't happy. Alice reckoned he had several hours of spit turning ahead of him, judging by the state of the pig, and she bent down to whisper something in his ear.*

Her heavy mourning dress, which had been so uncomfortable in the kitchen, was a blessing outside as the weather had turned chill of late but she took her time, picking her way carefully to keep her newly blacked boots as clean as possible.

She could have gone straight to the dairy but decided to go via the milking shed to see if Martha was there. Alice loved to watch her, softly crooning with eyes closed, small blonde head leaning against the cow's leg, patiently filling the pail with milk. A child of only a few years but, according to her mother, the cows stood still and produced more milk for her than anyone else. Suddenly aware of a presence, Martha started but settled back to her task as Alice patted her head and squeezed passed her to reach the dairy.

Jennet stopped what she was doing as soon as she saw who it was, took the jug and bowl from her and they fell into each other's arms, Alice no longer able to control her grief. "There, there child - you let it all out. I'm so sorry it came to this; your mother was such a good woman."

They both sat down on the bench, Jennet rocking and comforting her as she had done from the moment she'd held her as her wet nurse. In her heart she knew that the bond they shared was as strong as that with her own children but she was careful not to let it show in front of others. Alice, too, was aware from an early age to avoid public displays of affection and only sought Jennet when she was alone in the dairy.

The sobbing stopped eventually. Alice wiped her face and let out a big sigh. "There's so much to do, Jennet, I don't know where to start. Father is so heartsick he doesn't leave mother's chamber and everyone's looking to me. Have you been in the kitchen?"

Jennet shook her head, "No, I've too much to do here."

"Well," replied Alice, trying to secure a wayward chestnut curl, "You'd be wise to stay away. It's like Dante's Inferno in there and Cook is heart-broken and overworked in equal measure."

"Here, let me do it," Jennet took the hairpin from her. "Turn round."

Alice did as she was told. "I see your Martha's charming the cows to give every last drop of milk and it's just as well as I think we'll need it all. Cook is determined to produce the best she can for the funeral party. Anyway, that was my excuse for coming, she needs extra cream and butter if you have any. Oh, and have you got a little sweetmeat for Seth? I promised him something for spit-turning."

~ 10 ~
Late October 1985

Rob woke early, turned and reached over to Janie's side of the bed, only to find it empty and cold. He found her downstairs in the kitchen, poring over the House Book again.

"Hey, early bird, how long have you been up then?'

"Ages," she replied, not looking up from the book. "I woke really early and couldn't get back to sleep for thinking about this." She held her face up for a kiss. "I wanted to read some more." She stood up, filled the kettle and absent-mindedly left it on the draining board. Rob put it on the hob. He saw the builders pulling into the drive, so he left her to it and went out to have a word with them. "And look," she carried on when he came back in, "we didn't notice this yesterday. This little pen and ink sketch at the top of the page? It must be this place before the fire. See – it looks nothing like it does now from the front."

Rob leaned over her to have a look. "Oh, yeah. It looks wider, doesn't it, and not quite so tall? That's if it's to scale, of course." The kettle was dancing on the hob but Janie didn't notice. "I'll make the tea then, shall I?" he said.

"Mmm. And another thing, poor Thomas's second wife dies, too. So he's lost two wives and two sons and is left with just one daughter. That's so sad."

"Sad, but not uncommon in those days, I guess," and Rob put her mug of tea down next to her. She moved it carefully away from the book.

An hour later, on his way out to see how the builders were getting on in the studio, Rob found her still at the kitchen table in her dressing gown. "I thought you were going in to the office today."

"Oh, Christ." She looked at the clock, "Don't touch this, will you?" and raced upstairs. Moments later, she was back, carefully replacing the book in the archive box.

***

Rob called her later in the day. "Did you get a detention from Miss Hunter or will you be home at the normal time?

"Funny… normal time. Why?"

"Guy's just phoned. His parents have a horse running at St Cloud tomorrow, so he and Tash are catching the Portsmouth/le Havre ferry early in the morning to give the old man some moral support. As they haven't seen the house, they were wondering if they could come down and stay tonight and they'd be more than half way there in the morning."

"How the other half lives, eh? Yes, of course they can, it'll be fun, but I hope you've warned them that we're not exactly prepared for visitors…"

Janie left him with a list of things to do, the most important of which was to go and see Lorraine in the village shop to find something easy to cook for supper. Checking the booze cupboard came next on the list. Making up the spare bed? ….yeah, probably not. She'd just have to try and leave work early.

Lorraine, in common with most women, liked Rob. She sold him an oven ready chicken, large baking potatoes, ingredients for a salad, a frozen ice cream roulade, and suggested he cook the chicken before Janie got home. He looked at her blankly.

"You do know how to cook a chicken, don't you?"

"I know I stick it in one of the ovens, but I've no idea which one or for how long."

Lorraine looked at her mother, who'd popped in for a chat.

"I'm Lydia Cartwright," Lorraine's mum shook Rob's hand, "and I used to work up at t' Grange a while ago. If nowt's changed in't kitchen, then I know me way around. Do you want me to come and help you, lad?"

Not only did she find a roasting tin and do something extraordinary with the chicken, but she also scrubbed the potatoes, prepared the salad and left him with an idiot's guide so he couldn't mess up the cooking. She was in and out in about half an hour and brushed away Rob's heartfelt thanks with a breezy, "Think nowt of it, lad, it's nice to feel useful. And think on, if you want to know owt about t' house, then just come and ask."

Brilliant, he thought, how easy was that? He put the beers in the fridge and went back to the studio to see how the builders were getting on.

John Hobden (of Hobden & Son, Builders, Established 1916), over a foot shorter than Rob and built like a brick, was about 50 years old and strong as an ox. A third generation builder, there wasn't much he didn't know about old West Sussex buildings and he only employed people who shared his passion and work ethic. Rob knew they were lucky to get him.

"John, when you've got a minute, can you come over to the house. I've got something to show you."

"Aye. I'll be with you in two ticks."

And two ticks later, he popped his head round the kitchen door. "In here, is it?"

"No, come through, John. It's in the snug."

John leaned on the door jamb to heel off his work boots and followed Rob through the hall to the small sitting room behind the morning room.

"I want to know if we can do anything about that fireplace." Both men stared at the old electric fire, set in a repro Georgian fire surround.

"Well, I know what I'd do with it," murmured John, scratching his head underneath his cap. "I'd take the bugger out."

"That's sort of what we had in mind, too. We were just a bit worried, though, about what we'd find behind."

"Whatever it is, it's going to be better than that, isn't it? But this house is pretty old so I reckon you'll have a decent fireplace behind there. You'll be wanting an open fire?"

Rob nodded, and while John was having a good look around and knocking on the chimney breast, he repeated what Langridge had told them about the fire and the rebuilding of the front of the house.

"Aye, I'd forgotten about that. But this room's definitely part of the original house and so is this chimneystack. I wouldn't be surprised if there's an inglenook behind there – look at the width of the chimney breast, and the depth – it's definitely worth doing.

"Good, Janie'll be thrilled. We live in here most of the time and she wants an open fire for Christmas, that is, if you can manage it. How long do you think it'll take?"

"It's a job to say." This, they were to learn, was John's standard answer to any question involving timing or pricing. "We can do the work in here after we've finished your studio. It'll be tight to get it done before Christmas, mind, and it'll make a bit of mess, but whether it'll be working or not depends on the chimney."

"You think it could be blocked?"

"Could be capped off, or just blocked, or need sweeping. We'll have to get up there and have a look."

"And how much will it all cost, do you think?"

"It's a job to say."

***

Janie drove home from the station to find an Aston Volante parked in the drive and familiar voices floating through the open kitchen window.

"Aha, it's the lady of the manor. Home from a hard day's work in the smoke." Guy picked her up the second she got through the door and gave her a big kiss. Although matching Rob in height and build, his white blond hair contrasted so sharply with his friend's that he looked like a positive to Rob's negative.

Tash elbowed her husband out of the way. "Hello, darling. We've had the tour and we love your house – it's fabulous."

"Hey, it's great to see you both." Janie kissed Tash, kicked off her shoes and threw her jacket over the chair. "Ugh, I'm glad I left early, I've had a bitch of a day. I'm in desperate need of a drink and I see I'm already way behind you lot."

"There you go..." Rob handed her a large gin and tonic and bent down to whisper, "Sorry you've had a shit day, but everything's in hand here. There's nothing to do."

She frowned slightly. "Really?"

Guy, having been told to wait till Janie got home, was desperate to see outside, so they took their drinks and made for the walled garden just as the sun was sinking in the sky. The men were soon wrapped up in their own little horticultural world and, after ten minutes or so, Janie indicated to Tash with a tilt of her head and the two of them sneaked back to the house.

"I'm going to have a quick shower and change, Tash. Help yourself to another drink, won't you?" First, though, wary of Rob's 'everything's in hand here' remark, she went to check on the spare bedroom.

Surprisingly, she found the bed was made up with the Kelly's bed linen, the bathroom had heaps of fluffy towels and the windows had been opened to air the rooms. All she had to do was find some soap, bath bubbles and a spare loo roll. By the time she'd showered, changed into jeans and a shirt and made her way back downstairs, she'd worked it out.

"What time did you get here, Tash?"

"Oh, about four, I think."

"And how long did it take for Rob to show you the airing cupboard?"

Tash pulled a face and gestured with one perfectly manicured hand. "I offered, honest. We'd have had to remake it, anyway, wouldn't we? And it was the least I could do, dropping in on you at short notice." Janie gave a little, resigned nod and they both grinned. "Bloody men," Tash went on, "Guy left it to the very last minute to ring Rob, even though I told him to do it earlier in the week."

"Well, I hope he hasn't got you cooking too, has he? I can smell something."

"No, apparently that was all organised before we got here. He's just popped something in the oven while you were upstairs, but I'm sworn to secrecy."

It was dark by the time the men returned from looking round the studio. Rob checked his watch, removed a tray of jacket potatoes from the oven and said, "Right then, I'll get you all something to drink and then I want you out of my way while I get the supper on the table."

Tash bit her lip as Janie leaned over to whisper, "I'm so bloody hungry, I don't care if that's all there is, but I'm having the big one," before they cleared out of the kitchen and left him to it.

Rob was enjoying himself; it was a long time since he'd been able to surprise his wife. After Lydia had gone, he'd found a gingham tablecloth in one of the dresser drawers and some matching napkins, and he shoved a couple of household candles into empty wine bottles. He'd hidden everything in the larder. Once the table was laid, the candles lit, and all the food was ready, Rob called up the hall, "Come and get it!" and went to the head of the table.

There was silence as the three of them took their seats, exchanging bemused glances. A beautifully cooked chicken, still warm and smelling fantastic, with crisp brown skin, lay on a carving tray in front of the proud chef. The salad had bits in that, as far as Janie was aware, Rob didn't even know existed, and there was home made vinaigrette in a jug. The effect was slightly spoiled by an unopened packet of butter next to the plate of jacket potatoes and a bottle of salad cream.

Tash swept her hair over one shoulder and leant over the table. "Is that a lemon I can see inside the chicken?"

"Er, yes."

Guy's face was deadpan. "And you must tell me which herbs

have you used, Rob, 'cos it smells amazing."

"Okay, enough." Janie stood up and leaned across the table. "Who are you, and what have you done with my husband?"

He confessed; then they ate and drank and ate some more until there was nothing left.

"Rob Whittaker, you are shameless," Tash managed to get out between mouthfuls.

"Resourceful, though. You've got to give him that." Guy pointed to Rob with his knife.

Janie was just grateful. She proposed the toast to Lydia and resolved to ring her tomorrow – and grovel, if necessary.

~ 11 ~
Lydia, October 1985

Janie knocked on the door of the pretty cottage next to the village shop, and was surprised to find it opened by a very attractive, well turned out woman in her sixties. Not what she'd expected; and she was cross with herself for stereotyping.

"Mrs. Cartwright? I'm Janie Whittaker."

"Oh, Mrs. Whittaker, I'm right glad to meet you," and she took both of Janie's hands and led her inside. "Come in, lass, do…come in."

Immediately drawn in by the warmth of the woman, Janie smiled broadly, "Thanks, it's good of you to invite me round. And please, not Mrs. Whittaker, I'm Janie."

"Well, I'm Lydia, so that's all right then, in't it?"

The sitting room was as comfortable as its owner, and the two women settled down with tea and biscuits either side of the fire. Janie began with an apology. " I'm so sorry my husband threw himself on your mercy the other day, in such a shameless fashion I might add, but I was very grateful. I'd been working in London all day and then we had unexpected…"

Lydia cut her off. "Ee, love, think nowt of it. I were glad to do it; I get a bit bored now I'm retired, and I don't imagine your husband is ever short of willing female help, am I right?"

"That's the trouble, I'm sure he plays on it. Anyway, I have to tell you that we all appreciated your effort; the food was delicious, and Rob might even be able to cook a chicken now."

"Well, I think he's a grand lad." Lydia reached over and patted Janie on the knee, "You make a lovely couple and I'm so glad to see the Grange in such good hands."

Conversation came easily and Lydia's method of extracting information was as subtle as it was skillful. Before long, she knew something of Janie's background and all about Rob's early life in Brighton, his stint as a landscape gardener and his career as a graphic designer.

"Well, I'm pleased there's someone who can look after the garden. It'd be a right shame if it were to let go, wouldn't it? The Kellys loved that garden."

"We were thinking of keeping the gardener on anyway, because Rob's got loads of work on at the moment. Although, I suspect, he'd probably prefer to be doing the gardening, he finds it relaxing." They were both silent for a while, and then Janie continued, "Did you know that Dr. Kelly's ashes are to be scattered in the garden?"

Lydia put her hand to her mouth and shook her head slightly. "I didn't, but I'm not surprised. He'd want to be with Harriet, of course."

"Rob tells me you worked for them for a long time."

"Aye, I did. Thirty three years, including the time I worked for Harriet's parents."

"So, you'll know Tom had no close relatives in this country." Lydia nodded, her eyes filling with tears. "I'm sorry, I didn't mean to upset you. The coroner's only just released the body and Mr. Langridge is going to arrange a memorial service for him at St. John's. Then sometime after that we'll scatter the ashes. Would you like to be there for that?"

"I would. Yes, I really would." Lydia wiped her eyes. She sat back in her chair, screwed her handkerchief into a ball, and said, more to herself than Janie, "It feels like the end of an era, to me," and then she looked up. "I expect you're wondering how a Yorkshire lass ended up down here, aren't you?"

Janie was curious but, more importantly, she suspected Lydia needed to tell the story. She helped herself to another biscuit and listened in silence.

"I left Yorkshire and joined the Women's Auxiliary Army in 1940, when I were twenty-one, and ended up driving ambulances in London. I saw some terrible things, I really did, but I had the time of me life, as well. All the mechanics were men, so you can imagine, can't you?" Lydia winked and gave a dirty little chuckle. "They were desperate times – aye, they were that. Anyhow, when t'war finished, I were at a loose end. I didn't want to go back home and I couldn't get a job in London. There were too many returning soldiers, you see.

So, I answered an ad. in t'paper for a housekeeper at the Grange. All I knew was, that it were near Cowdray Park, where I'd done some training, and I liked it round here. Well, when I saw the size of the Grange, I nearly turned round and went back. I'd only ever looked after our little terraced house before and I'd got no experience. Although that was nothing to how I felt when I met Mrs. Parsons, Harriet's mother. She frightened the living daylights out of me and I were sure she thought I were a bit thick. Anyhow, she must have been desperate 'cos I got the job." Lydia paused to pour them both another cup of tea before continuing.

"Now, Harriet's father, the Brigadier, he were a different kettle of fish altogether. Me and him got on like a house on fire, shared war experience, you see, although we didn't talk about it much. He'd lost a leg towards the end of the war, and all the fiddling around with his falsey made him right grumpy, especially with Harriet. Any small complaint she made about post-war life and he were off to his study." She laughed. "He'd slam the door behind him. And his stump played him up a lot, so I used to dress it for him and this got me into his wife's good books 'cos she'd had to do it before I came and I can't imagine she were very sympathetic." She gave another little chuckle.

"Me and Harriet didn't have much in common even though I were only four year older than her. To be honest, I thought she were a right snotty cow. The Brig had made her get a job when he came home in 1944, and he told me his wife had kicked up a fuss about it. And then there was another big row shortly after I got there, and that ended up with Harriet jacking in her job and going off. Things were very rocky between the Brig and his missus for quite a while, after that. Harriet did come back after a few months but I'd married Frank by then and I wasn't living in."

Janie felt a little disappointed, "I hadn't imagined Harriet to be like that. Mr. Langridge painted a very different picture of her."

"Oh, don't get me wrong, it weren't all her fault. When I arrived, it became a sort of 'us and them' situation, if you know what I mean, and I didn't try too hard to befriend her. But the Harriet who married Tom Kelly was a much-improved version of the original, I can tell you that. I worked for her, on and off, until the year before she died and we got on very well; she became a friend. We didn't socialise, but we were definitely friends."

Lydia looked down at the balled up hanky in her lap and Janie waited, for she knew there was more. "Just before she died, we talked a lot about the past. It's inevitable, in't it? Her two brothers, Charles and Roger, had both been killed in t'war while the Brig was still out there fighting, and Harriet and her mother had to cope on their own. They didn't cope well, and when the Brig came back injured with, according to Harriet, 'his stiff upper lip well and truly intact', it weren't a happy household. And, like I said, I don't think I helped at first."

Janie said, "It can't have been an easy situation for you, either. Did you know about the boys' deaths?"

"Not at first. There were photos, of course, and lots of their stuff all over the place, and I used to dust and air their rooms, but, after a little while, it dawned on me, that no one talked about them. It was the Brig who first told me how they'd died, when I were dressing his leg one day; he were a very proud father. Harriet's mother never mentioned them."

Again, Lydia paused, as if replaying the next scene in her mind. "One day, when Harriet was away, I went up to do the boys' rooms, and I found Mrs. Parsons in Charles's room, lying on his bed and clutching a photo of the boys to her chest. Sobbing, she were. I were going to walk away, but something made me stay and I crept back in and closed t' door behind me. I didn't know what to say and she didn't speak – but she knew I were there. I went to sit on t' bed next to her, and I remember rubbing her back and thinking that this were the first time we'd ever touched each other. We stayed like that for ever such a long time, with me just stroking her hair and comforting her, and I cried, too. I'd just found out I was pregnant with our Lorraine. That was the turning point in our relationship, even though we never spoke about it." Lydia raised her eyebrows and pulled a little face. "We were Lydia and Lily after that. Harriet couldn't believe it when she came home, and everything changed for the better."

"I knew there'd have to be a happy ending," Janie said, "otherwise you wouldn't have stayed for thirty three years!"

"I'm sorry, lass, I do go on, I know. You didn't need to know all that."

"No, not at all," reassured Janie, "it's part of the history of the house and I want to know it all. I suppose Harriet married Dr. Kelly shortly after she came back?"

"No, it were a few years after. Tom had been through a messy divorce and his first wife, well, I mustn't gossip, let's just say, she weren't right for him, and leave it at that. Any road, he married Harriet and moved into the Grange and they looked after the Brig and Mrs. Parsons until they both passed on in the sixties. It was a happy house, even though they didn't… well, they all got on." Some instinct made Lydia cut her sentence short.

"Do you know, Lydia, you've painted such a vivid picture of them all, that I feel I knew them. When I get back, I shall be wandering round the house reliving all these tales, especially in the boys' rooms. You know they haven't been touched, don't you?"

"I do. I don't think Harriet had the heart to redecorate after her Mum and Dad went."

"So, when did you decide to retire?

"When I were sixty. It were the year before Harriet died and, if I'd known how ill she was, I'd have stayed on. But there you are, hindsight's a wonderful thing, in't it?

When it came time for Janie to go, Lydia kissed her on the cheek. "Thank you for listening to a silly old woman. And I'll tell you this; old Tom Kelly will be up there," and she pointed sky-ward, "as pleased as punch, that he managed to sell the house to you two. It couldn't be in better hands.

~ 12 ~
November 1985

"You do it, Rob, your handwriting's better than mine." Janie lifted the second House Book out of the box and put it on the table in front of her husband.

Rob turned the pages until he found the last entry. He read it twice. "Janie, come here. Come and look at this."

It read:

'Thomas Edward Kelly, died 15th August 1985

Oakwood Grange sold to Robert & Eugenie Whittaker, (blank)

1985'

Janie read it, "Langridge must have written that in."

"I don't think so. Look at the handwriting; it's the same as the hand that entered the death of Harriet. Tom wrote this. He'd planned his death down to the day. And the old devil was pretty sure we wouldn't back out of the sale, by the look of it." They sat there in silence for a long moment before Rob pulled himself together. "Right, I'm going to fill in the date and then, I think, you and I will start a new page. Eh, Mrs. Whittaker?"

Rob did it beautifully, and they both re-read their entry several times before making sure it was dry before they shut the book. To their surprise, they found it an emotional moment.

Putting the House Book back in its box, Janie idly flicked through one of the old account books before replacing them also. It was dated 1642. She sat down to read it and found the detail remarkable: everything bought and sold, from livestock to wooden spoons, every repair made, every person paid; it was all there. They were roughly in date order, and after a quick reference to the first House Book, she'd figured out who'd written them. The first farm account books were written by Thomas Crayford himself, the handwriting and dates matched, more or less, and then the majority were written in another hand, really quite difficult to read. She didn't have time to look through them properly now, so she rang Langridge to tell him she'd be returning the House Books as promised today, but would he mind if she hung on to the accounts? He didn't.

***

Rob had been late getting to London, his meetings had run on and on, and he'd been held up on the way home by an accident on the A3. He was not happy.

"Hi, darling," Janie pushed aside the account books and made a sympathetic face. "Let me get you a drink. Beer or whisky?"

"Whisky, a large one please. When did you get home?"

"Uh, usual time." She handed him the whisky. "There's some chili in the oven, when you're ready."

Supper over with, Rob pointed to the account books. "What are all those?"

"Just some of the old farm accounts. You remember, they were in with the House Books?"

She showed him the first few but, after a few minutes, Rob's interest was waning and he couldn't keep his eyes open. "I'm knackered, Janie. I'm going to bed, okay?" She didn't look up. "Don't be too long, eh?"

"No, alright. I'll be up soon." She was busy sorting out the rest of the account books, separating them into farm and household piles.

Then she found the notebook.

***

3rd September 1663

My 20th birthday. I have resolved to write a diary and today is the first entry. I do not expect I shall record faithfully every day if there is nothing interesting to report but rather that I should express my thoughts and describe events in my life, whether good or bad, if they be noteworthy.

Father surprised me by rising early and joining me for breakfast, foregoing his usual morning draft and instead taking tea! This was a rare treat, as was the meal, Mrs. Lynd providing lamb chops, freshly baked bread and cheese and my favourite curd cakes. Our birthdays are usually celebrated in a much less extravagant way and I was further surprised to learn that Father had already sent word to Henry that our morning round would be delayed today and that Cook had instructions for a birthday dinner and supper! I confess I was much relieved to find that he had not invited our neighbours as, although perfectly pleasant folk, they make rather boring supper companions.

Farm matters took up much of the day with only a short break for some excellent pease pottage and a sliver of venison pie. I left Father enjoying a quince cream with a third glass of sack. It is no wonder he complains of gout.

We took supper rather late, the highlight being a wonderful syllabub and a fine bottle of claret, and discussed how Henry and I plan to make the farm more efficient. Father does not seem convinced that change is necessary but is inclined to let us go ahead.

After breakfast, Father had presented me with my usual birthday books. This time they were 'Leviathan' by Thomas Hobbes, no doubt designed to further my political education, and the most beautifully bound and presented collection of Mr. Shakespeare's sonnets. So, it was rather surprising that, after supper, he presented me with another gift. It was my mother's jewellery box and we were both a little overcome as I handled each piece and we were lost in our memories.

We had intended to play a few hands of cribbage but it had been a tiring day and I could see that Father was in some pain so we retired to bed instead.

The jewellery box is now on my side table and, although my head is heavy with drink, I shall read a few sonnets before I blow out the candle.

I have been managing Oakwood for five years now but tomorrow, when I wake, I shall truly feel like its mistress.

~ 13 ~
The Diary

"I had to go back to the House Book to check, but there's no doubt, this is Alice's diary, Thomas Crayford's daughter. She was only fifteen when her mother died and she ran the house, and the farm, as well as doing all the accounts; they're in the same awful handwriting. It seems she was an old hand at it by the time she started this diary."

Rob picked up the copy Janie had made of the first diary entry. "How long did it take you to do this? I didn't hear you come to bed."

"Oh, I don't know, I think I got to bed about 3."

Rob nodded to the pile of account books. "Are there any others in there?"

"No, I've checked. This is the only one."

Promising to read it later, Rob was keen to get over to his new studio. The builders, electrician and plumber were finishing off in the office and the washroom, but the main studio was more or less done and he could get in to measure up for shelving and storage units. "No surprise what you'll be doing for the rest of the day, then," and he ruffled Janie's hair as he made his way to the back door. "Just remember, Miss Hunter thinks you're working from home, today…"

Janie ignored him, glanced at her watch, and decided to give herself another hour before heading up to her office. She drummed her fingers, wondering if anyone else had discovered

Alice's diary; it looked just like all the other account books and Langridge hadn't mentioned it. So…perhaps she wouldn't either.

She didn't have time for more transcribing, but she flicked through the diary to see how much damage there was, and how many years it covered. A name caught her eye, and she turned the pages back to find it again. 'Ann Bean', it was quite clear but, nevertheless, Janie found a magnifying glass to make sure. Still thinking that, perhaps, she had a false memory of something, she took the diary up to her office where all her University material lay in boxes waiting to be unpacked, and knelt down to try and find the right book. Seventeenth century literature had not been her thing, but the name Ann Bean definitely rang a bell. Forty minutes later, she found the reference, and as she sat back on her heels and started to read, her heart skipped a beat.

The phone rang, Janie was jolted back to the present, and the fax machine chattered into life. Ann Bean would have to wait

***

"Why are you looking so pleased with yourself," Rob said, as Janie came down the back stairs, grinning from ear to ear. "Don't tell me you've signed up the next Stephen King?"

"No, but I think I have made an exciting discovery. I've been busy all day, so I haven't had time to check it out thoroughly, but, when I have, I'll tell you all about it," and she dumped several text books on the kitchen table.

"Give me a clue. Is it to do with work, or this?" and he held up her transcript of Alice's first diary entry.

"That, have you read it yet?"

"I have, and you're right. Women in those days, or at least some of them, obviously did more than we give them credit for. Are you going to do the rest of the diary?"

"I want to, but I don't think I can. There's quite a bit of damage in some parts and, if anything, the writing gets more and more difficult to read, but I think I might be able to persuade an old colleague to do it for me.

***

"Professor Taylor's office."

The officious tone still grated on her. "Valerie, it's Janie Whitt... Mallory here. Is the professor in his office?"

"Janie Mallory. Gosh, it's a long time since we heard from you. Are you thinking of coming back?"

And how you'd hate that, thought Janie. "No, I'm happy doing what I'm doing. I just have something to discuss with the boss, if he's around."

"Well, he's very busy at the moment. It is end of term, you know. Just wait a moment, please," and then, a few seconds later, "putting you through now."

"Obersturmbahnfurher Charlton is still protecting you from underlings, I see, Professor."

He chuckled. "Ah, but she can't keep me from talking to my favourite protégée. How are you, Janie?"

Once the social chit chat was over, Richard Taylor listened carefully to Janie's description of the diary and the reference to Ann Bean, a known pseudonym of a seventeenth century character of great interest to him - Aphra Behn. "Is that the only reference to her?"

"It's hard to tell. The diary's not in great shape and the handwriting's really difficult to read, for me it is, anyway. I don't think you'd have any trouble though..." She let the unspoken question hang in the air.

"Janie, if you want me to look at it, I'd be delighted, because if it is Aphra, then it's a rare find. So much of her life is shrouded in mystery. Are you in a hurry for this?"

Janie laughed. "Only because I'm curious and impatient to know about Alice and Aphra and any other revelations the diary's going to throw up."

"Well, me too, but you know how crazy it is at the end of this term, and then it's Christmas."

They agreed to meet up again in January.

~ 14 ~
Oakwood Grange, November 1664

The household had retired a while ago and all was quiet. Only Thomas was awake, seated in his favourite chair with one leg propped up on a stool, his dog softly snoring by his side and the guttering candles casting chasing shadows over the walls. The fire was dying but it still provided some warmth and he saw no need to move either his bad leg or his dog to reach for another log.

Things were occupying his mind and he needed this time alone with only his dog, his pipe and a glass of port to go over his plans once again and consider his course of action. Of late, Thomas had felt that the time left to him may be short and, being a religious man, had spoken at length with his old friend, the Reverend Fawcett. They had both agreed that arrangements should be made for Alice.

Alice, the miracle child of his late middle age, first-born to a mother of 43 years of age and who was so like Anne that, if he didn't love her so much, he wouldn't be able to look upon her. Anne's death had been the turning point for him. Lethargy had crept over him, his eyes had lost their focus and old age had gradually overtaken him. It was fortunate indeed that Alice had been there, at first just to help with the running of the house, but eventually she had taken over the management and accounts of both the household and the farm. It's true that there had been tensions with Henry Durling who, at *first, had felt it beneath him to report to a young woman he'd known as a child and still regarded as one, but her willingness to take his advice and learn as much as she could about the farm, its practices and its workers, had brought him round. Most days, after dealing with Cook and any other household business, Alice could be seen around the farm, either on her horse or sometimes in the small trap which Durling had suggested was more suitable for a young woman. She much preferred to ride, insisting that all parts of the farm were more accessible on horseback, but the cart came in useful from time to time. Thomas knew there were many occasions when she wished she'd been born a man – and many occasions when Durling wished she had as well – but she hadn't. That was the problem.*

Thomas was not unaware that this arrangement was somewhat unorthodox but it had been expedient to ignore it, especially as everything seemed to be going so well and everyone was content. It was the Reverend Fawcett who had pointed out that, as far as the county was concerned, Thomas was still running things and that it was inconceivable that Alice, as a single woman, and Durling, a single man, could continue to manage the farm together after Thomas's death.

Thomas wondered, not for the first time, if he had been wise to allow Anne to educate their daughter.

Anne was a single woman of 41 years when she became his second wife. His first marriage, to Margaret, had been arranged by their families; they were, in fact, second cousins, and very young. Margaret was dainty and very pretty with not a thought in her head beyond dresses, parties and dancing and had not enjoyed the enforced confinements of her pregnancies. Their two sons had been sent away to school at the earliest convenience.

It had not been in Thomas's mind to wed again after Margaret died. Apart from producing two strapping boys, one of whom would surely take over the running of the farm one day, his marriage had given him little pleasure and Margaret's presence in later years had become like an itch he could not scratch. Her death freed him to pull down his house, a plan Margaret had vehemently opposed, and build a new home; a project that had invigorated him, consumed him and which had introduced him to Anne, the architect's daughter.

Having an interest in all things artistic, or, at least, that was the reason given, Anne accompanied her father as often as possible to Thomas's new house and, during the eighteen months it took to build, she and Thomas became very close. They married just as the house became habitable and Thomas experienced a joy and a passion that he had never dreamt was possible. Even more surprising to him, apart from the love he felt for her, was that, intellectually and educationally, Anne was more than a match for him. Their conversations were lively and stimulating and she encouraged him to take up reading again. Modest in all things, Anne rarely paraded her intelligence and keen wit, the exceptions being only to expose the pompous or the lying. The stupid, she felt, needed no help from her and she left them alone. Thomas did, once, ask her why she had remained unmarried for so long as it was surely not due to lack of offers. She merely replied, "Young men think only of themselves. They have nothing interesting to say until they reach middle age."

Having long resigned herself to childlessness, Alice's arrival came as rather a delightful shock to Anne. Thomas's sons had visited to congratulate their father and stepmother and, for two wonderful days in 1643, the family had celebrated, feasted and generally enjoyed each other's company. It was a golden time forever etched in Thomas's memory as, first Edward and then Richard, were lost fighting for King Charles in the Civil War.

Alice grew to be a willing pupil, soaking up every bit of knowledge Anne had to give, but the contempt she felt for 'womanly pursuits' such as sewing and sketching was entirely her own. Anne had tried, but failed, to interest her in these subjects and Alice frequently chose to accompany her father on his rounds of the farm rather than stay indoors.

Thomas drained his glass and placed it on the side table next to his wife's miniature. He picked it up, holding it very close for a few moments, although he needed no reminder of her likeness. The wavy chestnut hair framing a heart shaped face with a little pointed chin, the soft brown eyes and generous mouth – he saw these every day in Alice. "I do hope I'm doing the right thing, Anne," he said aloud as he replaced the miniature on the table.

Alice must marry. That was the solution Reverend Fawcett and he had arrived at, but persuading Alice of this was not going to be easy. The first problem was how to explain the urgency of a marriage without divulging his own ill health and the second problem was finding a suitable match. Although Alice enjoyed music and dancing at home, she was not keen to attend functions with the other young ladies of the area, whom she regarded as frivolous, and so there was little opportunity to meet eligible young men. In the five years since her mother had died, she had attended only two balls, celebrating the engagements of her cousins, and she wore a dress of her mother's altered by Jennet. Following each of these, several young men had attempted to pay court but Alice had politely, but firmly, rebuffed them and was not at all concerned that, at 21 years old, she was fast being considered a spinster.

The Reverend, keen to help his old friend who he knew to be completely out of his depth when it came to Alice, thought he had found a solution. Whilst visiting Chichester recently to congratulate his friend Joseph Gulston on his new appointment as Dean of Chichester Cathedral, Reverend Fawcett was introduced to William Harryman, the son of a mutual acquaintance. William impressed

Fawcett; he was a handsome man in his thirties, from a good family, a religious man and one who had suffered great loss. A few years ago his young wife had died in childbirth and the baby boy had also died some days later. William and his father, who had been bitterly divided over the Civil War - William and his in-laws were for Parliament and Mr. Harryman senior was staunchly for the monarchy - were reconciled in 1661 after the loss of William's family and after Charles II was restored to the throne. Shortly afterwards, Harryman senior died and William discovered that his inheritance had been woefully depleted as all but two of his father's properties had been sold to provide money for the Crown. As a gentleman of now limited means, his future was uncertain and he was contemplating a religious life.

Thomas could see the sense of an alliance between Alice and William. William was older, experienced and would provide the firm hand that Alice, in his opinion, would need. Their friends and neighbours would accept him as a gentleman, as long as he didn't parade his politics too much, and Alice would have the status and security she needed to enable her to stay at the farm. For his part, William gained a young wife, the prospect of a new family and a stable future. Surely, even Anne could not have chosen a better match.

~ 15 ~
Late November 1985

Gilbert Langridge had chosen the day well. The recent wet spell had been replaced by dry, very cold weather, but unusually for November, it was bright and sunny.

He'd debated long and hard with himself over the best time to scatter Tom's ashes. Logic told him that there was no hurry and that Spring might seem the most appropriate time to do it, although why, he couldn't say, unless you believed in rebirth. Summer seemed wrong, somehow, all that death strewn over so much life, and autumn was just too far away. No, he told himself, there was no point in delaying, Tom wouldn't have wanted to hang around, and would probably have been amused to know that his remains would be mingled with the mulch to ensure the growth of the garden come next year. He smiled a little smile, and why keep Harry waiting?

Sitting at his breakfast table and savouring his morning tea, Langridge's thoughts returned to the memorial service. It's true that Tom most likely would have hated the idea, but there was nothing in his long letter to indicate that there shouldn't be one, and anyway, a memorial service is for the living to pay their respects – not for the dead.

The vicar of St. John's was a new appointee and he'd had nothing more than a passing acquaintance with Tom, who'd stopped going to church when Harriet died. Langridge had noted the surprise on his face when he'd conducted the service to a full house, something the new vicar had only seen on Christmas Eve, and his relief that the solicitor had made most of the arrangements and delivered the eulogy. Tom's only living relatives were his estranged family in Australia and some cousins in Ireland, who had declined to make the trip, but it was no matter. From the pulpit, Langridge had looked out over the crowded pews and seen nearly the whole village; most local businesses had closed for the day, although the pub was one notable exception. He also recognised ex-patients from outlying villages, families who, in some cases, had known only one doctor for three generations.

He'd been a little nervous about the eulogy, with respect to both the content and delivery, but the response had been better than he'd hoped for and the anecdotes had gone down well. There were tears and laughter, and he was pleased to see that Rob and Janie, who'd slipped in at the back of the church, now knew how well Dr. Kelly had been respected and had devoted his life to this community. The solicitor had made a point of thanking the Whittakers at the end of his speech, for allowing Tom's ashes to be scattered in the garden at the Grange. It was time, he felt, that they should be acknowledged and welcomed.

Today, though, was going to be completely different and, possibly, even more emotional.

The early morning frost was fast disappearing as Langridge parked his car in the Grange's drive. It looked as if he was the first to arrive and he popped his head through the open garden gate to take a quick look at the garden before making his way to the back door. He stopped, reminding himself that this was no longer Tom's house but, as he turned to go round to the front, he saw Janie tapping the kitchen window and pointing the other way.

"Mr. Langridge, you are always welcome at my back door any day of the week. Come in. So far, only people peddling alternative religions and builders shovelling rubbish into the skip have used the front door."

Langridge laughed. "That's what happens in the country, no one stands on ceremony here."

Rob joined them in the kitchen and shook hands. "Good to see you again, Mr. Langridge. We thought you gave a wonderful eulogy last week, and wasn't it an amazing turn out? Nearly the whole village."

"With the exception of Stuart Burrows at the pub." Janie turned to the solicitor. "When we first went in there for a drink, he was really offhand with us when we started talking about Tom. What was the problem there?"

"It goes back a long way. Burrows had an 'understanding' with Tom's first wife, Mary Fletcher as she was then, who threw him over when she realised she could do better for herself and set her cap at the handsome young doctor. Tom was a single man in his thirties, and I know that there was considerable pressure put to bear on him by the senior in his practice, who considered that female patients wouldn't want to be seen by an unmarried man." Langridge's mouth turned down and he made a little gesture. "It was a different world in the forties, and so he got married. Inevitably, the marriage failed, and this presented an even bigger problem for the practice when Tom and Mary got divorced. It was ten years later, but there was still a stigma attached to divorce, especially for a professional person, but luckily, he was well established by then and the old partner had retired."

"Still," said Rob, "it wasn't an easy thing to do back then, was it?"

"Certainly not. There were only three reasons to grant a divorce; adultery, cruelty and desertion. Poor Tom agreed to be photographed doing the necessary, although I rather think that Mary was no angel, and the judge waved it through. Most villagers were sympathetic to Tom, but Burrows, of course, never forgave him for pinching his girl and 'ruining her life' as well as his."

Footsteps on the gravel drive caught their attention, and Janie went to open the back door to Lydia Cartwright and Mr. Hedges, the gardener, who was looking uncomfortable in suit and tie. Lydia made a beeline for Rob and was giving him a big hug when a second car turned into the drive, bringing Ludo and his father, Rupert Green, to complete the small party.

There was no ceremony. It was agreed by all, that each person would take their turn to scatter Tom's ashes in a different part of the garden, with Gilbert Langridge, who knew him best, taking the last turn. He scattered the remaining portion directly around the base of a standard rose given to Harriet by Tom on their silver wedding anniversary.

Instinctively, they'd all clustered around the bench where Tom had breathed his last, and they stood, heads bowed for a minute's silence before making a move to go.

Rob stopped them. "Just before you go, Janie and I want your opinion on something. It occurred to us that, with no gravestones in the churchyard for either Harriet or Tom, there's nothing tangible to link them to this place and this village they loved so much, and there should be." He reached under Tom's bench and unwrapped a plaque. It was a metal disc, about 15" across, delicately enamelled in pale blue, and with an inscription in black, which read:

In memory of Harriet and Tom Kelly, who loved this place.
November 1985

"We were thinking of fixing it to the wall in this garden, just over there. What do you think?" Rob laid it down on the bench and everyone but Langridge went to have a better look. There was a general buzz of surprise and appreciation.

"That's a wonderful gesture, both of you, thank you. I wish I'd thought of it myself." The solicitor reached up to clap Rob on the back and then, he too, went for a closer look.

Back in the warmth of the kitchen, there were scones and tea, and a rich chocolate cake, courtesy of Lydia. It was Tom's favourite and one she'd frequently made for the Kellys. Gilbert Langridge watched them all, chatting and sharing reminiscences, unsurprised that life in this house was continuing, as it always had, in an informal way in the kitchen. Eventually, there were thanks all round, hats and coats retrieved, and once Hedges had managed to prise Lydia away from Rob, everyone took their leave.

***

"Don't you go sloping off, Whittaker, when there's all this clearing up to be done." Janie threw a tea towel, which landed on his head. "Come on. I'll wash and you can dry."

"God, you're a hard woman." Rob snatched at the towel and whipped it across her rear. "I'm going to buy you a dishwasher for Christmas."

"I dare you."

Looping the tea towel round her waist, Rob drew her close and nuzzled her neck. She squirmed, then took his face in both hands, kissed him and flattened his hair where the towel had ruffled it. "Yeah, that's not going to work either."

They quickly managed to clear everything away, agreed that life was too short to put off getting a dishwasher, and decided that they would have to spend some time soon finalising the details for the next phase of renovations. As there was still a couple of hours left in the day for useful work, Rob crept out to the studio and Janie settled down with Alice's diary. It felt like a guilty pleasure

***

Rob rubbed his hands together, "It's bitter out there now," and pressed cold fingers against Janie's cheek.

"Go away. Why don't you make a hot drink to warm yourself up?" She looked up from her notes and grinned. "Mine's a gin and tonic, please."

Delivering the glass with a flourish, Rob looked over her shoulder, "I see you have a new toy," indicating a stand-alone magnifying glass.

"Mm. Easier than the hand held thing, but it's still slow progress, I'm afraid." She wrapped her arms round his thighs and rested her head on his side.

"Never mind. Your professor'll sort you out in the New Year," and he planted a kiss on her head and gently released himself when the kettle boiled. "Which reminds me," he said, over his shoulder, "you promised to tell me about your exciting find."

Janie stretched to ease out her back, released her hair from the clip and quickly massaged her head, leaving her with messy blonde curls. Rob felt the familiar hitch somewhere inside; she still had the power to stop him in his tracks, even when she wasn't trying.

"I'm not sure it is an exciting find yet. It might be just wishful thinking on my part, but I'll tell you what I'm hoping it is." She pushed the diary and notepad away from her and attacked the gin and tonic.

"In Alice's diary, when I was flicking through it, I noticed the name Ann Bean. Now, it may be nothing, but Ann Bean was one pseudonym, she had others, of a woman called Aphra Behn, who became a celebrated writer and playwright in the seventeenth century."

"Really? That must have been unusual, eh?"

"It was, hence one of the reasons she became famous," Janie gave him a sideways look, "and that wasn't the only reason she was famous, or infamous. It's fairly well documented that she was a spy for Charles II and spent some time abroad, but I read in one of my texts that she had difficulty getting paid by the Crown and fell into debt. Crucially, in 1667, there was a warrant out for her arrest, and guess when Ann Bean appears in Alice's diary? 1667."

"Ah, I see. Do we know what happened to this Aphra?"

"We know that, somehow, she got out of trouble and then supported herself as a playwright, as well as writing poetry and novels. Her plays were considered on the bawdy side, but I think they probably all were in Charles II's time."

Rob laughed. "She sounds a handful. I'd love to think this house played host to a woman like that. What a shame walls can't talk."

~ 16 ~
Early December 1985

The banging was driving her mad. On and on, it went, with monotonous regularity. Janie was feeling rubbish and regretted asking the builders to do the fireplace before Christmas. Nice idea, but the noise and the mess and the dust all through the house was difficult to cope with at the best of times, and this wasn't the best of times. She had a ton of work to do, a cold coming or, quite possibly, flu, the way she was feeling, and she'd just learned that Rob had invited his family over for Christmas, 'That's okay, isn't it, Janie?' Actually, it was okay, she got on really well with them, but it was all too much to think about at the moment.

She left her office, found an old rugby shirt of Rob's to put on over her jumper, went downstairs and poked her head round the snug door. "Cup of tea, John?"

The hammering stopped briefly and John pulled down his dust mask. "Lovely, Mrs. Whittaker. Two whites with two sugars each, please."

Waiting for the kettle to boil, Janie stood with her back to the range, arms folded, trying to stop shivering. She loved this kitchen, and the longer she worked in it, the less she thought about changing it. Their first idea, well her first idea anyway, had been to completely rip it out, range and all, but as the summer warmth faded, Janie began to appreciate the charms of the great hulk of metal behind her. It did feel like the beating heart of the house. She laughed now to remember her initial reaction to it; 'How can I cook on that when there are no knobs?' Well, she had learned how, and it was surprisingly easy.

Janie kicked the snug door to be let in, and she set the tray down on a dustsheet-covered table.

"Chocolate digestives, you spoil us, Mrs. Whittaker." John and his son downed tools at once. Janie stared at the gaping hole in the wall and the pile of broken rubble on the floor. "Don't you worry about the mess. We'll soon have all that cleared up when we're finished and you'll have a grand fireplace." He could see she wasn't convinced. "It'll be right, you wait and see."

A hot, lemon and honey drink and two painkillers later, and back upstairs in her office, Janie still couldn't make any headway with her work, but she wasn't overly concerned. The office in London was running like clockwork, her two new assistants were bright and keen and, although Joyce Hunter's role was now, primarily, Janie's PA and general gatekeeper, she also managed the office as she had always done and kept an eye on the new employees. This new Miss Hunter was also up to speed with all the technological advances in word processing and was the prime mover in updating office practices. Janie had given her a substantial pay rise, and the Joyce Hunter who greeted Antony Mallory on one of his rare visits to the office, was not only more confident, but had shed a stone in weight and looked ten years younger.

Janie made a quick phone call to tell her that she was taking tomorrow off and would be in on Monday.

Peace seemed to have broken out downstairs and Janie leaned on her desk, rested her poor aching head on her arms and gazed at the view through the window. Even in winter it was a beautiful sight; a hazy sun was burning the morning frost from the meadows and hedgerows, and the huge oak trees, markers of ancient boundaries, spread their black limbs against a grey sky. A dog fox made its way warily across the nearest meadow, stopped to scratch the ground, searching for any tiny morsel, and then, startled by something only he could hear, ran for the woods.

I love it here, thought Janie, especially just here, in this room. She knew she should probably go and lie down, but her office was so warm and cosy …

A waft of chilly air came and went just as quickly, and Janie half opened her eyes to check that the window was closed. Satisfied, she let her eyelids droop again, her face muscles relaxed, and, very soon, her breathing became slow and shallow. Behind her eyes, she was still seeing the meadows and the trees, but it was Spring and everything was alive and buzzing outside her window. Now she was looking down onto a garden that shouldn't be there, a kitchen garden with a gate out to the fields, and she could smell something, something familiar, but she couldn't quite put her finger on it. Perhaps it was the rambler tapping on the window. She felt such lightness in her body and such a sense of peace and wellbeing, that she didn't want to move, but the banging had started again so she rubbed her eyes and quickly ran her fingers through her hair. To her surprise, she found her 'short nap' had been more like two hours.

She knew what that smell was now, it was rosemary, and the daydream had been so real, that she fancied she could still smell it. Janie got up to leave the room but, a little disconcerted, she doubled back and opened the window wide. The garden was exactly as she knew it would be, lawn and shrubbery, and there was no rose round her window. Of course there wasn't. She pulled the casement to, with a bang, and rattled it to make sure it was tightly closed.

***

Feeling a lot better since her 'nap' and, completely at odds with how she'd felt earlier when bed seemed to be the answer, Janie now fancied a breath of fresh air. The beginning of December had turned very wintery, and she shrugged her thick waterproof over Rob's shirt, slipped into her wellies and made for the walled garden to see if Mr. Hedges (that still tickled her) wanted a drink.

Hedges, who appeared not to feel the cold, had the sleeves of his woolly, checked shirt rolled up and the tail firmly tucked into his thick baggy trousers secured by belt and braces. He whipped off a glove and wiped the dewdrop from the end of his nose when he spotted her coming through the gate. "No, I'm fine. Thanks anyway, Mrs. Whittaker." He indicated the tools stacked in the wheelbarrow. "I'm going to give this lot a good clean, oil 'em and hang 'em up so's they'll be ready for Spring, and then I'm off home. There's not much more I can do in here now, I've put it all to bed for the winter." He smiled at his own little joke, and his face wrinkled like so much brown paper.

"Thank you so much." Janie had taken to this old boy, and she flashed him one of her most radiant smiles. "I really don't know what we would have done without you these last few months. I can't tell you how much we appreciate you coming back to work for us." She made a mental note to send him something special for Christmas. "I'm not quite sure what arrangement you had with Dr. Kelly; do we give you a ring when we want you back or what?"

"No, there's no need. I'll know when the time's right and I'll just turn up, if that's all right with you. But, if there's anything you want doing in winter, like ditch clearing or log splitting or 'owt like that, then just give us a ring." He winked and nudged her with his elbow. "I'll be bored, so I won't mind coming over." Janie was left in no doubt that there might be another reason for him wanting to get out of the house.

"Right. Well, we'll see you in Spring then. Hopefully, Rob and I will both be spending a bit more time at home and you'll have some help. I'll be useless; I know nothing about gardening, but Rob's really keen to get into it again. You'll have at least one willing pupil."

Hedges trundled off to the shed and Janie sat on the bench where Tom had been found. It wasn't morbid fascination. On the contrary, she felt drawn to it at times when she needed comfort or reassurance, as if the spirits of Tom and Harriet were watching over them and confirming their right to belong in this place.

She heard a tapping off to her left, and saw Rob waving to her from his studio window. She saw him mouthing, 'Come here.'

He pulled her in through his office door. "What on earth are you doing sitting out there? You'll catch your death, you stupid girl, you should be in bed." He wrapped her in a bear hug and rubbed her back, before kissing each cheek. "You're cold, come with me." He led her through to the studio, and pushed her into a shabby old armchair he'd rescued from the house and placed in front of his log burner. "There, now I'm going to make us a coffee. Wait there till I come back."

She eased off her wellies and checked out the studio. He'd been working hard to get it all up and running before Christmas and it was looking great. Most of the storage and equipment he needed from the London studio was already in situ, much to Gilly's relief, as she was running out of space for her work, and he'd managed to put up the shelving since she was last in here. The log burner was brilliant, all thanks to John Hobden; it was so warm she was taking her jacket off as well when Rob came back. He was carrying a plastic bag and he pulled out an Italian espresso maker, a relic from his first flat, followed by a pint of milk, a bag of sugar, two mugs and a spoon.

Janie looked at him, "Coffee?"

"Oh, shit," and he was off again.

Janie was feeling so much better. She wasn't shivery any longer and the pain behind her eyes had disappeared. She went to the sink and filled the espresso maker just as Rob came back, panting. "Out of shape, Whittaker?"

"Not as fit as I used to be, that's for sure." He spooned in the coffee, screwed the top back and went over to the log burner. "I haven't tried this before, you're witnessing the inaugural firing of this thing, but John got this model because it has a hob on top. Look." He stood back proudly, one hand on his hip and the other pointing, conjuror's assistant style, to the hob. "Do you think it'll work?"

They were both a bit sceptical. Rob told her how much better she looked, and she'd just started to tell him about her weird dream, or daydream, when the pot started spitting and bouncing on the hob. "It's definitely worked, but I think you might have to turn this thing down a bit." Janie knelt down to have a good look. "There must be a damper or some way of regulating it."

"Yes, I'm sure there is, but you're not going to fix it now. Here, let's toast the studio with our very first cup of coffee. Cheers."

"Cheers. I must admit, I was wondering where you were going to heat the pot. I thought perhaps you'd bought one of those little electric plug-in hobs. But this," and she stretched her stockinged feet out in front of the fire, "is so much better. Next time I go shopping, I'm going to get you a little fridge so that we can have fresh milk all year round and chilled beer in the summer."

"We? Don't get any fancy ideas about moving in here, missus. You've got your own warm little office above the kitchen. I can't have you in here, distracting me."

"Okay, I'm off now," and she pulled her wellies back on. "I tell you what, though, have you thought of putting your museum posters on that wall over there? I think they'd look great…"

Rob pointed the way out.

***

As the banging had been replaced by a more bearable scraping sound, Janie made a sandwich for herself and took it back up to her office. Several faxes were waiting for her and she got cracking on the work that she'd abandoned in the morning. It went so well, she even got round to making a very tricky phone call to a publishing house that, in her opinion, was offering a less then attractive deal to her client. She played hardball and won. Nothing like success to make you feel good.

She was looking forward to next year now. A few months ago, she'd taken on a guy who'd been a sub-editor for a publisher, with a view to begin editing their clients' work, in-house. It had been a risk, but Chris was so good at his job, that they were already seeing an uptake on submissions from their first time authors. Janie's two assistants, both recent graduates, were learning fast and only bothered her when she was working at home if Miss Hunter couldn't help them. All in all, she thought, sitting back with a satisfied little smile, the business was ticking over nicely and she had no jitters about dropping her London days down to three after Christmas. Antony had raised his eyebrows at her decision when she had first mentioned it, but the business had changed so much in the last few years, and one look at the balance sheet told him that Janie knew what she was doing. As, apparently, did Miss Hunter, and he felt a little pang of guilt remembering how he'd done nothing to develop her talents. His wife would have been furious with him.

***

Rob found Janie in the kitchen preparing something for supper. "You're supposed to be ill. What are you doing?"

She stopped chopping and turned round. "As you can see, I'm feeling lots better. I took two painkillers this morning, had a little sleep and, since then, I've been okay." A quick glance at the clock and she carried on, "I hope you're not slacking, Whittaker. Have you finished for the day?"

"It's chilly in there now. The wood burner's gone out and we've run out of logs. I'll order some more tomorrow."

"That would have been a good excuse if you didn't have electric wall heaters."

Rob caught her round the waist and kissed the back of her neck. "How about I just wanted to spend time with my lovely, but poorly, wife...."

There was a cough, and John Hobden's son was standing in the doorway, not quite knowing how to attract their attention. Rob stepped away from his wife, "Yes, Kevin, did you want us?"

"Dad says he's got something he wants to show you, if you've got a minute."

~ 17 ~
Later

"There, I told you there'd be a decent fireplace, didn't I?" John Hobden, covered in a fine dusting of plaster and brick dust, leaned an elbow on his son's shoulder and they were both nodding.

"It's huge." Rob walked round all the rubble to get a better look. "I think it's even bigger than the one in the drawing room."

Janie joined him and they both stepped inside the inglenook and sat facing each other on the little wooden benches built in on each side of the hearth. "Very cosy, we look like a couple of bookends. I can't see a bread oven, though. There would have been one, wouldn't there, John?"

John shook his head. "Not in this room, and certainly not in the drawing room where you've got that lovely stone surround. No, any cooking going on in this house would've been confined to the kitchen, where your range is now. That fireplace was probably all stripped out when the oven was put in, but at least they left the bressummer exposed."

"They did?" Rob looked at Janie, puzzled, and she shrugged her shoulders, "What's a bressummer?"

Kevin pointed to the partially exposed oak beam, which acted as a lintel over the fireplace opening. "That's a bressummer; derived from 'breast, meaning mid-level, at the front, and 'summer' meaning a supporting beam, a term thought to come from the old French for a beast of burden." He turned to look

92

at John, who nodded and squeezed his shoulder in a rare act of fatherly pride.

Apart from receiving this completely unexpected piece of knowledge, this was the longest and most articulate sentence that either Rob or Janie had ever heard Kevin utter, and they were temporarily speechless. Kevin blushed and brushed the hair from his eyes. "Dad taught me that."

"Good knowledge, Kevin, I'm impressed," and to spare his embarrassment, Janie quickly stepped out of the opening, smacked the dust from her bottom and examined the part of the bressummer she could see.

John was keen to crack on. "Well, it's up to you two, whether or not you want it exposed. But, if you're asking me, it'd be a shame to leave it covered up."

They were all in agreement and the builders decided to work late, even though it was a Friday and they usually knocked off early. John wanted to finish chipping the plaster off the beam and part of the wall, and Kevin was set to work, wheelbarrowing all the mess out of the front door and into the skip, which was due to be picked up in the morning. It was seven o'clock before they'd finished and the Whittakers were enjoying a pre dinner drink in the kitchen when Kevin, once again, was sent to fetch them.

"Goodness, Kevin," Janie was wide-eyed in surprise when they reached the snug, "you can come and do my housework any time."

"We like to leave things tidy, don't we, lad?" Kevin nodded; he was getting used to the attention by now. "So, what do you think?

There were still some bits of plaster attached to the bressummer, but it was going to look really impressive, they could see that.

John chucked a damp rag to his son, "Give it another wipe down, so's they can see the marks," and as Kevin wiped, patterns emerged; daisy-like stylised flowers and what looked like letters, all along the length of the beam. John added, "Once it's cleaned properly and got a few coats of wax on it, those marks'll stand out more than they do now."

Rob was running his hand over the carving. "Someone's decorated this with their initials. I can make out M's, V's and W's. We could look in the House Book, Janie, to see who they might belong to."

"You won't find them there. Tell 'em, Kevin, you know a lot about this."

"They're apotropaic marks, or witches' marks," and, seeing the look on Janie's face, Kevin added quickly, "but they're nothing to get worked up about. It seems most people believed in witchcraft back then, and we often find marks like these in the houses we work in." He went over to the fireplace and pointed to the daisy-like flowers. "And you see this design here? That was meant to ward off witches and their …. Dad?"

"Familiars."

"That's it, their familiars, cats and suchlike. And these initials here, the ones that look like a W, those are two V's, not a W, and they stand for Virgin of Virgins. The M stands for Mary. So, whoever carved this was asking for protection from the Virgin Mary."

Rob said, "That seems weird now, doesn't it? Superstitious and religious at the same time."

Kevin was on a roll and was about to impart even more on the subject, when his father interrupted him. "As the lad said, there's nothing to be concerned about. In fact, it'd be a bit strange if we didn't find some of these marks somewhere in a house like this." He patted Janie's arm as he passed her on their way out. "Well, we'll be off now. Have a good weekend and we'll see you, nice and early, on Monday morning."

As John put his van into gear and pulled out of the drive, Kevin said, "I was just about to tell them about the cavity up the chimney. Why did you stop me?"

"Why do you think? Did you see that lassie's face? I'm not sure she's ready for whatever might be lurking up there. I'll talk to Mr. Whittaker next week, see what he wants to do."

"It's interesting though, isn't it, Dad? Have you ever seen so many marks as that, with such deep carving?"

"No, I haven't. Whoever did that, was a worried man, or woman. But I'm not sure a woman would have had the strength to carve oak like that."

~ 18 ~
December 1985

Rob had been catching up with Ludo to check that he was satisfied with all the new branding and that Gilly was providing him with everything he needed. It appeared that all was good; there'd already been a marked increase in enquiries from buyers and sellers alike and Ludo couldn't have been happier.

They'd had lunch in yet another lovely old pub in yet another lovely village that Rob didn't know existed and, on his way back home, found himself driving through Thatchling, where Janie had once shown him the cottage where her grandparents used to live. He stopped in the main street and turned off the engine.

He'd been a bit concerned about Janie recently. Each evening, she pored over Harriet's copy of the House Book, making a note of all the surnames and maiden names of past owners and servants alike, and had made an attempt to start transcribing Alice's diary again, even though her old professor had promised to look at it in the New Year. She'd laughed off Rob's suggestion that she was trying to find something or somebody to link her to the house with a "Well, you never know…but, really, I'm just interested in the social history of the place." He hadn't pushed it. Although Janie's Russian heritage was something she'd always known about, her Russian grandmother had made sure of that, Janie had never felt anything other than English, and Rob suspected that this research was all about her need to be rooted in this part of the country where she felt so at home. And that meant resurrecting the Richardsons, whether they had a connection to the house or not, and confronting the past.

Finding a convenient parking space outside the village shop-cum-post office, he decided that it was as good a place as any to start. A loud bell rang out as he ducked in through the low doorway and then skirted round a stand of Christmas cards to find the tiny post office behind a mesh screen offering little resistance to even the feeblest of would-be burglars. Whatever he was expecting, the person sitting behind the counter was not it. Chewing gum and reading a magazine, she eventually looked up and took an interest, "Help you?" Her dyed, white blonde hair with shocking pink tips was short and spiky and framed, quite possibly, a pretty face, but difficult to be sure under the thick layers of black eye make up and lipstick. She stood up and leaned on the counter, temporarily forgetting to look bored, and gave him a good view of what lay beneath the torn black tee shirt held together with nappy pins.

"Hi." Rob dimpled one of his most charming smiles.

"Hi, yourself."

"Er…I'm not sure you can help me. I was wondering if there was anyone here who might remember the Richardsons, who used to live in the village about twenty-odd years ago? Perhaps your Mum or Dad…."

"Nah, we've only been here five years or so. You could try The Bull, though. Grumpy old git who runs that place has been here since the year dot, he might know."

"Great, that's really helpful. Thanks."

"You're welcome. Sure there's nothing else I can help you with?" She cocked her head slightly to one side and gave him a look that left him in no doubt what was on offer.

Winking, in what he hoped was a fatherly fashion, he backed straight into the Christmas card stand on his way to the door, but even the sound of her laughter couldn't stop him from feeling smug. Good to know he still had it, even though the only urge he had was to see her cleaned up and in some decent clothes.

He checked his watch. The pub might still be open and he crossed the road and ran the hundred yards, hoping the landlord would be behind the bar. "Afternoon, sir. You look like a thirsty man. What can I get you?" Rob ordered a pint of bitter and answered the usual questions about who he was and where he came from, which led him neatly to the reason he was there. "Aye, I do remember the Richardsons. Nice family, lived up Mill Lane, she was a teacher and he was...um… Joe?" An old boy, sitting by himself in a corner, nursing the remains of a half, looked up. "You remember the Richardsons from up Mill Lane – what did he do?"

"He was a brewer."

"That's right, he was, I remember now. They rented that Mulberry Cottage from the brewery. Joe can most likely tell you more than me."

Rob ordered a pint of whatever Joe was drinking, and delivered it to his table. "Mind if I join you, Joe?"

Joe thanked him, supped his ale, and listened to Rob explaining how his wife needed to make contact with her grandmother and uncle, if they were still alive. Squinting through a cloud of pipe smoke, the old man could offer no information about where they were now, although he and his wife had been very friendly with Jim and Anna Richardson, back when their boys were growing up together. Rob asked if there was anyone else in the village who might know where they went to, and Joe said he couldn't promise anything but, if Rob wanted to leave his phone number, he'd make some enquiries for him.

"That's very kind of you, thank you." Rob borrowed a pen from the landlord and wrote down his name and address. "If you find anything out, I'd be grateful if you could drop me a line instead of phoning; I don't want Janie to know about this yet. If there's good news, I need to tell her when the time's right."

They shook hands and Rob thanked both the men again. The landlord waved him out and locked up after him. "Seems like a nice lad, Joe. You going to help him?"

"I might."

Joe reached into his pocket for his tobacco pouch and fiddled with his pipe, deep in thought. His son, Peter, and Mark Richardson had been great mates, both bright, scholarship boys but, possibly, not as clever as Fiona. Fiona, the shining light in Jim Richardson's life, was special and everyone knew it. Although she was two years older than Peter, Joe knew that his son carried a torch for her and was devastated when she married someone else, but they remained friends; Peter was a trainee barrister in London by that time and they occasionally met up for coffee. It was a terrible shock for everyone when she died, but for Jim - his whole world collapsed - and it was a very bad time for the family. After that, Joe reckoned the only time he saw a glimmer of the old Jim was when Fiona's daughter visited. He'd forgotten her name until this young man had mentioned it; Eugenie, that was it, or Janie, a pretty little thing.

Joe lit his pipe and clamped it between his teeth. What to do, now? That was the question. What was the right thing to do? If the Richardsons were still alive, would they now want to be reunited? Whether they wanted to or not, was it fair to deny this young lass her family history? He got up slowly, stretched out his back, and took the empties to the bar.

"Are you there, Ted? I'm off now."

Ted's voice came for the back room, "Alright, Joe, let yourself out, I'll lock up after you."

~ 19 ~
Mid December 1985

Rob was on a stepladder, hanging the now-framed museum posters on the long wall of the studio. They did look terrific, hard though it was to admit Janie was absolutely right about displaying the best examples of his work instead of just having them stacked in the racks. He'd also found a place that sold frames for LP's, and he was about to hang Taliesin's three albums alongside the artwork as well as others he'd done recently. Getting to be well-known now meant that prospective clients were more inclined to come to him, rather than the other way round, and he could see it made sense to advertise his successes.

He heard a knock on the office door and yelled, "Come in."

John Hobden stepped out of his boots and walked through the office to the studio. "By heck, it's cosy in here with that fire going, how are you getting on?"

"It's coming on well. I think I'll be able to start work in here after Christmas. And I have to say, that wood burner was a stroke of genius. I think Janie's a bit jealous."

"Is she out, Mrs. Whittaker?"

"Yeah, she's gone up to town. Did you want her for something?"

John went a bit closer to Rob and lowered his voice, even though they were alone. "No, I've got somethin' I want to show you and… I wanted to make sure the missus wouldn't be around."

Rob got off the steps and put down the hammer. "Sounds

mysterious, do you want me to come now?"

They slipped into their boots and made a dash through a sudden snow shower for the back door, where they slipped out of them again. Kevin was waiting for them in the snug.

"That beam's looking fantastic, Kevin. You've done a grand job of cleaning it up." Rob wondered if he was expected to say more. "And you've plastered, too. Excellent."

John said, "That's just the backing coat, I'll do the skim coat later and then it'll look the proper job." He paused, and then carried on, "That's not what we wanted you to look at any road. It's what's up the chimney."

Rob's face fell. "Oh, don't tell me the chimney's no good and we're not going to be able to have an open fire. Janie was banking on that."

"No, it's not that. You'll be able to have your open fire, perhaps not in time for Christmas, but once the hood's in place." John beckoned him over to the fireplace and shone a torch up the chimney. "Can you see that the stack narrows just up there? Well, there's a little ledge in either side just where the stack joins the bedroom wall and, around the time those marks were made on the bressummer, folks used to place objects on those ledges."

Rob straightened up. "You've found something, haven't you?"

John looked over to Kevin who removed a dustsheet from the table behind him.

"Bloody hell, what's that?"

"We found it on one of the ledges, behind a couple of bricks. It's a dried cat. Now you know why I wanted Mrs. Whittaker out of the way."

Rob was staring at the mummified animal; a flattened skeleton covered in dirty white skin complete with tail, and ears, still pricked up, over empty orbits. Its mouth was wide open in a silent screech.

"And that's not all," Kevin reached behind him. "We found this bottle and that old shoe on the other ledge."

Rob looked to John, "What's it all mean? Are we still talking witches here?"

John nodded and told him all he knew from research he'd done on the subject of witchcraft, both 'good' and 'evil', and from what he'd been told by his father and grandfather. It seemed that people used to believe that witches and evil spirits would enter a house through openings and, particularly, down the chimney. A single shoe in an opening had long been thought of as a good luck symbol to ward of evil spirits, but it possibly became something more like bait, when placed in a chimney, smelling enough of a human being to lure a witch into a dead end. Witches were thought to be unable to travel backwards and so they would be trapped forever.

The stoneware bottle was another spirit trap. It was quite intricate and had a bearded mask decorating the neck. John called it a 'bellarmine' or witch-bottle and, if anything, the explanation for this relic was even weirder than the shoe. It would have been filled with urine, usually from the person who felt they were under a spell or curse, and various objects placed in the liquid. John upended the bottle to reveal a handful of bent pins and nails which were intended to impale the evil spirit.

Fascinating though all that was, Rob wanted to know more about the cat. John said his father had found one a long time ago, but this was a first for him and he was eager to explain the current theory. It was thought that, being hunters in life and being more attuned to the spirit world than human beings, cats would retain these abilities after death and be able to catch spiritual vermin, perhaps witches' familiars.

"Interesting, isn't it?" Kevin was clearly charmed by the whole thing.

Rob was still staring at the cat. "What do we do with them now?"

John held up both his hands. "Well, if it were me, I'd put 'em back."

"You're joking."

"He's not. People who've removed them in the past have had nothing but bad luck."

John shot his son a sideways look. "He's exaggerating, Mr. Whittaker, take no notice. I wasn't going to show them to you at all, but I didn't want some chimney sweep pointing 'em out to your wife one day when you're not here. I think she'd be a bit discombobulated, wouldn't she? My advice is to put 'em back and I'll brick 'em in, unless, of course, you think she'd want to see 'em."

Rob rubbed his hands over his face and gave a loud sigh. "I don't know what to do now." He went over to the cat again. "Would she be freaked out by this? Possibly. Probably." He turned to father and son, waiting for instructions, and made up his mind. "We'll put them back on the ledges, exactly as they were, for the time being. You'll be back in the New Year anyway, doing the upstairs, and we'll brick them in then. That'll give me all over the holiday to decide whether or not to tell Janie about them, and if I do, and she wants to see them, then she can."

Back in the studio, Rob was still a little unsettled. Not particularly by the objects themselves, but more by what Kevin had said, and by the look his father had shot him. He didn't consider himself at all superstitious and was no believer in the supernatural, but Janie did admit to strange 'feelings' and was certainly open to the possibility that not everything could be explained by science.

He was grateful that John had followed his instincts and waited till she'd gone out.

~ 20 ~
A Week Later

Janie had been awake for an hour and couldn't get back off to sleep. She rolled over to read the clock, 2:24am, and groaned inwardly. There were so many 'to do' things going around in her head: Christmas presents, food lists, drink lists, bedrooms and bathrooms to sort out, decorations, logs, a tree. It went on and on, and she was getting nowhere.

Rob was snoring gently. She slipped out of bed as smoothly as possible and made for the door on tiptoes trying, but failing, to avoid the creaky floorboards. "Janie, y'alright?" Rob was a light sleeper but, reassured, he was back to sleep even before she'd found her slippers and left the room.

It was a cold night and she shuffled along the landing, wrapping herself tightly in her dressing gown, and made for the back stairs and the warmth of the kitchen. For a moment she thought she'd left the light on. The moon was huge and full and shining directly through the window, casting a silvery, otherworldly light over the whole room. It was quite beautiful. She filled a glass from the tap and leaned on the sink as she drank, gazing at the world outside. It was still as the grave and so quiet it felt like being under water. A barn owl flew into view on silent wings, its head swivelling to take in her unexpected form at the window, before continuing on its way. She could make out traces in the frosted grass and, unbidden, Grandpa Richardson's voice made an appearance. 'Well now, child, what's this then – rabbit

104

or fox, perhaps? Or do you think it might be a badger or deer?'

The house was going to be full soon, but there'd be no one from either side of her family. Antony and his friend, Helen, were away for Christmas and, anyway, her father preferred to celebrate on January 6th, a Russian tradition he still upheld. And who knew where the Richardsons were?

Janie's eyelids began to droop, but there was no point going back to bed for as soon as her head touched the pillow, she knew the merry-go-round would start all over again. She needed to start making lists. Rifling around in the middle drawer of the dresser, trying to find a pen that worked, she stopped when she heard a thumping noise coming from above. Calling up the stairs, "Rob, is that you?" she went up to check when there was no reply. The landing was empty, but there was a wicked draught coming from somewhere, and she made her way up the steep stairs to the attic rooms. There was nothing out of place, no windows open and no evidence of a trapped bird. Nothing. Back downstairs, she found a pen and was pulling out a chair when she heard it again, this time a definite scuffling sound from the back stairs, and then caught the merest hint of movement out of the corner of her eye. She jumped up and snapped on the light, heart in mouth. The kitchen immediately assumed its usual rosy glow, revealing nothing untoward, but it took Janie a little longer to settle. There was nothing on the stairs. Moon shadows and imagination, she told herself. Get a grip, woman. All sorts of creatures come out at night, don't they? Mice, bats, deathwatch beetles? She'd have a word with John in the morning.

The kitchen felt decidedly chilly now and she went to check the range. Please, God, she thought, don't let it pack up now, just before Christmas. But it was still on and the temperature was showing normal, so she put the kettle on to make a hot drink and warm herself up. Half an hour later, Janie was checking a satisfactory clutch of lists covering everything that needed to be done in the next ten days. Rob would be in charge of booze, tree, holly and mistletoe, logs and kindling, fairy lights and testing the drawing room fire. Lorraine at the shop said she could get anything, so that was the turkey, goose, fruit and vegetables sorted, and she even had a list for the milkman. Her own list was no shorter. Hampers had already been ordered for Hedges and the staff at Mallory's, but Janie still had to buy something personal for Joyce and, after her sister-in-law had dropped the bombshell that they always had Christmas stockings, adults included, she felt obliged to do the same or else Amy and Ollie would think it odd. So…stocking presents for four adults and two children, plus the stockings, and she still had to think of something for Rob.

It was nearly half past three, and Janie felt beyond tired, but she was taking the day off tomorrow anyway, so she wasn't bothered. At least her mind was clear now, so she could relax. She got up to put the milk back in the little fridge that had come with the house, and then went back to her list of 'things to do tomorrow' and added, 'buy fridge'. She also added, 'check to see if someone can service range next week', and then, 'get Rob to check the oil'. Her worst fear now was having nothing to cook on over Christmas.

Satisfied, she turned off the light, and made her way back to bed.

***

"Yes, okay, it's not that funny. I'd like to see what you'd have done last night, Rob Whittaker."

"What? When the hobnail-booted mice came running down the stairs?" Rob was grinning from ear to ear. "Anyway, what do you expect when you go wandering around in the dark in the middle of the night? Your imagination must have been working overtime."

"Oh, just bugger off and…have your breakfast or something." Janie shooed him off, took John Hobden's arm and led him into her office. "I want to talk to you sensibly, John," and then, so Rob could hear, "without the comic relief putting his oar in."

106

John laughed. "Okay, Mrs. W, what's the problem?"

Janie shut the door. "Every now and then, there's a little draught in here. It seems to spring from nowhere and then go, just as quickly. I've felt it sometimes when I've been sitting at my desk, and it's as if the window's open or someone has come in, but when I turn round, the door's shut." She gave the builder a little embarrassed smile, "Do you think I'm imagining it?"

John looked around the room, opened and closed the window and tested a few floorboards. "Well, I don't think you're imagining it, no, not at all. That window is pretty old and, what insulation there is, isn't worth having. So that's one possibility. Also, there's an airbrick, here, where the fireplace was. You can get a fair draught through one of those, if the wind's in the right direction. And, on top of that, these original floorboards have gaps between 'em."

Janie looked relieved. "Oh, good. I feel better already, what's the solution, then?"

"First off, I'll get Kevin to replace the insulation on that window. That's a must, because you'll get rain in through there if we get an easterly blow, and a fitted carpet'll stop the draughts coming up through the floorboards of course but, in my opinion, it'd be a bit of a shame, eh? You've got to leave the airbrick, anyway."

"You're right. I'm with you, I don't want a fitted carpet, but I might put down a bigger rug. No, I'll be satisfied if we just get the window fixed, and I'm happy to put up with the odd draught from the fireplace. Old houses are full of strange quirks, aren't they? That's one mystery solved."

John gave her a reassuring grin. "And the other mystery?"

Janie rolled her eyes. "Well, as you've probably already gathered from my husband, I was in the kitchen late last night, early morning really, and I heard noises on the back stairs. First, a thump, and then, I don't know what to call it, a scrabbling sound. Quite loud. I checked everywhere, but I couldn't find anything." John was silent. "I know Rob thinks I imagined it, but I didn't."

"Best bet, it's mice." The builder made a show of getting down on his hands and knees on the stairs, and tapping the woodwork. "Little buggers get everywhere, especially this time of the year when it's too cold for 'em in the fields. They can get behind panelling and skirting boards and, of course, they're active at night when there's normally no one around."

"Oh, okay. That's what Rob said it was, but I just thought it was too loud for that. So, should we do anything?"

John Hobden took his time trying to get back on his feet, carefully straightening each knee in turn. "I wouldn't, not unless they become a nuisance, and if they do, I can give you the name of a chap who'll sort you out." Keen to leave it at that, the builder started for the kitchen door, "And if there's nothing else, I think I've got some window insulation in the van, I'll go and get Kevin to start right away if it's convenient."

"Sure, carry on..." Janie was not entirely convinced by the mouse explanation but John was very familiar with this house and he'd tell her, wouldn't he, if he thought it was something else?

The back door opened and closed and she heard Rob's voice drifting in from the back lobby. "Well, well, well, what have we here? Are you there, Janie?" Moments later, he appeared in the kitchen with a ball of black fur nestling in his two gloved hands. "I think this is the most likely explanation for your midnight scare."

John turned back and he and Janie both went over for a closer look. The kitten lifted her sleepy head and opened her eyes. "Where did you find her? She's beautiful," Janie took the little cat from Rob and held her up for a closer look, "and she's got brown eyes. Look, have you ever seen that before?"

John shook his head. "Can't say I have."

"I found her in the back lobby, asleep in the corner, I didn't notice her on the way out. She must have come in through the cat flap in the night."

"Of course." She turned to John, "I'd forgotten we have a cat flap. Perhaps she was running around after mice last night, do you think?"

"Aye, perhaps." He left them to it and went in search of window insulation.

"What shall we call her, then? You've already decided it's a she."

Janie was sitting down with the kitten, who was remarkably still, curled up on her lap. "I'd love to keep her, Rob, but we can't. There might be some poor child crying its eyes out at this very moment at the loss of their pet."

"There's no collar, though. You'd think there would be if it belonged to someone."

"True, but I must be sure before we go giving her a name and assuming she's ours. I'm going to see Lorraine today, anyway, so I'll put a card on the noticeboard." Rob's mouth turned down at the corners. "Don't give me all that, Whittaker. You know I'm doing the right thing and, if she's meant to be ours, then she will be."

***

"No-one's reported a missing kitten," Lorraine took the postcard from Janie, "but I'll stick this up for a week anyway. There's not much that we don't hear about in here, so if it's not claimed by then, I think you can keep it."

"Thanks, I hope you're right. Also…I've got my Christmas food list here. Do you want to have a quick look to see if you can get everything?"

Being organised made Janie happy and, having given her lists to all concerned, she set off for Chichester, confident that she had everything under control, and was looking forward to a whole day Christmas, and fridge, shopping.

It went well and she had time to stop in at Petworth on the way back, to scour the antique shops for something special for Rob. For some time, he'd fancied buying an old easel for the studio to replace his current functional, utilitarian one, but they seemed to fall into two categories; ugly, heavy square Victorian ones, or more aesthetically pleasing, but flimsy, country pieces.

He'd given up looking. But Janie had just found the perfect one.

She'd stopped to look in the window of a smart antique shop, drawn by the open boxes displayed on a set of library steps. One of the boxes was an old set of watercolours and she went inside to have a better look.

A huge Great Dane eased itself upright and lazily sauntered over to greet her, followed by a small man in a tweed suit and spotted bow tie. "Don't be frightened, Ben's a softie. Can I help you?"

Janie tentatively patted big Ben on his massive head and squeezed past him. "I wanted to have a better look at your artist's box in the window," and she turned, pointed, and then changed her mind. "Oh, your library steps, it's an easel."

The fussy little owner came to stand next to her. "Yes, beautiful, isn't it? You don't see many of these, easel on one side and steps on the other. It's late Victorian, of course, and mahogany, but very fine; made by a top manufacturer, Hampton & Sons, London." He paused for breath, and then, his voice a little higher, "Might you be interested?"

She was, and she paid a good price, but it was worth it. The trouble was, at nearly six feet tall it was a bit difficult to hide, but Ben's owner promised to wrap it up very well and deliver it to her on Christmas Eve

***

Things were going so well, she made another decision, turned the car round, and drove to Thatchling.

St. Peter's, with its squat little Norman tower, was mainly Saxon built from flint and local stone, and sat neatly in the centre of its graveyard. The door to the church was locked, so Janie walked around the graves, looking at the names, but most gravestones were very old and difficult to read. She nodded to a gardener working in a far corner who shouted, "Afternoon, Miss. Are you looking for the Vicar?"

Janie picked her way through the graves to reach him, and

he whipped off his cap as she drew near. "Hello. I'm not really looking for the Vicar. I'm here to see if I can find my grandfather's grave, but I don't have a clue where to start."

"Ah, I see." The gardener drove his spade into the turf and wiped his hands on his trousers. "Well, I might be able to help you." Janie gave him the details she had and he pointed to the other corner of the graveyard. "A lot of the 1960's are over there, but I can't say I remember many Richardsons, it's not a common village name."

"Thanks, I'll go over and have a look." The newer stones were easy to read but the gardener was right, no Richardson among them.

She was walking out when she heard him call out, "No joy?" and she shook her head.

"I need to see the parish records so I guess I'll have to contact the vicar?"

Still eager to help, the gardener downed tools once more and led her to the church noticeboard where they found the vicar's phone number. "He's not ours, solely, you see. He does a few parishes. That's why it's locked, we've had a theft 'cos there's no incumbent." He wished he could think of something else to keep her there, but he couldn't.

Janie thanked him once more and left.

~ 21 ~
Late December 1985

Cat had taken up residence in Janie's office, either on the sofa or on a cushion on the hearth of the defunct fireplace. Occasionally, if the mood took her, she curled up on a similar cushion on the chair next to the oven in the kitchen. No one had claimed her, so she was now a Whittaker, but having had no other name for over a week, 'Cat' she was to remain.

Work at Mallory's was always slow before Christmas, and Janie had spent the previous afternoon trying once more to decipher the next page of Alice's diary. She'd given up at about four o'clock when her eyes were tired and Cat had jumped onto her lap to demand food.

Never one to be beaten, and feeling more up to the task in the morning, she decided to try again. The diary was where she'd left it, but she turned a few pages back and forth, and then went to the door and called down the back stairs, "Rob, are you there?"

From a mouthful of toast, came, "Mmmm?"

"Have you been in my office for anything?"

"No, why?"

"Someone's moved Alice's diary." She was at the bottom of the stairs now. "I left it open at a different page."

"Well I haven't been in there, and there's no one else in the house, so…are you sure?"

"Yes, of course, I'm sure," she said, irritably, "I was working on December 1664 and it's now open at July 1669!"

"Okay," Rob held up his hands in mock surrender, "but I'm not the guilty party. Could a draught have whipped over the pages?"

She shrugged. "I don't know. I can't say I've noticed any, anyway, since the window was insulated." She stomped half way up the stairs and then came back down again. "Sorry, didn't mean to snap."

Rob shook his head and went back to his breakfast.

Cat was sitting on the desk, tail flicking and brown eyes glinting, when Janie got back to her office. "Cat! No, not allowed," and she picked her up and placed her firmly on the hearth, stroking and petting her in case she'd hurt her feelings. Ridiculous, of course, she knew that, but she did feel very protective towards this little creature and wondered, not for the first time, if the strange brown eyes were some genetic quirk associated with muteness or deafness. Cat had never uttered a mew or any other sound.

The morning flew by with Janie lost in Alice's world of 1664. She felt a terrific sense of achievement, having transcribed the second entry, but even more than that, it was turning out to be a fascinating read. Although enjoying the academic exercise, she now found herself so impatient to know what happened next, that she couldn't wait to hand it over in the New Year.

The telephone rang and Janie picked up, praying it wasn't a work problem. "Janie, it's me, Barb. How's things? I was just ringing to see if there's anything you want me to do." Barbara. Lovely, sweet, biddable Barbara, married to Rob's brother, Dan.

"Thanks, Barb, but I think I'm all set. I intend to make very good use of you, though, once you get here. You know me, I've got a list of last minute things to do on Christmas Eve."

Barbara giggled. "It's going to be such fun. I can't tell you how much we're all looking forward to it, especially the kids. They keep telling everyone they're going to a 'big house' for the holiday."

"Well, we're looking forward to it, too. Try and come as early as you can on Christmas Eve, won't you, we're going to let the kids put the final decorations on the tree."

"Fantastic. We'll try to get there early but we're picking up Elsie on the way and, well, you know…" she let the sentence trail off.

"Is she getting worse?"

"Mmmm. You'll see for yourself soon. Dan thinks she's just getting a little forgetful, but I know the signs. I've seen it too many times before." Barbara had been a nurse before she had the children. "I'm hoping Rob will be concerned enough to talk to Dan. Don't mention it though, will you, Janie?"

"Course not, and don't worry about it. If we need to sort something out, we'll all do it together. Okay?"

"Okay."

"Oh, before you go, I've just thought of something we do need – your mince pies. I've bought some, obviously, but no one makes mincers like you. Bring as many as you like, they'll all go."

"Just as well I've made four dozen then. I've got a pudding too, if you want it…"

"What do you think?"

Janie was smiling when she put the phone down, but a loud, "Fucking hell" from downstairs sent her running to the drawing room. Smoke was swirling in the hall and she rushed in to find Rob frantically trying to open all the windows.

"Oh, my God. What's happened?" Smoke was still pouring out of the fireplace and Janie covered her nose and used the poker to try to move the logs from the grate.

Rob had found a big pair of brass tongs. "Move, Janie, I'll do that. Go and get me a towel."

With throats heaving and eyes streaming, they managed to put out the fire and the logs lay smouldering on the hearth. Janie wiped her eyes and handed over the towel, "Well, that was a success, so much for John saying this fireplace was a 'cracker'."

"No, it was my fault. There's obviously a nest up there. I saw some bits of branches in the grate but didn't put two and two together until the bloody thing started spewing smoke all over the place."

Janie grinned. "You didn't 'twig', then?" They were both kneeling on the hearthrug and Janie gave him a good shove.

He shoved her back. "That was terrible…"

They stopped laughing as a mighty 'whoosh' preceded another cloud of smoke and a thud, as a mass of twigs, feathers and soot landed on the hearth in front of them.

Coughing, Janie stood up and brushed the worst off her clothes, "I'm just going to ring the chimney sweep."

~ 22 ~
Christmas Eve 1985

"We think Ollie might sleep better if we could have Cat in our bedroom." Amy was holding one of Ollie's hands firmly; his other was clutching his flopsy bunny and his eyes were struggling to stay open.

Barbara left the table and went over to kneel down in front of her children. She stroked her daughter's hair. "It looks as though Ollie's been asleep already, Amy. Can you not get to sleep?"

Janie went to join them. "And I'm afraid Cat's asleep in her room, sweetheart, and she doesn't like to be disturbed."

Amy's eyes widened. "But she wouldn't mind being intersturbed for me."

Janie suppressed a smile. Cat had been so put out by all the visitors, and especially the children, that she had fled up to Janie's office as soon as she could get away. "I tell you what, do you want Uncle Rob to read you a story?"

Dan leaned back in his chair and stretched, "Good Heavens, is that the time? We'd better clear all these plates away pretty smartish. If Father Christmas catches us all up, I don't think he'll come in," and he stood up and started clearing the dishes from the kitchen table.

Amy ran to Rob and tugged at his sleeve. "Quick, Uncle Rob, we've got to be very quick." He made a show of looking at his watch, then scooped them both up and took the stairs two at a time.

By the time he was back, everyone was in the drawing room with glasses of Elsie's sloe gin and Janie's favourite chocolates, courtesy of Barb. They were all completely knackered.

It was the first time they'd used the drawing room, partly because the snug was cosier for just the two of them, but also because, with the Kelly's furniture in, it didn't really feel like theirs. Although once the fire had been sorted, and they'd got rid of all the furniture that didn't have a purpose, Janie had a better idea of what she was going to do with it. But right now, bathed in fireglow, it looked magnificent. Rob had bought a huge tree, which needed a bit of trimming to get it in the room, and it was standing in front of the window, draped in three times the number of lights he'd originally estimated. Heaps of presents were piled round the base. The rest of the room had been cheered up with as many vases as Janie could find to fill with holly branches, swathes of ivy, bowls of pine cones and candles. Simple, she thought, but effective, and sat back with a satisfied little sigh and a warm glow from the liqueur.

"This won't do." Rob clapped his hands to rouse them all, "What's the matter with you all? Don't you want to play a game or something?"

"Oh, God. I don't think I'm up to it." Dan waggled a finger at his brother. "It's all right for you. While you and Mum were hanging out in your studio, I was trying to wear out the monsters, which backfired, obviously, and the girls have been working their fingers to the bone in the kitchen."

"Anyway," Barb said, with her feet up on a stool and lazily waving her glass at Dan for a refill, "I want to hear more about this diary that Janie's found. It sounds really interesting."

"Seconded." Dan sat down next to his mother and pressed her to take another chocolate. "We want to know who lived here before and what they got up to, don't we, Mum?"

The consensus was for a reading and Janie went upstairs to get her notes. The door to her office was ajar and so she crept down the landing to check the children's room. Amy and Ollie were fast asleep and Cat was nowhere to be seen. Relieved, Janie went back to collect her notes and, glancing out of the window, saw 'her' dog fox on the lawn, standing quite still, looking towards the house. She loved to watch him and, as she leaned over the desk to get a better view, she saw him drop his head, slowly get down onto his belly and inch forward like a fawning puppy. My God, she thought, he's met his match, and she leaned even further forward to see what had brought him to his knees. Cat was sitting about ten yards away. Janie flew down the stairs and out of the back door. The dog fox had disappeared. Cat turned to look at Janie, stood and walked calmly towards her mistress, weaved around her legs, then led the way inside and curled up on her cushion by the oven.

"That's why they're called 'foxy', I guess," said Rob, after Janie had told them all what she'd seen. "He was lulling her into a false sense of security, just before he pounced."

Janie shook her head. "That's what I was afraid of at first, but, well, I know it's stupid, but it didn't look like that. A kitten would be instinctively afraid of a fox, wouldn't it? And, clearly, she wasn't."

"Let's face it, Janie. We have an unusual cat and, thankfully, one we needn't worry about. It's clear she can look after herself, even though she's still a kitten. Now, come on, everyone wants to hear about Alice.

First, Janie gave them a bit of background, explaining about Thomas Crayford building the Grange, the death of his two sons in the Civil war, his second marriage and the birth of Alice. She then read out her transcript of Alice's first diary entry, starting with; 'My 20th birthday…', and ending with, '… I shall truly feel like its mistress.

Although Janie found Alice's diary totally fascinating, she wasn't sure that others would, so was surprised and delighted to find that it had prompted a lively discussion; even Elsie, who was fading fast, joined in with comments on seventeenth century drinking habits.

"The thing is," said Rob, "that we assume, nowadays, that all women back then were largely uneducated or, at least, only given enough education to run a household. Yet, here we have Alice, a young woman of only twenty years, who has not only been running the household since she was fifteen, but helping to run a sizeable farm as well. Now, is that unusual or do we just not know enough about seventeenth century women?"

"It's unusual for a gentlewoman, surely." Dan was sitting on the edge of his seat now. "And I can't think there were many daughters who received 'Leviathan' for their birthday. I've read it, it's deathly boring."

Barbara joined in, "I don't think there would be many young women of her class who would want to look after a farm, either, but it doesn't sound like Alice found it a burden."

"And she did all the accounts," added Janie, "for the house and the farm. I've seen them, they're quite impressive."

A gentle snoring sound came from Elsie who was wedged between her two boys on the sofa, and Janie lowered her voice. "I seem to have put Mum to sleep. I'll save the rest for another time, shall I?"

"No, it's early." Rob eased himself upright without disturbing his mother, and went to throw another log on the fire. "I think we all deserve another little drink and one of Barb's excellent mince pies and then we want to hear what happens next. I haven't heard this yet, either, she's kept it very quiet."

"Okay, if you insist." Janie grinned at Rob and he winked at her. "There must be some pages missing because the next entry I have is fifteen months later, December 1664. Just think, 321 years ago, this very month, in this very house."

And she started to read.

Alice's Diary

December 1664

Last night, Father and I entertained the Reverend Fawcett and a young friend of his, William Harryman. Supposedly, he was just visiting, but my suspicions were confirmed after catching conspiratorial glances exchanged between the Reverend and my father. The realisation that I was being vetted brought a blush to my cheeks, which, I'm sure, did not go unnoticed. The men continued to discuss the church and Chichester where, apparently, Mr. Harryman has a home, and I had a chance to compose myself.

I have known for some time of my father's decline, despite his efforts to shield me from what I fear will be inevitable in a year or so, and I understand his fears for my future. Rather unwillingly, I admit, I am now coming to terms with the need for a husband and, in truth, I cannot go against Father's wishes at a time when he wants to see his affairs settled.

So, what do I think of Mr. Harryman? He is middling sort of height and build with a fine head of wavy, dark brown hair, which he wears very long, and he has a neat moustache and beard. His clothes are rather sombre in contrast to my father's; plain black breeches and coat but with an exquisite lace collar, fine silk stockings and black shoes with expensive looking buckles. He is a religious man, for certain, but one who does not deny himself some of life's luxuries. I know him to be in his mid thirties, but he could easily pass for several years younger, and he has a most attractive face and a rather disconcerting way of fixing one with his eyes when he speaks. Grudgingly, I must admit that if this is to be my fate – it could be worse.

Barbara was the first to comment when Janie finished reading.

"Well, she might not have been thrilled about the idea of marriage, but William sounds a bit dishy to me. Does she marry him?"

"I haven't got to that bit yet, but I have got an entry for March 1665, three months later. I'd like to read it to you, it's only short."

"Hang on," Rob interrupted, "you must know if she marries him. It's in the House Book, surely."

"It will be, yes, but I've made a point of not reading from 1663 to about 1735 when I reckon she'll be long dead. I want to hear her story unfold in her own words, otherwise it's like reading the end of a book before you've even started."

"Commendable will power, Janie." Dan applauded softly. "So, come on…we're all waiting now.

March 1665

William supped with us this evening, after which I made my excuses and retired. He is now talking to Father and asking for my hand in marriage. Father will, of course, give his consent but there is the marriage settlement to discuss before any formal announcement can be made.

Oakwood Grange is to be put in the hands of trustees and all incomes from the estate are to be used for the maintenance of the house and farm and for all our living expenses. Any future disposition of the estate is to be solely in accordance with my wishes. As William is bringing little to the marriage, he may be expecting such an arrangement, or this might be such an affront to his pride that he may change his mind.

I find I am rather fearful of the outcome

"Poor old William." Rob sat back with his arms folded. "If I've got this right, he's been completely outsmarted! After months of wooing, and finally asking for Alice's hand in marriage, he's just discovered that he'll have no interest in the property or the farm. Effectively, he's just going to be there to make everything look respectable so that Alice can continue as normal."

Dan agreed. "And he can't retract the proposal or else he'll look a cad and a bounder! Catch 22, I think you'll find."

Barbara and Janie looked at each other, open mouthed.

Barbara spoke first. "What makes you think he asked Alice's father first? She doesn't say that expressly."

Dan turned to his wife. "Actually, it doesn't really matter. The fact that the marriage settlement was discussed at all, means that they both knew a proposal was in the offing and, whether he backed out afterwards or whether he failed to propose as a result of the conversation, it would still be classed as 'ungentlemanly.'"

"Come on, girls, you must see that."

Janie was aghast. "Okay, you two, what about praising Thomas for ensuring that his only child isn't robbed of her home and her living by some money grubbing upstart? Because that's exactly what happened to lots of women in those times, especially in marriages of convenience. Without a settlement of this kind, everything Alice owned, and Alice herself, would become his property. Even if she had a dowry, a husband could take that without it being against the law."

"Anyway, I can't see why you're so concerned about 'poor' William," Barbara said, becoming indignant and raising her voice. "Even if it is a marriage of convenience, and we don't know that, they could be madly in love for all we know, he gets to live in a lovely home with a young wife who appears to look after everything, and that seems to be a distinct improvement on his circumstances."

"Yes, but the estate is never going to be his, is it? Alice 'gets' it, she says something about it being an affront to his pride, and I can understand that. He probably…" Rob was stopped in his tracks.

"Oooohhh, stop it." Elsie woke up and started waving her arms about. "Daddy, stop shouting, stop it. Mummy, don't argue with him, please…"

Dan was the nearest to her and he hugged her close. "Sshhh, Mum, it's all right."

She was clearly still distressed and Rob went over and knelt in front of her. "Just a dream, Mum. We weren't really arguing." He stroked her face and tried to get her to focus on him.

Barbara stepped up and took control. "I'm going to take you up to bed, Mum. You dropped off 'cos it's getting late; we're all going up shortly. Come on, up you come." Barbara, all bustling efficiency and clearly in 'nurse' mode, pushed the men aside and supported her mother-in-law, speaking to her in soothing tones as they made their way upstairs.

The remaining three sat in silence, Janie with her hand over her mouth, looking from one brother to the other, wondering who was going to be the first to speak. It was Rob who broke the ice. "How long has she been like this?"

Dan shook his head. "I don't think it's anything to worry about, she's often a little confused when she wakes up, and she's getting a little forgetful in her old age."

"Old age, Dan? She's only 68, for God's sake; I don't think that's old, is it? And it's more than a little forgetful; this afternoon in my studio, her head was all over the place, half the time she couldn't even remember where she was, never mind people's names. I'm really worried about her."

Dan dropped his head into his hands and stayed silent. His shoulders began to heave. Janie dashed to his side and wrapped her arms around him as he gave way to tears; Rob wasn't far behind.

That was how Barbara found them. Rob stood up and made way for her next to her husband. "Dan, darling, come on now," she forced him to look at her and kissed him. Turning to the others, she said, "It's Christmas Eve, guys, and this is a conversation we can all have at another time. Let's just make this a Christmas to remember for everyone, shall we? Mum, the kids and all of us, but especially for Mum."

There was nothing more to discuss. Dan was full of apologies,

Rob felt wretched and the two women did their best to make everything better. Barbara took her husband off to bed but Rob and Janie stayed up until the fire went out. She had intended to have a go at Rob for his defence of 'poor' William living in a house owned by a woman. After all, she'd owned their Wandsworth house, hadn't she? But now wasn't the time.

And anyway – it was Christmas.

~ 23 ~
Christmas Day 1985

Despite the amount of alcohol that had been consumed on Christmas Eve, none of the adults, with the exception of Elsie, managed to get to sleep before the early hours; only to be woken up before six am by the sound of small feet running along the landing and banging on doors.

"He's been, he's been, the mince pie's all gone." Ollie was clutching his pyjama bottoms and dancing on the spot.

Amy opened her parents' bedroom door. "Ollie's so excited, he's wet his pants, and I'm going downstairs now." She ran off, leaving Ollie who was swept up by his father, and whisked into the bathroom.

Although a rude awakening for the adults, the day improved after reviving mugs of tea and the joy of witnessing the children unwrapping their presents. It was a Christmas they all remembered for different reasons.

For Janie, it was a treat to be part of a normal, family Christmas, with three generations relaxed and happy and enjoying each other's company. It was a far cry from both the solitary Christmas she usually spent with Antony, and the grand, formal gathering held by Grandmother Malchikova on January 6th. As a child, she'd frequently had guilty thoughts about how wonderful it would be to spend the holiday with Winnie's family or the Richardsons, but now she was very much part of Rob's family and she had this house. Christmas would never be boring again.

Elsie was having a good day. It's true she wasn't participating as much as in the past, for whatever reason, but for most of the morning, she sat on the sofa, watching her grandchildren and linking arms with Rob. The confusion of the day before was not so apparent and her face radiated happiness.

Rob and his mother comprised the artistic and literary branch of the family, whereas Dan had been very close to his late father, sharing a passion for all things scientific and technical. He acknowledged that Rob was his mother's favourite, and it was not an issue for him. Looking at the two of them sitting like lovers on the sofa, Rob slouching in the seat so that their heads were nearly touching, Dan hoped against hope that Barbara's fears were unfounded. He suspected it was a vain hope. Seeing his mother several times a week, it had been easy to pass off her little lapses, but Rob's reaction had put paid to that, and it was a relief to know that he now didn't have to tackle this problem alone.

Rob was feeling guilty. Since their father died, Dan had always been the one to make sure that Elsie was okay, and Rob knew that, even though he'd have done the same if he'd lived closer, it didn't excuse him from having a go at his brother. But Elsie's behaviour had shocked him, and he'd lain awake most of the night, trying not to disturb Janie and attempting to get his head round the prospect of losing his mother bit by bit. He gave her arm a little pat and she turned to stroke his cheek before brushing some wayward curls from his forehead. It was a familiar gesture, but there was a vacancy behind the eyes that he'd never noticed before.

On the other hand, to see Janie throwing herself into all the children's games and so obviously having a wonderful time, made him very happy; bitter sweet, though it was. She and Barbara had become firm friends, despite being opposites in many ways, a bit like himself and Dan, he thought, and it was good to see them laughing and gossiping together. Being the most generous of souls, it was clear that Barbara was going to make sure Aunt Janie had full access to her niece and nephew.

The rest of the day passed in predictable fashion.

In spite of the rain, a walk was considered necessary to work off some of the kids' energy, and it certainly made returning to a roaring fire all the better. Dinner preparations were hampered by the inebriation of the cooks, but the food eventually made it to the kitchen table after much laughter and mopping of brows. Aprons were tossed aside and the men were delegated to take over. More games after dinner, and then, thankfully, two very tired children were packed off to bed and fell asleep as soon as their heads touched the pillow.

Trivial Pursuit was postponed till Boxing Day and, in common with millions of others, they all settled down to watch 'Only Fools and Horses'.

***

"Well, if I were you, I'd definitely follow it up." Barbara was unloading the dishwasher whilst her sister-in-law was putting everything away. "Wouldn't it be great to find out that you really do have a connection to this place?"

"Mmm. Celestine and Celeste, not exactly the same though, are they?" Janie picked up a serving plate, trying to remember where it went.

"No, but they must be unusual names for this part of the world, surely. And it's entirely possible that Celestine could become Celeste after a couple of centuries."

Janie went over to give her a hug. "Thank you, Barb. I don't like to talk to Rob about all this, I'm sure he thinks I'm bonkers, and I'm really not that desperate to find a connection, it's just that the name sprang out at me. And with Mum's middle name being Celeste, well, you know…"

Barbara hugged her back. "Yes, I know, you've got to find out."

***

"Do you like your present?" They were in bed and Janie threw an arm and a leg over her husband, and whispered in his ear.

"Are you kidding? It's perfect, just like you. And I love it." He turned sideways and wrapped his arms around her. "Thank you for making this a wonderful Christmas."

"Not just me, it was a truly corporate event, and so much fun. I have loved it." She paused for a second and added, "I'm so sorry about your mum, though. You know Barb wants her to go and live with them, don't you?"

"No, I didn't. Does Dan know?"

"He will soon. She's quite adamant that she can cope now that both kids are at school and she says it'll be easier than checking up on her every day. She has a point. Anyway, don't mention it until Dan does."

"What about her coming to live here?"

"I offered, but Barb won't hear of it. She's doubtful that Elsie would settle in a strange house away from Brighton, and anyway, we can't guarantee there'll be someone here all the time. What I suggested is that we have her here, now and again, to give them a break."

"You two have it all worked out, don't you? Thick as thieves, you've been, all day. And that reminds me, who's this Celeste I overheard you talking about?"

Janie found herself blushing, not that Rob could see in the dark, but then quickly realised she didn't have to mention the Celestine connection, or non-connection. "It was my mother's middle name, Fiona Celeste Richardson. We were just saying that there might be a French link somewhere, 'cos it's not really a common name, especially in the country."

Rob prompted her, "And…"

"And I've decided I'm definitely going to trace my family and, hopefully, find my grandmother and Uncle Mark. I didn't tell you this before, but I sort of made a start just before Christmas when I bought your easel in Petworth."

"Why didn't you tell me?"

"I was going to but, to be honest, I didn't discover anything.

I'm going to have to make an appointment with the vicar of St. Peter's, I think, although there's no gravestone for Grandpa and I don't even know if they were married there."

Rob rolled onto his back and let out a sigh. "I've got an admission to make, too." He told her about his spur-of-the-moment decision to do some investigating in Thatchling and his meeting with Joe. "I was positive it wouldn't come to anything, so I didn't tell you. Also, I didn't want to bounce you into tracing the Richardsons if you weren't up for it."

"Oh, darling," Janie climbed on top of him and covered his face with kisses, "you do think I should do it then?"

"Of course, I do. You may discover something nasty in the woodpile, who knows? I suspect we all have, somewhere in our family trees. That doesn't matter. If you want to trace your family back, then you have to start with your grandparents."

"You're right. Perhaps we can go back to Thatchling and talk to some more people. What do you think?"

"I think I'm not very tired now.

<h1 style="text-align:center">~ 24 ~
January 1986</h1>

John Hobden popped his head round the kitchen door. "Morning, Mrs. W., you off out, are you?" He held out a bunch of mail.

"Yep, I'll be out all day. Rob's in, though. He's in the studio sweating over a commission, he'll probably welcome a break if you need him." Janie swung her bag over her shoulder and took the post from him, "I'll take this over there now, it'll all be for him, anyway. Shall I tell him to come over?"

"Aye, if you don't mind. I'm just finishing off in the snug."

Going from the garden into Rob's studio was like going from the Arctic to the tropics. "Jeez, I don't know how you can work in this, it's stifling."

"It's just right," Rob grinned and posed in his short-sleeved tee shirt, "I don't like painting in lots of clothes. And it seems I'm not the only one who appreciates the warmth." Cat had followed Janie in.

"Has she been in here before?" Rob shook his head and they both watched as the cat circled the room, tail swishing angrily from side to side. "What do you think she's doing?"

"I don't know, but I hope to God I haven't got mice in here, not with all this paper around."

"Talk to John. He said he knows someone who'll sort it for you. Anyway, my love," and she pulled his head down to give him a kiss, "I've got to dash. I'm off to Oxford to see Professor

130

Taylor, bit of a scary moment, letting go of Alice's diary, but it's got to be done. And I've left a message for Rosie to see if she's free for lunch." She made for the door and Cat did likewise, "See you later..."

"Okay, have a good day, and give my love to Rosie. Tell her it's time she paid us a visit." Rob waved her off and stopped work to sort through the mail. The usual bills and work related stuff he tossed onto the desk in his office to be dealt with later, but he paused over one letter, addressed in old fashioned, copperplate handwriting, and took it with him back to the house.

John was waiting for him in the snug. "What are we doing then, Mr. W.? Are we going to brick up those cavities, or what?"

"Yes, we are, although I did bottle out of telling Janie about the cat and the other stuff. I just didn't see the point in the end." He raised an eyebrow inviting John to agree with him.

"I think you're right. All that messing about in the middle of the night unsettled her a bit, I know, but if there are any…" John searched for an appropriate word and was pleased with the result, "…any echoes of the past in this house, they're definitely friendly. And we don't want Mrs. W. thinking otherwise, do we?"

"Right." Rob pointed a finger to emphasise the point, and he was half way down the hall before he turned back. "You'll be starting on the bathroom next, won't you? Any idea how long it'll be out of commission?"

The cap came off and he scratched his head. "It's a job to say."

***

The unopened letter was still in his hand. There was no return address and, although the handwriting was elegant, the envelope was thin and cheap. He opened it and went straight to the signature. It was from Joe Wakeham.

Dear Mr. Whittaker,
    Since our meeting in 'The Bull' in Thatchling, I have given much thought to your request for any information

leading to the whereabouts of Mrs. Anna Richardson and her son, Mark.

I have to admit here, that I was not entirely truthful when I said that I could offer no information about where they are now. In my defence, I felt I needed time to balance the wishes of one party against the desire of the other, and the only person who could have helped me was my late wife. In the end, I was sure that my wife would have decided in favour of your wife.

I do know where the Richardsons went when they left Thatchling, but it is a long time ago and they may not be there now.

The address I have is: 26, Old Street, Sheringham, Norfolk.

I hope this information helps Mrs. Whittaker to find her family.

Yours sincerely,
Joseph Wakeham.

P.S. I remember seeing your wife when she was a little girl visiting her grandparents. She is very much like her mother, who I knew well.

Rob read the letter twice, replaced it carefully in the envelope, and propped it up against a vase on the kitchen table. He couldn't wait to see Janie's face when she read it.

***

"I'll take good care of this," Professor Taylor placed a hand on the Oakwood diary lying on his desk, "and I promise I won't show it, or mention it even, to anyone else unless you say I can. Until then, it will be just between the two of us."

"Well, thanks again. I'm so grateful." Janie got up to go and then sat down again. "Actually, I have another favour to ask. Even if it proves not to be Aphra Behn, would you mind…?"

132

"For you, Janie, never fear, I'll transcribe the whole thing. I can see how important it is to you and, as soon as I have anything worthwhile, I'll fax it over to you." He walked round his desk as Janie was getting up to leave, and placed both hands on her shoulders. "It's been lovely seeing you again. Married life agrees with you, I can see that. You look very...contented."

"I am." They smiled fondly at one another, Janie offering her cheek for a kiss, and then she left.

Walking down the corridor, she recognised the woman coming towards her, books tucked under one arm. "Oh, Margery. Hello."

"Janie Mallory. What on earth are you doing back here?"

Janie pointed back down the corridor. "I need some help from your husband on a manuscript I'm researching."

"I see." Margery shifted the books and hugged them to her chest. "Not trying to rekindle an old romance, then?"

Oh, shit, thought Janie, not now. Please, not now, but one look at Margery told her that a denial wouldn't cut it. "It was a long time ago, Margery," and then, after a stony silence, "I'm so sorry. What can I say?"

"Yes, well, I must admit I was a bit concerned at the time that your affair lasted so long but, since you left, he's had at least three other blonde students. So he's back to normal now." Margery's mouth smiled thinly but her eyes glittered with spite.

Janie pulled herself together, and faced up to the older woman. "I don't know what to say."

"Well, I don't want your pity," Margery affected a little laugh, "because there's no need. He still loves me and depends on me and, as you found out, there's no danger he will ever leave." She continued after a moment's pause. "We're just two ageing hippies, I guess, and sexual fidelity has never been high on our list of priorities. He even boasts about it sometimes, telling me things he shouldn't." She paused again, noticing with satisfaction the colour rising in Janie's cheeks.

There seemed no dignified way to end the conversation and Janie stood there, speechless. Margery broke the silence.

"Anyway, I hear you're married now," and in response to the younger woman's nod, "well, good luck with that." She patted Janie's arm before continuing on her way with a "Take care, now" tossed over her shoulder.

Janie left the building as fast as she could. Blinking away tears of humiliation, she crossed the quad and headed for the porter's lodge, narrowly avoiding a collision with a cyclist who shouldn't have been there. She picked up a message from Rosie, checked her watch and made straight for the pub.

She hadn't bought a packet of cigarettes for years, but she bought one now, together with a whisky, straight up, no ice, and by the time Rosie arrived, she was onto her second.

Janie parked her cigarette and stood to embrace her old friend, a petite brunette with a pneumatic figure, who immediately picked up on her mood. "Hey, since when have you been a solitary smoker?" She pulled out a chair and helped herself to one of Janie's cigarettes. "What's up? The aptly-named Dick hasn't upset you, has he?"

"No, but his sodding wife has. After all this bloody time, she decides to have a go at me." She ordered a drink for her friend and then gave Rosie a blow-by-blow account of her encounter with Margery.

"Ages ago, you told me, Janie Mallory - sorry, Whittaker - that the only way to sort out the upsetting crap banging around in my head was to apply logic. So, let's take your own advice, shall we?

Put simply, poor, jealous, abused Margery tells you three things:

1. She knew all along about your affair with her husband.
2. He's had several students since you finished your affair, and
3. Dastardly Dick told her all the sordid details.

So, in order, why be so upset that she knew?"

Janie ground out her cigarette, angrily. "Because I thought it was our secret, mine and Dick's. No one else was supposed to know, apart from you. But, all the while, bloody Margery knew, and Dick knew she knew, so it was their secret and now I feel like the stupid kid who wasn't let in on the joke."

Rosie took a long drag on her cigarette and blew a perfect smoke ring. "I see all that, but you've overlooked the fact that you only have Margery's word that she knew about it at the time. Okay, the other girls. I take it that's not a problem?'

"Correct. Dick had the next one lined up even before I left and, to his obvious dismay, he could see I wasn't jealous. I'd already come to my senses."

Rosie nodded and fixed Janie with a stare. "So, we come to the real crux of the matter, don't we? Sharing sordid details with his wife; this is what really bugs you."

"Bloody right, it does." Janie leaned forward on the table and lowered her voice. "The utter shit. The complete fucking liar. How could I have fallen for such a bastard? All those furtive fumblings and couplings in cars and dodgy hotel rooms – supposedly to keep it from his wife and the department – and all the while, not only did she know, but they were getting off on it! Either that, or the sadistic bastard was tormenting her."

Rosie called for another drink for herself and ordered a plain tonic water for her friend. "I'm not getting you another whisky, you've had enough for one lunchtime," and suggested Janie get something solid inside her. They shared a ploughman's and a packet of crisps. "Again, I reiterate - tautology, I know, be quiet - you don't know that she's telling the truth. Anyway, that aside, do you blame her for having a go at you?"

"Absolutely not. I feel nothing but admiration for someone who can wait so many years to get her revenge, and deliver it with such panache and self-possession that I felt this big." She indicated a gap of an inch between her thumb and finger before helping herself to a gherkin. "And do I believe she's lying? If you'd seen her, Rosie, no one lies as well as that without preparation."

"Yeah, but you know what? She just may have rehearsed that little speech over and over, on the off-chance that one day she'd have the opportunity to use it, you never know." Janie didn't look convinced. "Okay, so this is the biggy, how will all this affect your dealings with the Aptly-Named vis-à-vis your diary?" She held up a finger to stop Janie from answering straight away, "When you next see him, will you:

a.   Tell him about your meeting with Margery, call him a shitty, lying, little fucker who seduces young girls and makes a fool out of them, pick up your diary and storm out. Or…

b.   Tell him about your meeting with Margery and discuss how it's affected you. Or…

c.   Don't mention the meeting with Margery and, if he brings it up, just shrug it off as if it is of no importance. Because it is of no importance."

Rosie was holding up three fingers to indicate the options and Janie, now feeling the effect of the second scotch, couldn't help laughing. She pointed to the third finger. "I realise, of course, that c) is the strong, grown-up option, but I choose it only because he's a brilliant seventeenth century specialist who has agreed to help me with the diary – otherwise, it would be a), obviously."

Rosie banged the table, startling the only other customer at the bar. "Good! And don't you dare feel guilty about using him; this diary may help him steal a march on other Aphra researchers, don't forget that. In fact, even without Margery's interference, I reckon he's the one feeling a teeny weeny bit guilty, otherwise why would he offer to transcribe the whole thing if the Aphra connection is a red herring? He may still be fond of you, but I can't see him putting himself out for that reason alone."

Janie reached over to kiss her friend. "When did you grow up and become so wise?"

"I think it was when you left and I had to fend for myself. Also, you learn by your mistakes, and I've had a lot of those." They both sniggered, knowing that to be true. "Listen, darling girl, I have to fly now. I'm supposed to be delivering a lecture in fifteen minutes. Forget all this crap with Dick and Margery; it's all water under the bridge. Just go home and make love to your gorgeous husband, and give him a big, sloppy kiss from me."

"I will, and thanks for cheering me up. I don't know why I let it get to me so. Oh, and Rob says you owe us a visit, so ring and let me know when you can get away. Okay?"

***

"I think you ought to go to Oxford more often if this is the reception I get when you come home." Rob peeled her arms from around his neck, turned her round, and pointed to the table. "There's a letter for you there. It's addressed to me but it's really for you.

Janie read the letter. Her hand went to her mouth, and the tears that had been threatening all day, eventually fell.

~ 25 ~
Mid January 1986

Rob was swinging the axe with deadly accuracy, and the growing pile of split logs was easily big enough to last them for the next couple of months. He stopped when he heard Janie calling from the studio, "I've made you a cup of tea."

"I'll have it out here," and he started swinging again.

"This looks suspiciously like work displacement activity to me." She handed him the mug. "What's up?"

"No fooling you, is there? I can either sit inside to try and find inspiration, or I can find it out here, and this is more enjoyable."

"Okay," Janie rubbed his back, "but don't overdo it. I'll help you stack them in the garage later. I'm going back to the office now, do you want anything?"

Rob looked at her over the mug and shook his head.

The phone was ringing as she reached the kitchen and she hurried to pick it up, but she wasn't quick enough. It was probably Guy and she needed to tell him that they couldn't make it this weekend, so she rang him back.

"Sorry, darling, it wasn't us," Tash answered the phone. "Guy will be really disappointed, we were so looking forward to seeing you both. Promise you'll come as soon as you can. He's bought some wonderful stuff, there's bound to be something that you'll want for your place. Trade price, obviously." Guy and Tash were now living on his parents' estate, dealing in architectural salvage as well as still taking on landscape design projects.

"I know, we're disappointed too, but we've both got heavy work loads at the moment and deadlines looming. We'll be working all weekend. I promise we'll be up to see you soon, and we'll need a van by the sound of it!"

When Janie rang off she went upstairs to see how the builders were getting on with the new dressing room and en suite. Thankfully, this work wasn't producing anywhere near as much mess as the fireplace and John reckoned that the electricians and plumbers would be in soon for the first fix. She stayed chatting for a while, discussing where exactly they were eventually going to knock through to the bedroom, when she heard the fax machine spring to life.

"Sorry, John, excuse me. That's something I'm waiting for," and she dashed off to her office. Cat looked up and stretched out on her cushion. Janie stroked her while the pages were still rattling out of the machine. "I'm sorry, Cat, but I can't work in here with all the noise going on. Come over to the studio with me." Cat blinked a few times then rolled over and went back to sleep.

Janie stacked the pages and flicked through them to make sure that Joyce had sent everything she needed. Of course she had. They had a whole slew of new young writers currently; everyone in the office was excited about it and working hard to get the best out of them.

She was halfway down the front stairs when she heard another fax coming through, but she had enough to deal with for one afternoon, and went down to check the post. Nothing from Norfolk. It was two weeks since she'd posted her letter to the address Joe had given them, and she was feeling a little despondent.

***

Rob chopped logs until there were no longer any to chop. It was getting dark, too late to stack them in the garage and, anyway, Janie could tell by the set of his jaw that it would be wise to leave him alone. Her work had gone really well without interference from the builders, Rob and her office phone, and she picked up all her papers to go back to the house. Passing Rob on the way, he said he was going back to the studio for a few hours. She didn't argue with him.

Cat welcomed her back, weaving silently around her legs and rubbing her face on her jeans. Janie picked her up, cradling her like a baby. "You are a funny little thing, why don't you speak to me, eh?" Dropping the cat back to the floor, she caught sight of the fax she'd ignored earlier. It was from Richard Taylor:

Dear Janie,

As it's a bit quiet here, before the rabble return at the weekend, I made a start on your diary and managed to dash off a couple of pages, which I'm sending now.

You were right – it's really quite difficult to decipher, even without the poor condition of the book itself, and there are some big gaps. At first I thought there were pages missing, but maybe not. Alice, herself, wrote that this was never meant to be a diary in the strict sense of the word. I've paraphrased, as I think you said you had too, to make it more readable and I think I've got the names right – but you can check those with the House Book probably.

I admit I was surprised. Your Alice doesn't appear to bang on, ad nauseam, about everyday stuff - believe me, I've read several ladies' diaries and most are deathly boring - there's a reference to the Great Plague and some other interesting bits. If the rest of it is in the same vein, I shall enjoy it, whether or not Ann Bean is Aphra.

I know I said it before, but it really was lovely to see you again after all this time. You look just the same, possibly more confident and a bit more sophisticated now that you're a successful literary agent, but certainly no older. Your Mr. Whittaker is a lucky man.

I shall send you the next installment as soon as I can. Like you, I'm eager to find out more about Ann/ Aphra, but I shall resist the temptation to transcribe out of sequence.

Regards,

Dick

Janie's first reaction was to snort with laughter. 'Confident' and 'sophisticated' would not have been the adjectives he'd have chosen if he'd seen her after Margery had finished with her. It appeared that he knew nothing about that, thank God.

She was about to settle down to read when her phone rang. Frustrated at being interrupted, she snatched up the phone, "Yes?"

"Mrs. Whittaker?"

It was a rather weak, tremulous little voice, and one she didn't recognise. "Yes. I'm sorry; I thought it was someone else. Yes, I'm Mrs. Whittaker."

"My name's Mrs. Elliott. I live in Old St, Sheringham, and you wrote asking about Mrs. Richardson. I've tried a few times to get you."

Janie eyes widened and she sat down at her desk. "Oh, Mrs. Elliott, thank you so much for phoning. Yes, we've been out a lot recently."

The voice at the other end was a little less wobbly now. "Well, as you've probably gathered, Mrs. Richardson doesn't live here anymore. And I'm sorry to tell you, that she passed away two years ago; that's when we bought the house."

Janie received the news like a physical blow and could only say, "Oh, no," even though Rob had tried to get her to face up to the possibility.

"I'm so sorry, Mrs. Whittaker. I wasn't sure whether it would be better to hear it in person or read it in a letter. It was my husband who said I should ring."

"You're very kind. It's extremely good of you to take the trouble and I do appreciate it. I don't suppose you know anything about her son, Mark, do you?"

"That was another reason for ringing you." Mrs. Elliott was happy now that the bad news was out of the way. "I made some enquiries at the post office for you, and it seems that Mark moved to a cottage just down the coast in a little place called Arnby-next-the-Sea. He's in the phone book and I tried to ring him but I think he's been disconnected. I can give you his address, though."

Janie scribbled it down, repeated it to make sure she'd got it right, and thanked Mrs. Elliott again, for taking so much trouble.

Alice's diary was temporarily forgotten. Janie dashed over to the studio to find Rob.

***

Only when supper was cleared away, and her letter to Mark was written, did Janie remember the diary. Rob was in a better mood, partly due to seeing Janie so happy and partly due to some progress with work, and he listened attentively while she read the transcript aloud.

Alice's Diary

May day 1665

Jennet persuaded me to join her in gathering May-dew this morning before sunrise. She swears it will reduce my freckles but I fear that is a false hope.

I attended the festivities on the green this afternoon.

Martha made a lovely May Queen and was a popular choice judging by the whoops and cheers as she was carried aloft through the crowd. I swear I saw tears in Edmund's eyes. The Green Man was a lad from a neighbouring farm who, I think as far as Edmund was concerned, was paying too much attention to his duties.

Reverend Fawcett sought me out to congratulate me on my engagement and I suggested that he could seek a second profession as a matchmaker. Despite the jolly occasion, he seemed a little low as he was very concerned for his relatives in London. The latest report of the increase in the numbers dying is very worrying.

Father was in a bad mood this evening and, once again, raised the subject of an Engagement Ball. William is firmly against the idea but I may be able to talk him round.

***

Wedding Day, October 15th 1665

It has been a joyful day.

Jennet fussed over me all morning, determined that everything should be as my mother would have wanted, and I was happy to let her. She dressed me in my new silk gown, terracotta silk with an ivory underskirt and ribbons, which I wore over an old shift of my mother's. I borrowed one of Jennet's handkerchiefs and, for 'something blue', we decided on the pearl necklace with a sapphire drop and matching earrings. Father slipped me a silver sixpence.

My usual hairstyle was not deemed suitable so we spent a good half hour trying to tame the curls into something more elegant. I'm not sure we succeeded.

Edmund bowed very low and winked at me as he handed me into the carriage with my father and I took this to mean that I met with his approval.

It was a small gathering in Church with only a few relatives from both sides, some local friends and neighbours and our oldest servants. But, as I walked out with my handsome new husband, there, just outside the church, were all the estate workers waiting to throw handfuls of wheat and rose petals, and Gabe, dear little Gabe, looking for all the world like his brother Seth, gave me a four leaf clover. I later discovered that it had been cleverly constructed from two of the more common kind but it is the thought that counts and I shall press it and keep it forever.

The festivities are over now and everyone, apart from the few relatives staying here, has gone home.

Jennet helped me to undress and unpin my hair and she laid out a new nightshift for me – one that she has made herself. It is fine linen with lovely lace edgings and the stitching is so small I can hardly see it. She must have been working on this for so long and it is yet another present that I shall treasure for always. She has just left after offering a few words of womanly advice.

I am writing this whilst my father and husband (how strange that sounds!) finish their pipes and brandy by the fire.

I am nervous about what lies ahead tonight.

***

December 4th 1665

It is true what Jennet told me. The first experience of intimacy is painful but it does become easier.

I know it has only been a few weeks but everything is not as I expected. I fear something is not right and I cannot confide this to Jennet, as I am not able to find the words.

***

December 30th 1665

Father died today. I have entered it in the House Book.

I should not feel alone – but I do.

***

"Ah ha," Rob was grinning. "So he's accepted the marriage settlement then, and Thomas survived to see his daughter married. Who's this Janet person she talks about?"

Janie was looking in Harriet's copy of the House Book. "It's Jennet, not Janet, and according to this, she's a dairymaid. Her surname is Sandford, so she's related somehow to Edmund Sandford, who's a groom, and, if I'm not reading too much into it, I think Martha, the May Queen, may be his daughter."

"The way Alice writes about her, Jennet sounds more like a friend than a servant."

"Yes, I thought that. Perhaps she's been with the family for a long time and, since Alice has no mother, she's become like Winnie was to me." Janie rested her chin on both hands. "Anyway, that aside, it seems as if there's a bit of needle between Thomas and his prospective son-in-law. What do you think?" Janie made a little grimace.

"You mean just because he didn't want an Engagement Ball?"

"Mmmm. I mean, it seems a little churlish to me. We know William's religious; Alice says so but, unless he had a real Puritan streak, it seems unlikely he would object to one on religious grounds alone. I'm wondering if he's just being cussed because he's been outmanoeuvred by the marriage settlement."

"I think you're reading far too much into this."

"I don't think I am. Alice is happy on her wedding day; it seems to me that she's fallen in love with her new husband, but, only three months later, she's miserable. What do you think is the matter?"

Rob shrugged his shoulders. "I don't know. Perhaps he's got some weird sexual perversion?"

"Perhaps. Or perhaps, for him, it's a marriage of convenience and, for her, it isn't. We'll just have to wait and see how it all pans out..."

~ 26 ~
Oakwood Grange, February 1666

I t was over. Again. Exactly the same as before, and all the times before that. Alice resolved that tomorrow night, or whenever he next came to her, it would be different. She would be different. Her body had woken up and she desperately wanted to share in the act of lovemaking, although what they had done so far could hardly be described as making love.

It wasn't clear to her if William enjoyed the act or merely felt it was his duty, but it was clear that he didn't expect her to enjoy it. And she didn't, yet, but she wanted to, very much. She wanted to kiss him passionately, press his skin against hers, feel his hands on her body and wrap her arms and legs around him to draw him deep inside her. She wanted him to stay all night and for them to wake in each other's arms. She didn't want him panting into her neck and holding her hips still as he pumped away. She didn't want to stifle her moans and she didn't want to be thanked with a chaste kiss before he left for his own chamber. She had seen more passion between her parents outside their bedroom than she had witnessed inside hers. Even glimpses of furtive May Day couplings had shown her that both parties usually found it pleasurable.

Her increasing frustration and William's apparent lack of awareness was making her depressed and tearful. How could he *not understand? Did he love his first wife so much that being with Alice felt like a betrayal? Was she not sufficiently attractive? Perhaps he needed a little encouragement. She intended to find out.*

***

The floorboards creaked as he entered the room. As usual it was late, but Alice had stayed awake, waiting, sitting on the edge of the bed. As William placed the candlestick on the nightstand, she slipped the nightdress from her shoulders and let it fall to her waist. The candlelight played across the mounds and valleys of her body to great effect and William seemed transfixed, not meeting her eyes and not speaking, but eventually resting his hands on her shoulders. He was already aroused and Alice reached under his nightshirt to hold him for the first time. His eyes closed and his breathing became heavy, his hands moved to her breasts and she knelt up, drawing his head down so she could kiss him.

Seconds later she was flat on her back on the bed. "Cover yourself, Alice. You should be ashamed of yourself," and he threw the counterpane over her. Turning away, he tried to compose himself, picked up the candlestick and, without making eye contact, made his feelings perfectly clear. "Respectable married women do not display such lustfulness. We are not beasts in the field. In the eyes of the Church, marriage and procreation are for the begetting of children. You forget yourself." And he left.

At least she now had the answer.

~ 27 ~
Norfolk, February 1986

Janie pulled over to look again at the map Mark had sent her. It had already taken her well over an hour longer than anticipated to get there, the rain was making it hard to see where she was going, and she was still worried that this meeting could go horribly wrong. Her anxiety level was hovering near maximum.

The track she was aiming for appeared to be less than a mile away, so she waited until there were no cars in her rear view mirror and then pulled out and crawled, leaning forward and squinting through the rain-lashed windscreen. According to her uncle, the track was unmarked and difficult to spot, but it lay off to the right, about a hundred yards after a telephone box. She saw a splash of red shimmering on her right hand side, let out a huge sigh of relief, signalled and pulled onto the track.

If there were a word less flattering than 'track', Janie thought, then it would apply to this. There was no knowing how deep the potholes were as they were full to the brim with water, so she weaved around them as best she could, hoping to avoid a puncture. The track ended in a small parking area, large enough for about four cars, and she nosed in next to a Citroen 2CV, the only other car there. Off to her right was an angry sea crashing onto a deserted beach, barely fifty yards from her car, which was rocking gently from side to side. Straight ahead were three white, terraced cottages, accessed by a tiny path, and she sat staring at them for several minutes before reaching for her bag and pulling up her hood. The wind whipped the car door as soon as she released the handle and she dropped the keys trying to hold on to it. By the time she'd found them in a puddle, locked the car and tiptoed her way down the path, she was wet through.

The old man standing in the doorway, waiting for her, was a shock. Janie reckoned he was only just over sixty, but the thin, ever youthful-looking Uncle Mark she remembered had not aged well.

"Little Janie," he said, in a voice which had deepened only slightly with the years, "you haven't changed a bit. I would have recognised you anywhere."

With rain dripping off her eyelashes and nose and her hood pulled down over her hair, she suspected she did, indeed, look more like her twelve year old self than the confident, smart, professional woman she hoped she had become. "Uncle Mark, I'm so sorry I'm late, I completely misjudged how long it was going to take."

They both stood there, a little awkwardly, Janie dripping over the floor, until Mark helped her off with her wet things and they moved into the kitchen.

"I love your cottage. Do you live here alone?"

"Yes, apart from the cat," and he shooed it off a chair so that Janie could sit down. "I moved here when mother died, about two years ago. It suits me, being on my own, the other cottages are holiday lets so I don't really have neighbours, and I love being able to walk the beach every day." The wind was screaming around the house, and Mark grinned in his familiar, lob sided way. "It's not always like this."

Conversation stalled. Rescued by a whistling kettle, Mark busied himself with the teapot and Janie found it easier, talking to his back. "As I said in my letter, apart from meeting you again, it's Grandma I wanted to talk to you about, Uncle Mark. Well, not just Grandma, I know next to nothing about this side of my family, but perhaps we could start with her?" She was aware she might be gabbling.

Mark put a steaming mug in front of her and took the chair at right angles to hers, spooning sugar into his tea and stirring slowly. "She died of cancer in the end; I told you that, didn't I? It wasn't quick and it wasn't pretty and I couldn't do anything to help her."

"I'm so sorry." Janie reached out a hand and gave his a little squeeze. "I'd very much like to visit her grave, if that's possible. I have wonderful memories of her."

Mark looked at her and nodded. "Yes, I'm sure you do. Perhaps, if the weather calms down a bit."

The subject of Janie's last visit was hovering over them like a spectre at the feast, but it was too soon to bring it up. Instead, Mark reminisced about his sister, fleshing out her character with tales from their childhood and teenage years, in a way that hadn't been possible when Janie had been a child. Janie found herself laughing and crying. It was Mark's turn to squeeze her hand. "You're very much like her, you know."

Janie grinned, "Apart from the hair."

"Apart from the hair."

"Tell me, Uncle, where did Mum's middle name come from? Celeste - it's a bit unusual, isn't it? Is there a French connection somewhere?"

"Not that I know of. But it is a family name. Your Grandma's middle name was Celeste, too, but I don't know who she was named after."

"I've been after this information for ages," Janie said. "I've been trawling through parish records, and you've told me more in two minutes than I've managed to turn up in weeks."

"Well, perhaps you've been looking in the wrong place. Mum was born in Petworth, so there won't be any records in St. Peter's, if that's where you've been searching. You need to go to St. Mary's, Petworth. That's where your great grandparents are buried; I'm sure you'll find everything you want to know there."

Mark was finding his stride and, as more memories of his grandparents came tumbling out of him, the years fell away and the younger man showed himself again. Janie, chin propped on one hand, listened and encouraged him with smiles and nods. It was as if a big, empty space inside her was gradually being filled with a history she never thought she'd hear.

There was a loud crash outside. "Christ, what was that?"

Mark got up and went to look through the kitchen window. "No panic, it's just the back gate banging open and the bins have gone flying." He reached for his cagoule and stepped into his boots. "Back in a mo."

A quick glance at her watch, and Janie puffed out her cheeks, wondering how she was going to cover everything she still wanted to talk to Mark about, before she'd have to set off for home. Absentmindedly, she picked up and washed the mugs and swilled out the teapot while she was waiting for him to come back.

"It's blowing a hooley, out there. Black as night already and I can't see this rain letting up." Mark shrugged off his cagoule, "I don't think we'll be going to see Mother's grave today."

She was dreading the journey back, even if she started now, and that wasn't going to happen because she'd resolved to stay until she got some answers. "Right, well, I think I'll find somewhere to stay tonight. I really don't fancy driving home in this. There must be a B&B around here, isn't there?"

"There are several, but they're not open out of season. Anyway it's not necessary, you can stay here. I've got a spare room if you don't mind sleeping in a single bed."

Janie didn't, but she did need to phone Rob and, because Mark's phone wasn't working, that meant driving back down to the main road and the telephone box she'd passed earlier; Mark took her in his 2CV. Rob had been worried about her all day, not able to concentrate on his work for wondering how she was getting on, but the minute he heard her voice, he relaxed. She kept it brief because Mark was waiting in the car, "I'd better go, darling. I'll tell you all about it when I get back.

"Okay. And, Janie – promise me you'll leave in good time tomorrow."

A fish and chip supper at a local pub was followed by a couple of whiskies to prepare them for the drive back to the cottage. Janie slept like a log.

Morning dawned clear and bright, and Janie woke early to the sound of Mark, clattering around in the kitchen. She accompanied him on his usual pre-breakfast walk on the beach and then surprised herself by polishing off a huge fry up.

The cemetery wasn't far away. Mark detoured through the little town so that Janie could buy some flowers and he could show her the house where he and his mother had lived when they left Sussex. She couldn't imagine them there; Mulberry Cottage it was not. The cemetery gates loomed and they drove in slowly, so as not to waken the dead, and when they reached the grave, Janie read aloud the inscription:

'Anna Celeste Richardson, widow of James and mother to Fiona and Mark.

Sadly missed. Born July 1899. Died September 1983.'

There was a little knot in her throat with the effort of holding back the tears. They stood next to each other, in silence, until Janie reached out and took her uncle's hand. "What happened, Mark, was it my fault? I've got to know."

***

She set off after lunch and made good time on the way home, although she couldn't remember much about the journey. Her head had been too full of Mark's revelations, and her joy at discovering so much family history had been marred by what she had just learned. Seeing her sorrowful little face, Rob had immediately stopped what he was doing, sat her down in the snug and listened.

"It sort of was my fault, Rob. I knew it." Janie sat back in the chair and covered her face with her hands.

153

"Just start at the beginning."

"Okay. This is the quick version. Mark was suspended from his school for, allegedly, interfering with a twelve-year-old girl. He didn't – he's not that way inclined. He'd landed this plum job at a posh boarding school and he was eager to be the best he could be. This little girl was a challenge; she was being bullied and her work was suffering, so he decided to give her special tuition but, stupidly, didn't tell anyone. Rumours began to circulate about their 'relationship' amongst the other girls, the bullying got worse, the headmaster questioned Mark about the extra lessons, and her parents removed the girl from the school. A psychiatrist became involved, the police visited the school and Mark, poor, innocent Mark, was sent home." Janie paused for breath. She reached for one of Rob's cigarettes and inhaled deeply, before continuing.

"Apparently, Grandma believed Mark, but Grandpa was less than sympathetic. Reading between the lines, and knowing what Grandpa was like, I suspect he didn't take kindly to having a 'pansy' for a son, and now he was wondering if Mark was something even worse. Anyway, the police didn't pursue the case but, of course, Mark lost his job and no reference was forthcoming. End of career." Janie flicked her cigarette. Rob remained silent, sensing the difficult bit was to come. "This was the time when yours truly enters the picture. Mark was home, kicking his heels with nothing to do except write poetry – imagine how that went down with his father – when I turn up for my annual holiday. He takes me fishing. I remember the day well because we had such a wonderful time. I caught two or three fish, we cooked them over a little fire and we had a picnic lunch. It was very hot, so hot that I decide to have a dip in the river. Mark tried to stop me, but I took off my sundress and went in in my knickers. I remember him watching over me in case I got into trouble and laughing as I fooled around in the water.

Grandpa watched us coming back, hand in hand, apparently. I don't remember. I do remember Grandma seemed cross that night when she put me to bed, and I couldn't understand why she was so upset that I'd thrown my wet knickers away."

"Oh, bloody hell, poor Mark." Rob shook his head. "It wasn't your fault, Janie."

"Yeah, but it doesn't make me feel any better. And the story gets worse. My grandfather is now so convinced that I'm in danger from his son, that he has a breakdown and blows his brains out."

"No!" Rob was really shocked. "I suppose that clears up the mystery of the funeral?"

"Exactly. And they left without telling us because, according to Mark, although Grandma wanted to believe him, her instinct to protect me was stronger. Also, she couldn't face the prospect of my father finding out about all of this." Janie thumped the arm of the chair in anger. "One stupid fucking mistake, a seed of doubt, and three lives completely ruined!"

Rob went over to give her a hug. "It's in the past, Janie. I know it seems very raw to you but, for Mark, this is all over and done with. It sounds to me like it was a relief for him to get it all off his chest, to someone who he knew would believe him. And now he has a family again, if he wants it.

~ 28 ~
Petworth, Late February 1986

The vicar of St. Mary's was in an accommodating mood. "Come in, my dear."

"I really didn't want to disturb you, vicar," Janie was feeling a little awkward, "I only came to browse round the graveyard and find your phone number to make an appointment. I can come back another time."

"No, don't do that," he smiled and took her by the arm, "this is a good time to catch me. No meetings or societies today, and it's too early in the week to start thinking about the sermon." He gave her a little wink. "All the records are kept in the sacristy, I'll just go and get the key."

He was gone long enough for Janie to wander in and appreciate the beauty of the church, a sublime mixture of ancient and Victorian architecture. She was studying some old coffin plates taken from the tombs of members of the Percy family, when he returned.

"This way," he waved, and she followed him to the sacristy. "Your grandparents were Richardsons, I think you said? I'm afraid there's no shortage of Richardsons in this town, it may be a difficult search."

"Luckily, I'm trying to trace my grandmother's side of the family first, and her maiden name was Stedman so, perhaps, that may be a little easier, do you think?"

"Ah yes, another Sussex name, but not so many of those."

He gave her an encouraging smile. "Here, have a seat and tell me what you know about your grandmother."

"Her birth name was Anna Celeste Stedman and she was born in 1899, married James Richardson in the early 1920's, gave birth to my mother in 1923 and my uncle in 1925, and died in 1983. My uncle thinks Anna's mother's name was Lily Celeste Stedman."

"Well, that's enough to be going on with." The vicar rubbed his hands together and turned to the leather bound parish records. "If we start with her baptismal record, then we can find out both her parents' names. Right, this is the one we're looking for." He placed the book in front of her on the table and a cloud of dust motes rose into the air. "Start in 1899, but remember that these are baptism records, you might find the entry in 1900, or not at all; some folks never baptized their children. If that's the case, then we'll try to find her marriage record."

Janie opened the book, closed her eyes and inhaled the familiar smell. What alchemy exists, she wondered, to produce such a seductive scent, simply from paper, ink and glue?

"Another bibliophile, I see." The vicar patted her on the shoulder. "No need to tell you to be careful with the pages. I'm going to leave you to it now, I have a few phone calls to make, but I'll come back in what? Shall we say, an hour? I'll be just through that door if you need me."

The entries were very clear and easy to read, unlike Alice's diary, and after half an hour's search, Janie had found her grandmother's baptism record. She was so thrilled, she spoke out loud, "Yes, yes!" and the vicar popped his head round the door.

"Success, I take it?"

"Yes, it's so exciting. Could I borrow a pen and paper, please? I didn't come prepared."

Anna's parents were shown as Lily and Robert Stedman. There was no mention of Lily's second name but there was no doubt she'd found the right couple. All she needed to do now was find the entry of their marriage so that she could discover Lily's maiden name, and that meant trawling through all the records backwards from 1899. Given that Mark could remember his grandmother, it seemed unlikely she was born before 1860 and therefore, probably married no later than 1880. Janie was looking at the possibility of searching through nearly twenty years of records and she made a start but, after half an hour, she decided to leave it for another day. She felt she'd taken up enough of the vicar's time already.

All was very quiet in the next room, and Janie put her ear to the door before knocking gently. The soft snoring noise she heard became a grunt, followed by a chair scraping the floor, and the vicar appeared looking a little bleary-eyed. She explained that she'd need to return, if that was okay, and the vicar ran a hand through his tousled hair. "Come back, by all means, my dear. I've got a card here," and he fished around under his cassock for his trouser pocket. "Just give me a ring to make sure I'm around."

They shook hands, and Janie ran back to her car, clutching the piece of paper that signalled the start of her search. Exciting though it was to find her family, she couldn't help hoping that, somewhere in her search, round about 1790, she might discover a Celestine Palmer.

~ 29 ~
March 1986

It was half way through March and, for a month or so, Rob and Janie had barely seen each other. Everyone at Mallory's was working flat out and Janie hadn't even made it home some nights, sleeping in Antony's flat instead so that she could work late and make an early start. Rob, too, had been forced out of his studio, in an attempt to nail down a commission that he desperately wanted; one that was perfect for him, but would mean many more trips to Germany.

At first, Janie had relied on the Hobdens to feed and water Cat, but there were occasions when no one was at the Grange and Lydia was drafted in to fill the gap.

"Don't be silly," Lydia had said. "As I told your husband last year, it's jolly nice to feel that I can still be of some use to someone."

Janie had given her a little tour of the house, showing her all the alterations, and Lydia had approved wholeheartedly before promising to come back in the afternoon to see to Cat.

At four o'clock exactly, Lydia turned the key in the back door and called Cat, who padded silently down the back stairs and jumped onto her cushion by the range, lifting her head to be stroked.

"You are a funny little thing, aren't you, with your brown eyes?" Lydia loved cats and stroked behind Cat's ears and under her chin. She could feel the vibration of a purr, but there was no perceptible sound. Once the food and water were down and Cat had nipped out of the cat flap, Lydia settled down at the kitchen table with a magazine and a cup of tea and decided to stay for a couple of hours to give Cat some company. She hadn't been sitting for ten minutes when Cat climbed onto her lap and went to sleep.

Lydia was just thinking about leaving, when she heard a car in the drive and Cat shot off her lap. Looking through the kitchen window, she saw Rob getting out of his car and went to open the back door. "Janie said you wouldn't be home till later. I've just been cat-sitting for a couple of hours."

"Hi, Lydia. I managed to catch an earlier plane. Is Janie going to be late then?"

Lydia nodded and saw the disappointment in his face. "She said she'd ring if she had to stay over, although she wasn't planning to."

Whilst Lydia was slipping into her coat, Rob dumped his jacket and bag on the floor, and went straight to the fridge. "Well, it looks like a cheese sandwich unless there's something in the freezer."

The look on his face told Lydia that there wasn't. "Right, mister. No arguments. You've got fifteen minutes to shower and change, and by that time, your supper'll be on t' table. Look sharp." She took off her coat and shooed him out of the kitchen. He knew better than to argue and, anyway, he was hungry.

The smell was enough to drive him downstairs in double quick time. A mushroom, onion and cheese omelette was just about ready and, together with a bit of salad and a glass of white wine already on the table, Rob thought he'd never seen a sweeter sight. He'd had a crap day with no time for a proper meal. "Marry me, Lydia, I'll dump Janie."

She delivered his plate to the table, gave him a gentle cuff round the ear, and picked up her bag. Through a mouthful of food, Rob said, "Don't leave me now. If you've got nothing better to do, stay and help me finish this bottle of wine. Go on, get a glass, and have some of this omelette, there's plenty for two."

Lydia didn't need asking twice. There was something about Rob she found hard to resist, and there was no one at home to talk to. She declined the food but went to get a glass.

They chatted companionably whilst Rob finished his meal and, no sooner had he cleared his plate, than the phone rang. Lydia got the gist of the conversation and heard the edge in Rob's voice; Janie wasn't coming home. He returned to the table and poured the remainder of the bottle into both their glasses. "Oh, Rob, no, I'm tiddly as it is. I'm not used to drinking wine."

"Well, it doesn't matter does it? You don't have far to go and I'll walk you home. A bit of night air will do me good." He looked miserable.

The wine had loosened Lydia's tongue, and she found herself saying things that, normally, she wouldn't have said. "I know she didn't want to stay up in town tonight. She told me she wanted to be here when you got back."

"Yeah, I know. She said there's something on that she can't leave to the others, but still…I came home early specially." He reached for a cigarette. "Everything was so great just after Christmas. I was working in the studio most days and Janie only went up to town three days a week; we thought we had it cracked. And now, we're both so busy, we may as well be back in London, we'd probably see more of each other.

"Are you complaining about being successful, Rob Whittaker?"

He grinned at her. "I know, I don't know when we're well off, I can see it in your face. And you're right. We've just got to ride this out and hope that, in future, we're not both manically busy at the same time."

Lydia changed the subject. "I had a tour of the house this morning. I love the fireplace in the snug, and your whatchamacallit, en sweet, that's going to be fabulous. I must say you've managed to get cracking straight away, even though you are busy."

"Did you see the witches' marks?"

"Aye, I did." Lydia chuckled. "Someone had a right go at that, didn't they?"

"Janie didn't seem worried, though, did she?"

"Nah, not at all. Why? Do you think it upset her?"

Rob stubbed out his cigarette. "I wasn't sure. Mind you, she was a bit rattled when she heard a commotion on the stairs in the middle of the night, but," he reached down and lifted up the little cat, "that's when we found you, wasn't it?"

"That would be the back stairs then, would it?" Lydia was busying herself with her handbag.

"Yes." Rob waited for her to say more, and when she didn't. "Lydia?"

"Nothing. I'm just going to wash these things up and then I'll be off."

She made a move but Rob reached for her hand. "Tell me, otherwise I'll be imagining all sorts of things."

Lydia sank back into the chair. "I've had too much of that," and pointed to the empty bottle, "I shouldn't have said anything."

"You haven't, yet."

She gave a big sigh. "Mrs. Kelly, Harriet, told me that, when she was young, her brothers used to frighten her to death with stories of things that went bump in t'night. But they were always playing pranks on her and no one else took any notice of them. Of course, their bedrooms were near the back stairs, whereas Harriet's was where your 'en sweet' is going to be. It was the Brig who put an end to the teasing when he saw Harriet getting upset." Lydia fiddled with her hankie.

"Is that it?" Rob was grinning.

"No. When Harriet first became ill, she had very unsettled nights, and she used to creep downstairs and sit reading in the kitchen, with a cup of cocoa. She heard it, not once, many times. It frightened her at first; I think we're all frightened by something we can't explain, aren't we? But once she realised there was no harm in it, she just accepted it as part of the house."

"And that's it – promise?"

"I promise. No one knows what it is. But, I can tell you this, Janie didn't imagine it, and it had nowt to do wi' Cat."

When Rob returned from walking Lydia home, he decided to do some nighttime investigating for himself, but the business trip had left him exhausted and he slept for nine straight hours.

***

Mallory's had so much work on at the moment that Janie didn't know whether she was coming or going. Her staff was quick to learn, she had no complaints, and Joyce was brilliant at calming everyone down when things promised to get out of hand, but there were certain parts of the job, like checking final submissions and negotiating with high profile publishing houses, that only she could do. She knew Rob was pissed off because she hadn't really been home for ages, but she couldn't help that, he'd been away, too.

It was nearly the end of March and, in about two weeks' time, they'd need to be ready for the London Book Fair. Joyce would organise the stand, as usual, but both her new assistants would need some hand holding and it would mean staying up in town for three nights. With a bit of luck, things would calm down after that.

Janie did admit to herself that she felt very conflicted about things at the moment. She was thrilled that the business was going so well; she derived huge pleasure from knowing that she'd made her father proud and she was still ambitious. On the other hand, if she could spend every day with Rob in the Grange, she would die a happy woman.

Bloody Rob. If he'd only phoned her to say he was catching an early plane, she would have moved heaven and earth to get home. She wasn't a bloody mind reader.

~ 30 ~
The Next Day

Rob spent the whole of the next day in his studio. He'd come away from his meeting in Germany feeling a little confused about exactly what his clients wanted, and whilst that was frequently the case, yesterday he'd felt pretty devoid of ideas himself. Perhaps it was just that he was tired, or grumpy. He certainly felt better after his nine hour sleep and several cups of coffee, and ideas that were merely vague the night before, now started to crystallise into something he could get excited about.

At five o'clock, he phoned his client in Germany. They wanted to see what he had as soon as possible and Rob agreed to fax over his outline ideas. He was buzzing and so sure that he'd nailed the brief, that he ran over to the house, crashing through the kitchen and taking the stairs up to Janie's office two at a time.

There was already an incoming fax waiting in the tray. It was several pages and Rob picked them up, stacked them neatly and went to place them on Janie's desk. He could see it was from her old college and he knew it would be the next installment she'd been waiting for; the covering letter was hand written and headed 'From the Office of Professor Richard Taylor'. Rob had no intention of reading it until his eye caught the signature at the bottom.

He read the letter:

My Dear Janie,

I'm so sorry it's taken me a couple of months to get round to your diary again – you've been very patient – but I can assure you that I'm nearly as keen as you are to see how it all unfolds.

This Hilary term has been a nightmare; everyone except me seems to have succumbed to 'flu and I've had no time to myself. However, Easter break is now upon us and your diary is high on my list of priorities.

In the meantime, I'm sending a couple of entries. Not much, I know, but you may find them interesting.

Perhaps you might collect the next batch in person? We didn't have much time to talk on your last visit and I'd like to take you to lunch at our favourite Italian restaurant – for old time's sake?

Regards,

Dick

Rob sat down heavily in Janie's chair and read it again. This was the guy she was always so cagey about. Dick, the one who he'd always assumed was a student like her, and the one, he reckoned, who'd broken her heart. His thoughts became muddled and he tried to remember if she'd said anything about him at all; he didn't think she had.

He felt winded and sat for some time staring out of the window, feeling desperately alone, even Cat had deserted him. His mood had changed in the blink of an eye and, suddenly, nothing seemed to matter. He sent his fax.

***

It was Friday, and Janie left work early, confident that they were ahead of schedule and she wouldn't need to work over the weekend. She picked up her car at the station and drove straight to the supermarket. Knowing the cupboard was bare and that Lydia had stepped into the breach, once again, to administer to her poor abandoned husband, she stocked up on several frozen meals as well as ingredients for all Rob's favourite dishes. She was going to spoil him this weekend. Feeling reckless, she invested in several good bottles of wine, some flowers and a few bars of his guilty pleasure, Caramac.

Yes, I know, she told herself, I'm the one feeling guilty; still a little indignant, but definitely guilty. Above all, she was just looking forward to spending the weekend together, alone, no visitors. Just the two of them curled up together in the snug. The new hood over the fireplace was in place and appeared to be working a treat, but this would be the first opportunity to try it out properly, and they weren't short of logs.

As her car pulled into the drive and he heard the horn sound, Rob went to the back door. Janie climbed out, beamed at him and waved. "Hello, I'm back. Can you help me with the shopping, please?"

He waved back, stepped into his boots and went to help her, but she knew, just from the way he walked towards her, that he was still pissed off with her. A little peck on the cheek and the absence of eye contact put her back up at once and, after all her good intentions, she found herself spoiling for a fight.

Dumping the shopping on the kitchen table, Janie spoke to his back. "What's the matter, Rob? Has something happened, or are you still cross that I wasn't home last night, even though you said you wouldn't be back till late?" She had one hand on her hip and the other on the corner of the table.

"You have a fax upstairs, Janie, from Professor Taylor." He turned round and placed some of the wine bottles on the table. "Richard Taylor, also known as Dick." This time he looked her straight in the eye.

Janie was wrong footed. This was the last thing she expected, her cheeks flushed and it was her turn to look away. "Oh, for goodness sake, Rob, is that all?"

"Is that all?" He'd gone from quiet and sad to loud and furious at a stroke, and Janie jumped involuntarily. "I'm sorry, but is it stupid of me to think there might be something going on?"

"There's nothing going..."

"The mysterious Dick, who you never spoke about? The old flame who you were with for years, and you never thought to mention that he and your professor are one and the same person. The same person you've been meeting and chatting to on the phone and who now, apparently, is keen to see you again and take you to your favourite restaurant. Am I being stupid?"

"No. I mean, yes." Janie was flustered and near to tears. She couldn't believe how quickly everything seemed to be falling apart.

Rob moved to stand right in front of her. "So which is it?"

She still couldn't look at him, and sat down at the table, with head in hands. Rob sat next to her and waited, more worried than angry.

She stood up. "I need a drink." Rob shook his head, so she fixed herself a gin and tonic and returned to her seat, where they sat facing each other, and she began.

"So you see," she said, when she'd finished, "not so much guilt as shame that made me keep quiet. I knew what he was like before I embarked on the affair, I gave no thought to his wife, who I knew, and I was stupid enough to think I was different. My father never knew all of it, either." She took both his hands in hers and kissed them. "I finished the affair, Rob, when I grew up. He did not break my heart; we worked together afterwards, as friends, for over a year, and we've had no contact between then and now. That's all."

Rob closed his eyes and said, "Promise?"

"Cross my heart." Janie tugged on his hands to make him look at her. "And whilst we're on this subject, and being completely open and honest with each other, I'll tell you what happened when I took the diary to him in January."

She recounted the sorry tale of her humiliation at the hands of Margery Taylor, playing it a little for laughs, and told how Rosie had put her back together again over a couple of whiskies and a ploughman's lunch. To her relief, Rob was managing to smile. "Well done, Margery. You deserved that."

"True."

"I remember that day," Rob went on, "it was the day Joe's letter arrived."

"And the day I took Rosie's advice to forget all past follies, and go home and make my gorgeous husband glad he married me."

"I don't recall you cooking that evening…"

***

Lying in bed later that night, Janie reflected on the benefits of a good row. They had started to live their busy lives in isolation, no longer talking and sharing their problems as they had always done before and, for a while, they had ceased to be a couple. She shuddered to think how easy it was to drift apart and pulled Rob's arm across her body to draw him closer.

She was very nearly asleep when she felt the brush of his lips on the back of her neck.

***

Waking early, Janie crept out of bed and made straight for her office. Cat was sitting on the window sill, looking out across the meadows, when she entered, but leapt over the desk and stretched high against the back of the chair to greet her mistress. Janie swept her up, together with Dick's fax, and went downstairs to the kitchen.

She read the short, transcribed entries that Dick had sent, and then read them again. The lines were few, but spoke volumes, and Janie found herself to be deeply affected by them.

She took a cup of tea up to her husband.

Alice's Diary

February 1666

Jennet knows there is something wrong. She knows that

this dark mood and the evidence of tears are not solely because I am grieving for my father.

How can I tell her that my husband thinks me a wanton and not a respectable wife? He says 'of course' he cares for me but his manner has changed and I do not feel loved. I feel dirty and humiliated and I shall not risk debasing myself again.

He has not returned to my bed even though I am not unclean.

March 1666

I am forgiven. This vessel is with child.

William is overjoyed and harmony appears to be restored. I shall need Jennet with me in the house – Martha will have to take over in the dairy.

March 1666

William is being very gentle with me and rather overprotective, although this is understandable considering his previous experience of childbirth. It does, however, make me feel more like an invalid and less like a perfectly healthy young woman with child. Jennet tells me that the sickness and lethargy will pass soon and I shall be full of energy again. That may be so, but I suspect that William will be against me walking or riding about the farm as before. Surely, though, he cannot object to my taking the trap?

I shall raise the subject with him tomorrow.

~ 31 ~
Oakwood Grange, March 1666

"It is out of the question, Alice. You must see that." William's face was thunderous as he snatched Alice's boots from Jennet's hands. "You can leave us now, Jennet."

Jennet bobbed a curtsey, "Yes, master," and she left Alice's chamber, closing the door on her way out.

"I need some fresh air, William, and taking the trap means I can look over the farm with Henry. There are orders to check, repairs to be assessed and so much else to be discussed..."

William cut her off. "Driving the trap can be dangerous, anything could spook the horse and cause an accident. Anyway, you needn't worry about the farm. I have already told Durling what I want doing and I'm waiting for him to give me an idea of the cost and quantities involved. It's all in hand."

Alice looked aghast. "But we haven't discussed this. Has Henry spoken to you about our plans for rotating the crops this year?"

William finally lost his temper. "Really Alice, farm management is not a suitable occupation for a lady, especially one who is soon to be a mother. Do you think I am not capable of running the farm as well as you do? Why can you not amuse yourself, as do other ladies of your station, with needlepoint or lace making?

Alice's face had drained of all colour and she was having difficulty containing her anger. "That is because I do not enjoy such things, as you well know."

"Well, what about drawing? I am happy to engage a sketching tutor for you if you wish."

"I do NOT wish," Alice stood up to face him, fists clenched at her sides, and was now shouting, "and nor do I wish to spend more time at the harpsichord before you suggest that. I'm so sorry that I do not measure up, in so many ways, to your idea of a model wife but you knew what I was like before you married me."

William was taken aback but soon recovered. He wagged a finger in her face. "This, Alice, is what comes with filling your head with ideas and education not fitting to a young woman. If our child is a daughter, I do not expect you to make the same mistake your parents made with you." Alice was speechless. "You must understand that I have to be master in my own house."

They glared furiously at each other and Alice opened her mouth to say something but thought better of it and looked away. William, though, heard the unspoken words loud and clear. He left her, slamming the door behind him.

Jennet, who'd lingered on the landing pretending to fold some laundry, had heard every word and, once William had disappeared down the stairs, she let herself into Alice's chamber without knocking. Alice rounded on her, tears of anger showing on her cheeks. "Did you know about all this, and didn't tell me?"

"No, I know the master's been about the farm a lot but I thought you knew." Jennet looked miserable. "It wasn't until yesterday when Henry came to see me that I knew something was amiss. He wants to see you as soon as possible."

Alice wiped away her tears and reached for Jennet's hand. "I'm sorry. I'm not blaming you. Please tell Henry that he should come here tomorrow after his morning round. It'll be quite safe, the master *is going to Chichester to inspect his property."*

*****

"Miss Alice, may I speak freely?" Henry Durling was not comfortable in the Grange, even though William was far away, and he was feverishly feeding the brim of his hat through his sweating fingers.

"You may, Henry. You know you can, but first let's go to the kitchen and get Mrs. Lynd to find us some refreshments."

Cook ushered out the kitchen maids and made her own tactful exit after Alice and Henry were provided for. The farm manager relaxed in the more familiar surroundings and Alice waited for him to begin. She heard his complaints in silence, nodding every now and then, to encourage him to get everything off his chest.

Last night, Alice had lain awake, replaying the scene with William over and over in her head. She had started by feeling outrage but the longer the night wore on, the more she felt that William should, perhaps, be more involved with the farm, especially given her condition. Jennet's advice, too, was making her rethink her position, 'Marriage is give and take, Alice. It's that simple.' By this morning, she was still smarting from the things he'd said and the way he had gone behind her back but she'd resolved to be more supportive of him.

"Henry, I know this period when I'm not around as much might be difficult, but the master is a proud man and we must allow him to make the final decisions. He will make mistakes, as I did at first, but he'll learn and we must try to mitigate any damage without calling into question his authority. Rest assured, Henry, that no one will blame you if one or two things go wrong. I shall try to still be involved but, as I said, the master is a proud man." Alice smiled at him and hoped that she'd sounded sincere.

Henry looked far from convinced. "Alright, Miss Alice, as long as you know what's going on; but it's not the same as working with you."

"I'm sure everything will work out," Alice reached out and laid a hand on his shoulder, "but there is one thing that still worries me and that's the state of the farm cottages. I want to inspect them myself and I think you and I should go and do it now, straight away. Please go and tell Edmund to prepare the trap."

***

William returned from Chichester in a black mood and although Alice tried to engage him in conversation about his trip, his answers were terse and offered no information. He was obviously still furious with her but she sensed that his day had not gone well either.

"I hear you've been riding around the farm with Durling, Alice. I thought I'd made my feelings about that quite clear yesterday." William glared at her.

For the first time, Alice felt a little intimidated which made it easier to stay calm and to try a more conciliatory approach. "Henry was driving, William, not I, and it was only a very short trip to look at the cottages, that's all." She paused and went over to link her arm through his. "I was quite safe."

William looked sideways at her. "And the purpose of this visit?"

"Well," said Alice, " I know you've been very busy and I don't suppose you've had time to inspect the cottages, but the roofs are in a bad way and if we don't repair them before winter, the damage next year will end up costing us more."

William pondered this for a moment, surprised by her change in attitude and, for the sake of restoring some harmony in the house, decided a compromise might be in order. "Very well, Alice, I shall go and look myself and, should some basic repairs be necessary, then I shall give the order." He patted her arm.

Alice smiled up at him, sweetly.

173

~ 32 ~
Petworth, Early April 1986

The young man waiting at the church door was nothing like the vicar. Tall and thin, sporting a suit and dog collar clearly designed for a fatter person, and with neat blonde hair, he peered at Janie through pale watery eyes. "Mrs. Whittaker, I presume."

She nodded, smiled and held out her hand. The curate hesitated before offering a brief, limp handshake but no returning smile. "This way." Janie followed him to the sacristy, as he talked to her over his shoulder. "The vicar sends his apologies. He's been called away on church business and has left me in charge today. I believe you've been here once already." He made it sound like an accusation.

Janie glared at his back as she followed him into the record room and placed her bag on the centre table. "I'm looking for the marriage record of my great grandmother, Lily, to Robert Stedman, probably in the 1890's. It'll be in that book there; would you mind getting it down for me, please?"

The curate made a production of getting a bunch of keys from his pocket and squinting at the labels before finally selecting the right one and opening the bookcase. Dragging the book from the shelf, he was clearly surprised by the weight of it, and delivered it to her with a thump, before taking a seat at the end of the table.

Fifteen minutes in, Janie was finding it difficult to concentrate. She could see him at the edge of her eye line and knew that it would only take one more sigh or ill-disguised glance at his watch, before she lost her temper. Chin propped on one hand, and without looking up from the book, the tone of her voice underlined just how pissed off she was. "If there is something more pressing that you need to do, I could always arrange with the vicar to come back at a more convenient time."

The curate's chair dropped back onto all four legs, and his pale face reddened alarmingly as Janie now looked sideways at him. "Oh, no, no," he stammered, "take all the time you like." At once deflated and embarrassed, he stood up and straightened his jacket. "I'm supposed to stay here with you but, as you know the vicar, I'm certain it'll be alright if I leave you to it." He made his way to the door and Janie followed him with her eyes. "I do have something to do in the church…but I'll pop back to see how you're getting on." He shot out of the door.

Janie relaxed into her task, feeling no guilt.

As luck would have it, she found the entry on the very next page, and knew that her search in Petworth had come to an end. Lily's maiden name was Remmant and the record stated that she was from Fittleworth. More importantly, it showed that her middle name was also Celeste, confirming Mark's assertion that it was a name handed down through the family.

Janie copied all the details, closed the record book and replaced it in the bookcase. Slipping into her coat and shouldering her bag, she made her way down the corridor to the church and peered in to find the curate giving the flower ladies the benefit of his advice. They all turned to look at her. She gave them a broad smile before addressing the curate. "Excuse me, I'm sorry to interrupt, but I found the entry I was looking for and I've replaced the register in the bookcase."

"Good, good. I'll just go and lock up then." He strode ahead up the aisle and Janie followed after turning to smile goodbye to the flower ladies. She caught them shaking their heads and smirking as they went back to their arranging.

***

On her way home, Janie detoured to Fittleworth, only a few miles down the road, and found the vicar's phone number pinned to the noticeboard of another St. Mary's church. She really wanted to wander round the gravestones, but she knew that the next search was going to have to wait till the Book Fair was over; she just couldn't spare the time.

Pulling into the drive, she could see the lights were on in the studio and went to see Rob before getting down to real, pressing work.

"I'm home..." Janie dumped her bag and coat just inside the door, the temperature, as always in the studio, was just sub-tropical, and went to give him a backwards hug as he was sitting at the drawing board.

"Easy, girl, I'm in the middle of creating something sensational for my new client. I can't afford to be distracted." He grinned as she delivered soft, little kisses round his neck, then swiveled his seat round and pulled her on to his lap with a growl. "What can I say? I'm easily distracted."

"Either that, or I'm just too irresistible." She beamed and planted a kiss on his mouth before getting off his lap. "Anyway, I'm not stopping, I've got a ton of work to do before next week."

"How did the search go?"

"Really well. I was in and out in no time, which was just as well, as the lovely vicar was away and his young, jumped up curate was in charge and he really pissed me off. I found the marriage record, Lily's maiden name was Remmant and she came from Fittleworth, so that's my next search once the Book Fair's over."

"Hey, that's brilliant. You're making progress."

"I know, I'm really pleased. Anyway, I'll leave you in peace now. See you about 6pm for drinks, and it'll have to be something from the freezer for supper, I'm afraid." Janie went to pick up her bag and coat.

"Oh, I nearly forgot," Rob had turned back to the drawing board, "your professor rang."

Janie stopped in her tracks. "Was there a message?"

"Yes. He's very excited about the latest transcript he's done and he wants you to ring him." There was nothing in Rob's voice to indicate he was still rattled by the whole 'Dick thing' but Janie couldn't see his face.

"Right…"

"And he told me that I was a very lucky man and that you were his most able student." He turned to look at her. "Of course, he didn't say in which department you were the most able…" Rob saw the stricken look on Janie's face and burst out laughing. "Joke."

"I hate you, Rob Whittaker."

"No, you don't. Tell me what you think of this before you go." He moved so that she could see the drawing board clearly.

"It's crap." She flounced out of the door, banging it behind her, and pulled a face at him as she went by the window. He was still laughing.

She grinned to herself as she made her way to the back door. It felt so good to be back where they were a few months ago, before the pressure of work and travelling had disrupted their lives, and she hadn't acknowledged, until now, just how anxious she'd been about the whole 'Dick thing'. No more secrets, she resolved, no matter what.

Up in her office, with a warm Cat on her lap, Janie was in two minds about what to do first; ring Dick or Joyce? It was still the Easter break but, with a bit of luck, Dick might be in his study in college, and she really didn't fancy ringing him at home. Get a couple of hours work in first, she told herself, and then ring Dick later; she could always leave a message.

She and Joyce had such a good working relationship that Janie only had to mention a plan of action and she knew it would be executed perfectly. Mallory's main focus at the Book Fair was to interest foreign publishers in the translation rights to their authors' books, and Janie wanted to make sure that her assistants were up to speed with who's who and what they currently published. Joyce was to provide the necessary weekend homework for the staff to avoid any embarrassing situations.

These same foreign publishers also expected to be wined and dined – and not all at the same time. This meant an exhausting round of entertaining on three consecutive nights after long days at the fair. Joyce knew the numbers for each night and Janie gave her a list of acceptable restaurants and left her to get on with it. An hour later, she'd made good progress on her own preparations for the following week, and went downstairs to feed Cat and make herself a cup of tea.

She was feeling a little nervous about ringing Dick. He'd mentioned lunch in his last fax and, although she didn't want to, she felt it would be mean spirited to refuse as he was doing her such a favour. (She could hear Rosie's voice saying, 'What? You're doing him a favour, if it really is Aphra.') And then, she'd have to tell Rob, who might, or might not, be okay with it. Oh, bloody hell. She rang.

It went to answerphone and Janie had just started her message when Dick picked up the phone. "Janie, you got me just in time, I was on my way out."

"Sorry, do you want me to ring tomorrow?"

"No, I've been waiting for you to call." Janie heard him sit down and put his case on the desk. "And it's good news, I'm convinced your Ann Bean is Aphra."

Janie gave a little shriek of excitement. "Oh, my goodness. Really?"

"Really, I'll send it all over to you first thing on Monday when Valerie opens up the office. The first three entries don't mention Ann Bean, but you'll find them interesting reading and I'll say no more about them. They take us up to September 1666. Then, rather disappointingly, there was a whole chunk of pages all stuck together which I tried to winkle apart but it was no use, and then several more sections too feint to read. As it happens though, from my point of view, it doesn't matter, because, in the next vaguely decipherable entries, Alice talks about a visit from a family friend called Thomas, who happens to be a colonel. Then, there's what is obviously the first mention of Ann Bean.

I can't make out the month – it may be June – but the year is definitely 1667 and, as you pointed out, that is very significant. And I'm pretty sure this colonel is Thomas Culpepper and that, too, if you remember Aphra's background, is also significant…"

***

"…because Aphra's mother was employed as a nurse for the Culpepper family in Kent, and some reports quote Thomas as saying he regarded Aphra as a foster sister; there was only two or three years between them." Janie was explaining to Rob why Dick was so sure that it was Aphra who had been a guest at Oakwood Grange.

Rob leaned forward on the kitchen table "It seems a bit tenuous though, doesn't it?"

"Not when you consider that in 1667, Aphra was deeply in debt because, despite working abroad as a spy for the Crown, she was never paid and had sold every personal item she possessed, just in order to exist. She accepted a loan from a chap called Edward Butler so that she could pay her way back to England and petition the King for her long overdue salary. Unfortunately, she got no response, Butler wouldn't wait any longer, and a warrant was issued for her arrest."

"So her friend, Thomas Culpepper, arranges for her to go into hiding?"

"Exactly. In fact there were several warrants out for her, over a year or so, and she was eventually thrown into jail for a short time until some unknown person paid the debt. I think that was either 1668 or 1669. Dick's desperate to read the rest of the diary to see if it all fits in with what's already known about her and, of course, to see if there's something we don't already know."

Rob was smiling at her. "Look at you, all excited about it. You can't wait to read the rest, can you?"

"No…but it'll have to wait till the Book Fair's over now." What she didn't add was that it was Alice's story she was so desperate to read, not Aphra's.

<h1 align="center">~ 33 ~
After the Book Fair</h1>

The Book Fair was over. It seemed to Janie that it had been more energy sapping than previous years and she was now looking forward to a long relaxing weekend. Truthfully, what she was looking forward to was seeing Dick's latest offering, which was waiting for her in a fat manila envelope when she got back from London.

The diary had seduced her. She was drawn to Alice's world, into seventeenth century lives played out within these walls by people who had trod the same boards and left their DNA in the grain of the same woodwork. Sometimes, she even fancied she could feel their presence.

Alice's future worried her, as if it were something that could still be changed, and one sentence kept repeating itself in her head, 'This vessel is with child', laying bare all Alice's disappointments and fears.

It was with some apprehension that she started to read…

Alice's Diary

March 1666

After all the recent disagreements over the running of the farm and my part in it, William and I have tentatively agreed on a way forward. I shall remain indoors looking after myself but continue to do the farm accounts. At least, this way, I can still keep abreast of what is going on. William will run the farm.

My main success is getting William to agree to repair the farm cottages' roofs. The repairs will be more basic than I would have liked but it is to be hoped that they will be sufficient to keep the workers and their children dry over the winter.

I am trying hard to be the wife William wants but I cannot change the way I am. Although he has never spoken Eleanor's name, I fear I am found wanting, in so many ways, when compared to his first wife.

July 1666

My baby came this morning, four months early. He was quite blue and quite dead.

I didn't think it was possible to feel such loss for a baby I never knew.

William visited me after Jennet had cleared everything away and he was very tender, but this is his second dead son and I cannot bear his sorrow.

September 1666

We have news today of the devastation caused by the great fire in London. Some are saying that it was arson and not an accident as was originally reported, and that either foreigners or Catholics are to blame. Thousands of people are now homeless and desperate with no belongings, no shelter and little food. For this tragedy to come so soon after the plague is a cruel blow to the city indeed.

It makes me ashamed. For weeks now I have been miserable and very poor company, lying abed till late, which is very unlike me, and finding no pleasure in anything. Jennet is always telling me to count my blessings and she's right – I am so very fortunate and have much to be thankful for.

June(?) 1667

We had a surprise visit from Thomas today!

I was in the garden as he rode in on a big, beautiful grey, tossed the reins to Edmund, dismounted in his usual flamboyant style and swung me around as he used to when we were children. He kissed me and apologised again for not being able to attend our wedding but was looking forward to meeting William and hoped that Mrs. Lynd was still keeping our kitchen.

As we had several hours together before William returned, we spent the time in childhood reminiscences and exchanging all our families' news. I told him all about William and warned him about his past allegiance to the Parliamentarians but Thomas's view was that the past was the past.

William, to my surprise, acted in a most deferential manner towards Thomas and persisted in calling him 'Colonel' despite being told, more than once, that Thomas would suffice.

It seems that Thomas caused quite a stir among the housemaids who were taking their time over his room, hoping to catch his eye, and even Mrs. Lynd was charmed into producing special dishes for supper. He was always one of her favourite visitors.

Supper was very convivial. William had produced several

good bottles of wine from Father's cellar, Thomas was at his most charming and there was much laughter at his anecdotes and tales of court life.

I retired early but Thomas and William are still continuing in conversation over a pipe or two in the study.

It strikes me how dull we have become when one visit from an old friend can make such a difference to our mood.

June(?) 1667

It appears that William, also, has been seduced by Thomas's easy manner and I would not have believed it unless I'd seen it with my own eyes. They are so different; Thomas, a military man for the King and a man of fashionable London tastes, and William, with his old Parliamentary leanings and plain dress. But, this morning, they were discussing all manner of things amicably, from Christopher Wren's plans for rebuilding London to Thomas's interest in Science, and I was pleased that William was now calling him just plain Thomas.

It appears that last night after I had retired, Thomas asked William if we could accommodate a friend of his, a Mrs. Ann Bean, and her companion, for, perhaps, a few months. Mrs. Bean finds herself in difficulties through no fault of her own and her situation is precarious. For reasons Thomas would not divulge, Mrs. Bean cannot be seen in London at present and needs somewhere quiet to stay. I suspect there might be a man involved. By all accounts, Mrs. Bean is cultured and amusing and William agreed, without consulting me, that it might do me good to have some female company. It appears to be a 'fait accompli' but I was pleased to agree to the arrangements, as I feel sure that any friend of Thomas's will be a friend to me.

I find myself quite excited by the prospect.

July 1667

They are here! Mrs. Bean and Elisabeth Turner, her companion, arrived late morning in Thomas's coach with a large number of trunks and chests together with a couple of horses for their convenience, supplied, no doubt, by Thomas.

I have been in a state of anxiety for the last two days, driving Cook and the housemaids to distraction with my demands, but was pleased, at last, that the house was looking its best when they arrived.

I decided, this morning, to present myself, also, in as good a light as possible and wore my best day gown and cap. It was to no effect – I still looked like a poor little house sparrow in contrast to the two exotic birds who stepped from the coach. It has been ten years since I was last in London and I had no idea that fashions had changed so much.

My first impressions:

Mrs. Bean is handsome, I think some would say very handsome, with light brown curly hair, charmingly arranged in long ringlets. She has a clear, pale complexion and large fine eyes. She is, perhaps, a little older than I, and a few inches taller. Her dress is of a wondrous mid blue satin with paned sleeves lined with the same dove grey fabric trimming the neck and the under petticoat. The bodice is long and so very tight that I wonder how she breathes. The neckline is rather wide and low, exposing her lovely shoulders.

Miss Elisabeth Turner is slightly younger, I think, with very dark hair in a much more modest style. She has something of a foreign appearance with a darker complexion and large, arresting eyes. She, too, has a satin gown of similar style but hers is rose pink. To my eyes, she is by far the more beautiful.

Mrs. Bean was quickly established in the best guest room with Tansy to settle her in. I showed Miss Turner the other available rooms and, to my great surprise, she asked if she might have the small bedroom by the back stairs. As I suspected, she is used to warmer climes, and this room is small and warm, being immediately above the kitchen. She was also charmed by the view and, I must admit, it probably does have the best outlook of all the rooms. It struck me as strange that she should take a room so far away from her mistress but, perhaps, I do not as yet fully understand their relationship.

William is still on the farm and has not met our guests yet. I am interested to see his reaction.

October 1667

Mrs. Bean (or Ann as she says I must now call her, though I cannot in front of William) has once again returned to London for a few days but, as she has no need of her on this trip, Elisabeth remains here and I admit that I am pleased to have her all to myself.

We spent a very pleasant morning together practicing a duet on the harpsichord with which we hope to surprise William on his birthday next week. Our playing is coming on much better than our singing.

Ann has entreated me for so long to abandon my coif and allow Elisabeth to dress my hair but I have always resisted for fear that I would look ridiculous. Today, though, without her influence, I trusted Elisabeth to arrange my hair in a modest style. I was very pleased with the result and felt years younger but replaced my coif before William came home. I felt sure he would not approve.

This afternoon, Elisabeth played her lute for me and taught me a new song in French. To my surprise, I discover that she is quite fluent. I have not spoken French since Mother died but now I have the opportunity, I am keen to improve.

Perhaps William will be pleased now that I have found pastimes that are more to his liking.

October 1667

Ann has returned from London but she has lost her former gay mood and spends much time alone in her room. Elisabeth attends to her and says there is no need for concern as she is not ill, but offers no explanation and I am beginning to suspect that her situation may be more complicated than at first I imagined.

I notice that she has sent several letters today, including one to Thomas.

January 1668

There was a letter for Ann today, which may have brought good news as she rose earlier than of late and was in a happy and mischievous mood.

She kept us amused with shocking tales of her travels in

the Americas and then, when Elisabeth had finished dressing my hair, insisted we take parts in a piece she is writing for the stage.

As William was away on business today, we three partook of a light midday meal and left the table in high spirits. Ann entertained us with some bawdy rhymes of her own devising, but Elisabeth and I were incapable of matching her for quickness and wit.

We spent the rest of the afternoon in French conversation. Ann has a good knowledge of the language, but her accent is lacking whereas mine is improving greatly. She eventually retired to her room and Elisabeth and I carried on without her, taking advantage of William's absence. He has no talent for languages.

William will be home in time for supper and we are all looking forward to a splendid meal.

~ 34 ~
Oakwood Grange, January 1668

"Ladies, I have come to tell you that supper is about to be served." William swept into the room and executed a little bow. "Shall we go through?" He stood aside to allow them to pass, faltered slightly and reached for the door handle to steady himself.

William escorted each one to her place at the dining table. His unusually jolly mood and heightened colour could only mean one thing and Ann, who was sitting opposite Elisabeth, raised an eyebrow as they exchanged a look. Alice, who had started the evening in high spirits, was now silent and fiddling nervously with her napkin.

When everyone was served with food, William opened the conversation. "Well, ladies, I trust you've had an enjoyable day?"

"Mr. Harryman," Ann began, "we have, thank you. I think we would all agree that we've had a most entertaining day. You may possibly think us frivolous but we have laughed so much this afternoon that my sides are still aching."

"And what was the source of all this merriment, may I ask?" William drained his glass and immediately refilled it. He topped up Ann's glass but the other two were still untouched.

Elisabeth shot a glance at Ann and replied first. "Mrs. Bean was regaling us with tales of her travels in South America."

"And Elisabeth and I were trying our hand at composing poetry but our efforts were laughable compared with Mrs. Bean's," Alice managed to add. William insisted on hearing some of their efforts and they duly obliged with Ann resisting the temptation to recite some of the more bawdy verses that had so amused them earlier.

William raised his glass and saluted Ann, pushing away his plate and leaning back in his chair. "Why, Mrs. Bean, a poet and a traveller; you have been keeping all this very quiet. Were you in South America with your husband?"

There was an uncomfortable pause. Thomas had suggested that this was a subject to be avoided. Alice and Elisabeth concentrated on their food but Ann turned to look him squarely in the face, the smile on her lips never reaching her eyes. "No, sadly, my husband is no longer with us. I went to the colony of Surinam with my parents, for business reasons, but it came to nought and we returned to England." And with that, she, too, drained her glass.

By the time dessert was served, Alice had rescued the situation by getting William to discuss his recent trip to Chichester and the arrangements for rebuilding the cathedral spire. Ann was clearly becoming bored with his monologue. She and William had matched each other glass for glass all evening, although they all knew he'd had a head start, and Elisabeth, recognising danger signs, prepared to excuse herself and break up the party.

"Elisabeth," Ann looked at her pointedly, "it's far too early to retire and, anyway, I wish to hear what Mr. Harryman has to say about his wife's hair." She turned towards him and smiled sweetly. "Elisabeth has spent much of the morning creating those lovely curls; do you not think Mrs. Harryman looks quite the picture?"

William, who had chosen to ignore his wife's appearance with a view to discussing it with her later, stumbled a little over his words. Alice could not meet his eyes.

"I...I can appreciate the...er...artistry, madam, but I feel that such refinements are rather out of place for a married woman who... who... spends all her time in the country. I prefer Alice in a coif. It is a more sensible option."

Ann visibly bridled. "Well, I think she looks quite charming, although I agree that, even in a coif, she is still a beautiful young woman. It seems to me, Mr. Harryman, that such a lovely young bride should be shown off whilst she is still in her prime, dressed in satins and pearls and admired by all. Or do you wish to keep her to yourself?"

William forced a small laugh and appealed to Alice, who looked close to tears. "Mrs. Bean thinks I am forcing you to accept this quiet country life, Alice, but we must put her right." Turning to Ann, "Alice has never been interested in fashion or balls or any other social activity. In fact, before we were married she was only ever concerned with the farm, education and other serious matters. I am indebted to you, Mrs. Bean and Miss Turner, for diverting her from business affairs but I think neither of us wishes to be part of smart society." William raised his eyebrows in Alice's direction for her cue to speak.

"Dear Mrs. Bean, William speaks the truth. I thank you both for your efforts to make something of me but I fear I am a lost cause." She attempted a weak smile to Ann and a silent plea to drop the subject. "I fear I am quite the country mouse."

William passed around the port and even Alice and Elisabeth accepted a glass, hoping that all danger had been averted. It was a vain hope. Ann drank hers down in one with no apparent ill effects apart from her inability to abide by the good manners of a houseguest.

"Your wife's loyalty does you great credit, Mr. Harryman, but I have seen the pleasure she derives from singing and dancing and there is no opportunity for such diversions in this small community."

Alice started to say something but Ann continued speaking over her, "and today, when we were play-acting and she was dressed in one of my gowns with her hair curled, why, I have never seen her look more alive and more lovely. I wish you had seen her."

Alice groaned inwardly. "William, it was only..." she began, but he silenced her.

"Play-acting, Alice, in my house?"

"Really, Mr. Harryman, " Ann seemed satisfied now that she had succeeded in provoking him, "it is only a little play that I am writing. It's called 'The Forced Marriage'. There is really nothing shocking about play-acting – everyone in London goes to the theatre these days – and women are no longer barred from the stage. It is quite respectable."

"That, madam, is a matter of opinion," William replied, furious. "Sit down, Alice. We have not finished our discussion."

"Well, perhaps," Ann continued, "when I am re-established in London, which I hope will be soon, I can return your hospitality and you and Mrs. Harryman can experience a play for yourselves."

William downed his second glass of port. "I, too, hope that your return to London will be soon, Mrs. Bean, as I fear our company is far too dull for you."

At this point, Elisabeth chose to stand and Ann took the hint. William rose as they made their 'Goodnights' and swept past him. Alice was left to face the music alone.

✳✳✳

Ann and William bumped into each other in the hall the following morning. Ann was on her way out for an early morning ride and her riding habit did little to alter William's opinion that this woman was no suitable companion for his wife. Apart from the petticoat, the whole outfit was more suited to a man.

Ignoring his obvious distaste, Ann struck a pose and smiled broadly. "Dear Mr. Harryman, I fear I owe you an apology for my outspoken remarks last evening. I could blame your excellent wines and generous hospitality for my intemperance but I know that I only have myself to blame. I am a terrible guest. Please forgive me."

"Madam," William replied, managing a thin smile, "think nothing of it. I'm sure I was equally at fault."

Ann inclined her a head a little and gazed up at him through long lashes. "You are very kind and I really am most grateful to you for accommodating us for these past months. However, I'm sure you will be pleased to learn that I plan to go to London soon for a month or so but, as I shall have no fixed lodgings, I should be most grateful if Elisabeth could remain here."

Both parties delivered these pretty apologies with good grace, but neither meant it and, of course, they both knew it.

~ 35 ~
April 1986

Rob poked his head round Janie's office door. "You found the post then?" He indicated the envelope next to her. "I guessed who that was from."

Janie noted her husband's reluctance to use Dick's name and cocked an eyebrow in his direction. "You're right, it is. He knew I wouldn't get round to reading it for a few days, so he posted it instead of faxing and added a whole raft of facts about Aphra that I'd forgotten, if, indeed, I ever knew them."

"Has he finished the whole diary, or is there more?" He shooed Cat off the sofa, sat down next to her and put his arm round her.

"There's quite a bit more, I think, but he's now in no doubt that our Ann Bean is Aphra Behn. He's transcribed more since I last spoke to him and it's all here; her trip to Surinam, her playwriting, her ability to speak French, her trips to..."

"She went to Surinam?"

"Yeah, I'd forgotten about that," and she picked up Dick's notes. "He says here that she went to Surinam with her parents. It was an English colony at the time and it's thought that her father had been given a post there. Unfortunately, the poor man died on the voyage, but the remaining family carried on and lived there until the Restoration of the monarchy. While they were there, Aphra became an avid reader, of French literature as well as English, and that's when she began writing."

"So, how did she get into the spying game?"

"Well…are you sure you want to hear all about this?" Cat had jumped back onto the sofa and was trying to lie down between them. Janie firmly moved her to her other side.

"Course, I do – it's fascinating. I'm just going to get a cigarette. Do you want anything?" Janie shook her head.

He came back, cigarette in mouth and carrying two mugs. "I thought you'd want one as soon as you smelled the coffee," and he sat down on her desk chair, facing her.

"Mmm, thanks." Janie took the mug and looked back at Dick's notes. "To continue, shortly after she got back to London, Aphra met a wealthy Dutch merchant, called Mr. Behn, and married him. They led a charmed life, attending what was considered a very racy court, and some say that the King, Charles II, was very taken with her beauty, conversation and wit. Anyway, when Mr. Behn died a couple of years later, possibly of the plague, Aphra found herself in dire straits and, probably because of her Dutch connection and facility with languages, was recruited as a political spy and sent to Holland."

"Why was she sent to Holland?"

"Because relations between the Dutch and the English were very poor at that time and we were gearing up for the Second Dutch War; it was all about trade routes, I think."

Rob squinted through the cigarette smoke. "And we know the rest, it didn't turn out to be a good move. How old was she when all this was happening?"

Janie flicked back to the beginning of Dick's notes. "She was born in 1640, so…that would make her 27 or 28 when she was in hiding here."

"Remarkable. And then she become a famous playwright afterwards?"

She consulted Dick's notes again. "Yes, here it is, her first play was performed in 1670. It was called 'The Forc'd Marriage' and, Dick's particularly excited about this, he thinks there's a reference to it in the diary. But, until he's finished with the whole thing, we won't know if she was still here then, or not. It seems unlikely, though. Her troubles were over in 1669, because some unknown person paid her debts, and Dick reckons she returned to London then."

"Is she really famous, though?" Rob stubbed out his cigarette. "I bet most people have never heard of her."

"I guess it's probably only literature students who know about her, mainly because she's the first woman credited with earning a living through her writing. And she was prolific. Not only did she write plays, but also poetry, novels and short stories and she was celebrated in literary and social circles alike for her skill and wit. She was also famous, or infamous, for her unconventional lifestyle and her string of lovers. She never remarried."

Rob was grinning, "Do you think she carried on in our bedroom?"

"Well, no, seeing as how the major rooms were destroyed in the fire and our bedroom was built much later. Also, if what I'm reading about William Harryman is true, then I think it extremely unlikely that Aphra's lovers would have been welcomed."

"I see. Interesting, is it?"

"Well, I think so, but I'll tell you about Alice and William later. Do you want to know what happened to Aphra?"

"Sure, is there more?"

"Only that she died when she was 49 and, to answer your question about whether or not she was really famous; she was buried in Westminster Abbey."

∗∗∗

After Rob had gone to make a few phone calls, Janie took another sip of coffee and pulled a face. Heaven knows what he'd done, but it tasted weird and she put the mug down and left it.

She was beginning to really dislike William Harryman. A cold man, a Parliamentarian with a puritan streak, he appeared to have no scruples about marrying into a Royalist household. Janie mistrusted his motives and wondered if Alice's mother would have allowed the match.

Her heart went out to Alice. Intelligent and capable, warm and passionate, and so soon to be disillusioned after falling for the man she married, nevertheless, she still seemed eager to please him. Would the miscarriage bring them closer together? Janie felt it might.

Five years ago, she and Rob had been in a similar situation. They hadn't been living together for very long and the pregnancy had been an accident. Despite that, when the miscarriage happened, the sense of loss had so surprised them both that it was a huge factor in their decision to get married. They'd planned to have lots of children.

A sudden burst of activity in the magnolia outside the window interrupted her thoughts. It had been a bitterly cold April, one of the coldest, and this reminder that Spring wasn't far away made her want to get out in the garden to see what was stirring. Not today, though. Last week at the Book Fair had been exhausting; talking all day long as well as keeping an eye on her assistants, it had been a chore to drag herself out every evening. She lay down on her little sofa, pulled up her knees and closed her eyes.

Cat, from her vantage point on the rug next to the sofa, watched as her mistress drifted into sleep.

Tableaux featuring three women, with no narrative to connect them, shifted in and out of focus as her brain sifted and processed information before laying it down in memory banks. She knew instinctively who they were. They couldn't hear her when she tried to attract their attention but, just before they drifted away, one turned her head, looked straight at her and said 'hello'.

Janie woke with a start, the woman's face still clear in her mind. Not Alice, she knew that. Alice had freckles, so her hair must have been some shade of auburn. Aphra, by all accounts, had curly, light brown hair. Janie reached for the diary to find the right page. 'Very dark hair…a foreign appearance with a darker complexion and large, arresting eyes.' This was Elisabeth Turner, she was quite sure of it. Reading further down the page, she noticed something she'd missed before, probably because she was so wrapped up with Aphra.

This room, her office, was Elisabeth's bedroom.

~ 36 ~
Oxford, Late April 1986

"It's changed a bit in here." Janie looked around the restaurant and could find little to remind her of the old bistro. "What happened to the checked tablecloths and candles in Chianti bottles?" she added in a whisper.

Dick helped her off with her coat and whispered back, "I know. It's a shame, but it's still run by the Berardis and the food's just as good as ever."

The younger Berardis, no doubt responsible for the revamp, were now all front-of-house and Janie didn't recognise any of them, but after an explosion of rapid Italian, their mother burst out of the kitchen to welcome 'il mio professore' with kisses on each cheek. It was clear that this was still Dick's trysting place of choice. Janie couldn't help a little smile, but then was completely floored when Mama Berardi turned to her, put a hand on her shoulder and said, 'linguini alle vongole?'

"It's been years. How on earth did you remember that?"

Mama Berardi shrugged. "Cosi bella, come potrei dimenticare?"

Janie's Italian wasn't good, but she got the gist. "You are kind, and I'm not even going to look at the menu. If you still do linguini with clams, then that's what I'm having."

Dick handed back his menu. "Make that two, and a bottle of Pinot Grigio, please."

"So," Dick rested both elbows on the table and leaned forward, "how's life treating you, Janie?"

She settled back into her chair and crossed her arms. "Very good indeed. It can be hectic at times, both of us working flat out, but we love living where we do. We wouldn't change it."

Dick leaned back to allow the waiter to pour the wine and then raised his glass in a toast. "To you and Rob."

"I'll drink to that. Thank you."

"Any plans for a family?" Dick nonchalantly unfolded his napkin and placed it on his knees.

"We did have plans, but it never happened, and it's not something we think about anymore. Marriages often work without children, or sometimes because there are no children. You should know that."

Dick gave a little snort. "The reason my marriage works, if it does, has nothing to do with children, or the lack of, and I certainly wouldn't hold it up as an example to anyone."

"That's true." Janie took a sip of wine and grinned as she replaced the glass on the table.

Dick hitched his shoulders, raised his eyebrows and gave a comic grin. "I did think about propositioning you again, of course, but I knew I wouldn't stand a chance and, anyway, your husband sounds a very decent bloke. We had quite a chat. He knows about us, obviously."

"What did you talk about?

"You, what else?" Her serious face made him chuckle. "No need to worry. He was a little offhand to begin with, that's how I supposed he knew, but the more we talked, the more I think he realised he had nothing to fear from this pathetic, ageing Lothario." The shamefaced grin again, and then he reached out for her hands. "We are still friends though, aren't we, Janie?"

It was on the tip of her tongue to say it had been a close run thing, but she suddenly felt so sorry for him, she just squeezed his hands instead. They pulled apart as their food arrived.

After digging in and savouring the first mouthful, Janie steered the conversation back to the diary. "So, don't keep me in suspense any longer. Have you found out any more interesting facts about Aphra?"

Dick dabbed his mouth before replying. "Not really. I think the fact that she went into hiding at your house, whilst dodging arrest warrants, is the significant revelation. Then there's Elisabeth Turner. I can find no mention of her anywhere else, either by name or as a travelling companion, but I'll keep researching that." He turned back to his pasta. "Apart from that, the diary does a great job confirming everything that we already know about Aphra, but it doesn't appear to add anything significant. Not so far, anyway."

"Oh, that's a shame. Is there much left to transcribe?"

"The last entry is January 1671, so I've a way to go. The pages I've just given to you take us up to May 1668 and Aphra has just returned to London. It may be she doesn't go back to the Grange at all." He refilled her glass and sensed her disappointment. "On the other hand...I know you don't want me to tell you what's in there," he pointed to the envelope he'd given her, "but there's a lot going on in your house, and Elisabeth Turner is proving to be a very interesting lady."

"Really?" Janie looked up from winkling out the last of the clams. "I'm quite keen to find more out about Elisabeth, especially as I now know that the room I'm using as my office was her bedroom. You will let me know if you manage to discover anything about her, won't you?"

"Sure." Dick was signaling for more bread. "Can't let all this sauce go to waste, even though there's enough garlic in here to keep me safe from evil spirits for the rest of my life."

Janie laughed. She thought about mentioning the fireplace with the witches' marks but decided against it. Instead, she talked about Alice. "You probably think this is silly, but I like to read Alice's diary when I'm quiet and on my own. At first, it didn't seem to matter, but now, reading it to others feels a bit like a breach of confidence. Even Rob - I give him the potted version." She shot him a glance to see his reaction. "I feel I know her so well, Dick, that I hear her voice when I read her words."

"I don't think it's silly, not at all. Apart from me, and I don't really count, it's highly likely that you're the first person ever to read her words. Two young women, both married, and who, despite a gap of 300-odd years, have inhabited the same house. It would be odd if you didn't feel empathy – and a reluctance to share her." Smiling fondly, Dick offered the bottle, but Janie declined and he filled his glass with the remainder of the wine. "What about William?"

Janie rolled her eyes. "Rob and I fundamentally disagree about William. He thinks the poor man was shafted by the marriage settlement, stripping him of his pride, and confining him to the role of sperm donor.

Dick made a gesture to indicate that that was a perfectly acceptable point of view. "And you?"

"Oh, I could go on, but the short answer is that I think William married for status, money and a family, in that order, and so far, at any rate, has been disappointed in all three. Alice was a means to an end, and it was her misfortune that she actually fell for him."

"So you think William was using Alice, and Rob thinks Alice was using William? Interesting. I make no comment, but I'll be interested to know what you think after reading the next lot."

***

The late train home was quiet, and Janie found herself alone in her carriage. She pulled the envelope out of her bag and started to read…

Alice's Diary

January 1668

Last night over supper, tensions between William and Ann, which have become somewhat strained of late, finally came to a head and words were exchanged. The wine was partly to blame. Apologies were delivered this morning, so Elisabeth tells me, but Ann is leaving for London in the next couple of days and may not return for several weeks.

I must confess that this is a relief, as William's sour moods have become something of a trial recently and Ann's presence has not helped.

I am hoping that my news will cheer him, for both Elisabeth and I think that I am with child again. The prospect fills me with joy and fear in equal measure but, this time, Elisabeth will be here to help me.

February 1668

The sickness has been so bad these last few days that I have not left my bed. Neither food nor liquid will stay down and I have a headache that will not go away. This is worse than before and, this time, there is a pain in my lower back, which makes every position uncomfortable.

Elisabeth has much experience as a midwife and has promised to make a tonic to help the sickness. She and Jennet have been out collecting herbs today and tomorrow they hope to find the other ingredients at the market.

I hope it works.

March 1668

Elisabeth's tonic is fermenting in the kitchen and I should be able to start taking it tomorrow. I don't know what I shall do if it doesn't work.

I had a very strange experience this afternoon. Elisabeth

asked if I was prepared to let her touch me as she felt she could help rid me of my aches and pains. Jennet was with us and she nodded encouragingly, so I agreed. Elisabeth asked me to take off all my clothes and lie face down near the edge of the bed and this I did, feeling a little nervous and glad that William was out on the farm and there was no chance of him finding us like this.

Other than my mother and Jennet, no woman has ever touched my body and I feared that I would find it unnatural. I need not have worried. She used small, gentle, circular motions on various parts of my body and then laid her hands on the small of my back. At first I felt a warm, soothing glow and then a curious feeling under her hands as though something were moving. Elisabeth then turned me over, covered me with a quilt and asked me to lie across the bed with my head overhanging the edge. She sat close by and rested my head in her lap. I closed my eyes and felt her trace little patterns over my brow and temples with gentle pressure and, before long, my head felt so very heavy and she cupped it in her hands. A beautiful, peaceful calm overtook me; I could feel the tightness in my head relax and I do not know how long I stayed like that.

Jennet and Elisabeth must have moved me but I don't remember. I awoke in the early evening having slept for four hours, feeling refreshed and free of all pain.

I even managed to eat the coddled egg that Jennet brought to me a little later. She is full of respect for Elisabeth who, she says, knows 'the old ways' and says that I should not be afraid but trust her to help me.

I do trust her. I know Elisabeth would never harm me.

Still – I shall not mention it to William.

March 1668

Ann has summoned Elisabeth back to London, just when I need her here. She has promised to return as soon as she is able, at any rate, before baby is born.

April 1668

It is a week since I lost my baby. Another boy.

I cannot stop the tears, not even when I'm asleep. My pillow is damp each morning and my heart breaks anew. Jennet is more like a mother than ever, fussing over me and fretting about my lack of appetite.

The loss of our first baby seemed to bring William and me closer together; we shared the sorrow. This time it seems very different. Is it true that all I see in William's face is disappointment when he looks at me? Or is it that guilt and shame have given me a warped perspective on everything? For I do feel guilt even though logic tells me that I have nothing to feel guilty about. I have rested as much as any woman can and my appetite did improve once Elisabeth's tonic took hold.

It is surely a woman's main purpose in life to produce children – some would say that it is the only purpose – and my failure to do this does cause me shame.

May 1668

The trustees paid a visit today, wishing to speak to us on urgent business.

Even up here in my chamber, I heard William's raised voice and, soon after, the sound of departing horses. William was furious that, even though he told them that I was indisposed, they insisted on speaking to both of us together and will return tomorrow afternoon.

As my husband has shown nothing but irritation at my unwillingness to leave my chamber, due to my low mood and lack of energy, I am rather suspicious that now he would prefer it if I were to remain there.

May 1668

I am partly to blame for what has occurred. I should never have relinquished the farm accounts after my first pregnancy. I should have tried to work with William on farm matters instead of amusing myself with my new friends and assuming that he would cope.

And now this is the result of my weakness. The trustees have been very clear; Henry and I are to manage the farm together, as we did before, and William is to have no more involvement. His pride is deeply wounded and I can sympathise with him for having to undergo such a humiliating interview, especially in front of me, and the outcome seems very hard on him. However, I was dismayed at his refusal to acknowledge that he had a part to play in the failure of the farm and his willingness to blame everything and anyone else has made me see him in a different light.

I wonder how much of his behaviour is down to his drinking. Or is this the true nature of the man I married?

~ 37 ~
Oakwood Grange, May 1668

The trustees had gone, no doubt relieved that the acrimonious meeting was over.

Alice was sitting at the table in the dining hall, the farm accounts spread out before her, her heart beating a little too quickly with the shock of what had just been revealed to her. She was already feeling fragile on this, the first day she had dressed properly and received company for weeks, but now all colour had drained from her face and she felt quite faint.

William, on the other hand, was furiously pacing around the table, one moment cursing the trustees, and the next, with his hands on the table, glaring at Alice and attempting to deflect any criticism that may be coming his way. It was the first time Alice had seen him in the cold light of day for some time and she was struck by the change in him. His face, once so handsome, was now slightly bloated and somewhat flushed and the calm, controlled manner, which had almost come to define him, was completely absent.

Incapable of dealing with the situation, Alice announced that she was retiring to her chamber and that they should discuss everything the next day, when William had calmed down.

Back in her room, Jennet brought her some food and a little brandy, made no comment on what she had undoubtedly heard, but *asked if there was anything she needed.*

"Yes, Jennet. You should find the farm accounts on the table in the dining hall. Please bring them to me, along with the household accounts, some paper, a quill and some ink. Oh, and several more candles, please. I think I shall need them."

Although she and William had agreed that Alice should attend to the farm accounts, she was so indisposed after her first miscarriage that William had assumed responsibility for them, as well as the farm. Consequently, this was the first time that Alice had seen them for some time and she berated herself for her weakness in not insisting on a return to their agreement. They made shocking reading and the trustees were right to be worried. She was worried. Grain yields were down, cattle numbers were down, fewer itinerants had been hired and, most shocking of all, the farm workers wages were in arrears. It seemed that expenditure on maintenance was the only item to increase, perhaps, Alice thought, because she had made such an issue about the farm cottages. He must have decided to completely re-roof them, after all.

William's explanation of a series of unfortunate incidents plus idle workers, poor market prices and unfavourable weather conditions, could not wholly account for such a decline in so short a time. This was farming; things rarely ran smoothly and overcoming problems was part of the job. Alice pored over the accounts until late into the night and decided to visit Henry Durling in the morning.

Despite her lack of sleep, Alice rose feeling quite alert and with a sense of purpose she hadn't felt for some time. She breakfasted in her room, left the house without seeing William, and made for the stables.

"Here you are, Miss Alice, she's all ready for you. Are you sure you'll be all right?" Edmund helped her up into the saddle but hung onto the reins tightly until he was sure that Jennet had been right when she said that Alice was determined to ride today.

"I shall take it steady, Edmund. I don't intend taking any fences today – you can rest assured about that. It's a beautiful day and some gentle exercise in the fresh air can only be good for me. Now, if you would strap that bag to the back of the saddle for me, I'll be off."

She didn't go directly to find Henry but, instead, trotted around the farm inspecting fences, farm buildings and cottages. She checked the grain store, spent some time with Gabe in the chicken run and looked in on Martha in the dairy. Despite her worries, it amused her to see one of the village boys escaping through the milking parlour door as he heard her horse, and thought it was a good job for Martha that it was she, and not Edmund, who'd caught her. Not willing to put it off any longer, Alice turned round and backtracked to the field where she'd seen Henry with the cattle. She called him over and they arranged to meet back at his cottage.

***

Seated opposite each other at Henry's kitchen table, Alice felt the weariness of the man, noted how thin he had become and how deeply etched were the lines on his face. Henry found it difficult to look at her.

The trustees had sought him out on their first visit when they had been unable to see Alice, and he was well aware of the purpose of this meeting.

"Let me say straight away, Henry," Alice began, "that I do not hold you responsible for these figures," and she laid her hands on the papers she'd taken from her bag. "I am not here to apportion blame. I know it's been difficult for you recently and I know that no-one works harder, or is more loyal, than you."

Henry met her eyes for the first time. "I don't want to speak out of turn, Miss Alice, but even though I've only ever known this cottage and this farm, there have been times this last year when I *would have left if it weren't for you and the memory of your father." Henry lowered his eyes again. "And I couldn't speak to you. I didn't want to add to your troubles."*

The tears came without warning and she quickly dashed them away. "Right, well things are going to change now," and she reached across the table and gently shook his hand to make him look at her again. "I have great plans, Henry. There will be exciting times ahead. Do you remember our plan to copy the Dutch?"

Henry wiped his nose on the back of his hand. "What, you mean like planting turnips instead of leaving fallow fields?"

"Exactly, that is what we're going to do. I want us to meet again next week with your plans for all the fields. And we'll need to build a new barn because, once we have the fodder, we'll try keeping the stock through the winter. Just think – milk, butter and beef all year round, Henry, and not just for us, but for market as well. Plus we'll get valuable manure for the fields. We're going to make this work."

"But the master…" he let the rest of the sentence hang.

"Is not your concern. You will answer only to me."

Something resembling a smile twitched the corners of Henry's mouth. "It sounds grand, Miss."

"I know that this is a lot to take in now, but I want to outline my other plans and I want you to consider them carefully because, next week, we will discuss it all in detail, together with any ideas you may have."

Alice's plans involved getting the maximum out of all areas of the farm and every worker, not to work them to death, but to give each man responsibilities and training. Seth and Gabe were currently at the beck and call of all the hands, doing a bit of everything, and they would still lend a hand when help was needed, but Alice wanted Seth to take sole charge of the piggery and Gabe was to learn everything about chickens. Alice was going to speak to Chicken Nan in the village. A short apprenticeship for Gabe in exchange for free cream and butter should seal the deal, and Seth's cousin was already a pig man at a neighbouring farm so he should be able to get all the help he needed. She knew this was a risk, but the fact that most of the workers were still here, even though they hadn't been paid recently, spoke volumes for their loyalty.

Alice felt that Henry had enough to think about now but, next week, she was going to tell him about importing a Dutch bull to improve their stock, the expansion of the dairy and her desire to find new markets. Oakwood was to become a proper business.

"Before I leave, I want to ask you about something in the accounts." Alice spread the papers before him although she knew he couldn't read very well. "There is a purchase here for roofing tiles. It's quite a large sum. I assumed that these were for the farm cottages but I saw today that no new tiles have been used. Do you know anything about this?"

Henry looked at her, puzzled. "I've seen no roofing tiles, Miss. If I had, I'd have used them straight away. The cottage roofs are in a bad way."

Alice was now feeling quite uneasy but decided to plough on. "And here, there's an item for labouring in October. Why did we need to employ people in October?"

Henry shook his head. "We've had no labourers, just the usual itinerants at harvest time but even they didn't stay long. The master stopped them foraging and trapping in the woods and so they moved on."

There was no more to be said. Unwilling to pursue an exercise causing embarrassment to both of them, Alice packed the accounts back into the bag and headed back to the stables. Edmund ran out to meet her and lifted her down. "Are you all right, Miss Alice? I'm not sure this was a good idea, you're looking awful pale."

Alice forced a smile. "I really don't know who's worse, you or Jennet. I'm quite well, thank you," and Alice took the bag he handed to her. "Edmund, tell me. Is everything all right with the horses and the stables? Do you want for anything?"

"No, Miss. I think we're more than all right."

"Good, I'm glad," and she turned to go.

"There's just one thing though, Miss, now you're asking. It's the saddler, Mr. Stapely."

Edmund paused and Alice turned back to face him. "What about him?"

"He hasn't been paid, Miss, for the master's new saddle, boots and tack. It's been a couple of months now…"

Alice thought for a moment. "Well, you tell Mr. Stapely to present his account directly to me and give him my apologies. I'm afraid the master has been rather distracted and overworked lately and it must have been overlooked."

"Right you are, Miss, and can I say how good it is to see you out and about again and I'm sorry for, you know, your trouble."

Alice was taken aback for a second or two until she realised that he was talking about the baby.

$$\sim 38 \sim$$

End April 1986

"One generation further back, then. Aren't you pleased?" Rob was driving them back from Fittleworth where he'd been helping Janie go through the church records.

"Yes, course I am. It's just that I'm a bit disappointed that Lily's mother doesn't have Celeste in her name."

"Why?"

"Because I'd like to find the original Celeste, the one whose first name was Celeste or Celestine, surely there must be one somewhere along the line." Janie hadn't meant to mention Celestine, but now she had and she could see the little puzzled look on Rob's face. An explanation was overdue and she took a deep breath. "There's a Celestine Palmer in the House Book. She married Miles Lyckfold in 1812 and they had seven children, but it seems they didn't have much luck. Their eldest son, also Miles, died at the Battle of Vitoria in the Peninsula war – he was only 17 – and then, in 1815, they abandoned the Grange after the fire which destroyed the front of the house. Several of their children were killed in the blaze. Miles survived because there's an entry for his death some years later, but there's no record for Celestine."

Rob gave her a knowing, sideways look. "Now I understand."

Janie waited, but he left it alone. "Anyway," she said, a little defensively, "even if I were to prove a link between my family and Celestine, her connection with the house ended there in 1815.

Whether Miles lacked the money to renovate, or whatever, we'll never know, but the house passed to Miles' sister, Grace, who was married to a George Parsons."

"Ah-ha! Harriet was a Parsons." Rob's face dimpled; pleased he'd made the connection.

"Correct. George and Grace rebuilt the house, adding the Georgian façade and reducing the overall size. He was a military man and, I can't remember how many times it was passed from father to son, but they were all military men, ending with the Brigadier, Edward Parsons, Harriet's father. He inherited in 1918, I think."

They turned into the drive, Rob yanked on the handbrake, and turned to face her. "I don't know how you remember all that stuff."

She grinned. "Because I'm fascinated by the history of our house and because I've read Harriet's copy of the House Book loads of times, always from the back to the front, so I don't inadvertently read anything about Alice."

"That reminds me," Rob said, "You promised to give me the low-down on 'what Alice and William did next'."

****

When she'd finished reading, she laid the sheets on the kitchen table. Rob widened his eyes and puffed out his cheeks. "Poor Alice, she doesn't have much luck, does she?"

For some reason, it mattered very much to Janie that this had been Rob's first reaction, and that he hadn't tried to excuse William. "I've just found this upstairs in the fax tray." She waved another piece of paper. "I haven't read it yet. Dick sent it as soon as he saw it; he says 'you'll see why'."

She read it aloud.

Alice's Diary

May 1668

My husband appears to be avoiding me. I did not see him this morning even though I was up at his usual time. Edmund tells me he left very early.

I had an interesting and productive meeting with Henry and we have already started to make new plans for the farm. There are just about sufficient funds in the farm account to cover these and I'm hopeful that the trustees will approve. Worryingly, I have discovered that several items in the account are suspect – mainly relating to building material and labour costs – which have clearly not been spent on the farm and neither, to my knowledge, on the house. Also, the extent of unpaid wages and bills is far greater than I had thought.

I cannot let this pass. I must have it out with William if, and when, he returns.

May 1668

The scales have fallen from my eyes. No longer will I defend or make excuses for William's behaviour.

The roofing tiles and all the other materials plus the labour costs were all for his property in Chichester. It is apparent to me now that the trustees already knew this and that is why they will not tolerate his further involvement in the farm. It is a clear breach of the trust.

And it is a clear breach of my trust.

I have sent a message to the wine merchant reducing our monthly order. I have been meaning to do this for some time.

~ 39 ~
May 1986

Passing by the kitchen window, she saw Rob and John Hobden at the table, studying plans. "I'm home," she sang from the back lobby, scooping up Cat and joining them in the kitchen. "Hi, John. What's going on here, then?"

Rob stood to give her a kiss. "No need to worry, we won't be making any decisions without your approval. John's come up with some great ideas for our new guest bedroom and bathroom; come and have a look."

Janie had already flopped down on the chair by the range, Cat on her knee. John stood up and laid a hand on Rob's arm. "No, listen, I've got to be off, anyway. I'll leave these with you, and Mrs. W. can look at them in her own time. There's no rush, we can discuss it again on Monday." He winked at her and Janie gave him a grateful smile.

Rob saw him out and she heard him lock the back door before going to the larder to get a beer. "Do you want anything, Janie? Gin and tonic?"

"No, I don't think so. What I need is a restorative cup of tea."

Leaving his beer on the table, he put the kettle on and then bent down to have a good look at her. "You look knackered. Did the kids wear you out?"

"Not really. We took them to the beach for a kick-about but they amused themselves mainly, while Barbara and I took turns to sit with Elsie." Rob was making her tea and made no comment.

"I don't know how Barbara's coping, Rob. Mum's much worse."

It wasn't something he wanted to face, she knew that, but it was clear that her sister-in-law wouldn't be able to manage for much longer. Sooner or later, the brothers were going to have to make a decision. "Barbara was asking if you could pop down sometime soon, like, this weekend?"

Placing the mug on the range beside her, he knelt down and Janie wrapped her arms round him and rocked gently. "Please ring Dan," she whispered.

Eventually, he stood up. "I will. I'll go down. I promise."

***

Water lapped over her ears and she closed her eyes, detached from everything but the sound of her own breath. In and out, in and out, heart rate slowing as her body relaxed. The bath was huge and old, an extravagant house-warming present from Guy and Tash, and took nearly a whole tank of hot water to fill, but nothing felt quite so decadent as when lying full stretch in it, with a glass of wine on the side. Unlike most cats, Cat had no aversion to water, and watched her mistress from a chair next to the bath.

Janie replayed the day's events. Although Barbara had prepared her, it was still a shock to realise that Elsie was having difficulty remembering her other daughter-in-law. On the other hand, she'd had a brilliant time on the beach, laughing at the children playing, even if she couldn't distinguish her own grandchildren from the others. Delivering Barbara's message had been tough, but Rob was going to find the visit even tougher.

She topped up the water from the hot tap and lay back once more, unwilling to join the real world just yet. As was happening more and more, her thoughts drifted back to that other world, Alice's world, which was beginning to occupy much of her waking hours. The fact that William was turning out to be the shit she'd always suspected, filled her with sorrow rather than satisfaction. Her heart ached for Alice. It seemed increasingly unlikely that their marriage would have a happy ending. And then there was

Elisabeth, the mystery woman: background and status unknown, multi-talented and, latterly, Alice's trusted and valued friend; probably, servants aside, her only friend.

Elisabeth, with her thick coils of shiny, black hair and knowing brown eyes. A woman who'd looked directly at her, smiled and said 'Hello'.

Janie was reconciled to the possibility that there may be nothing else to discover about Aphra, but she knew she'd be really disappointed if Elisabeth had disappeared for good, and Dick hadn't seemed hopeful about uncovering anything about her, either.

With no hot water left in the tank, Janie reluctantly stepped out of the bath, wrapped herself in a towel and shoved Cat aside to retrieve her dressing gown. She was in no mood to cook, so Rob had booked a table at the new Indian in Petworth and she was looking forward to wearing something other than work clothes or jeans. So…that'll be her new top and the flattering, but rather tight, black trousers she bought last Christmas.

Except that she couldn't fasten the black trousers.

***

Rob popped his head round the door and found her sitting on the side of the bed, staring into space. "Hey, what's up? Have you changed your mind about going out?"

She looked down at the gaping fly and the button, which had no chance of reaching its buttonhole. "I can't get into my trousers."

"Well, put something else on then. Come on, we'll have to get moving in ten minutes," and he started to back out of the door.

"Did you notice I'd put weight on?"

Recognising this as a possible no-win situation, he steered as diplomatic a course as was possible. "Perhaps a little bit of weight, a bit more rounded here and there, but it suits you. I like it." The dimples were working overtime.

"Oh, very good, Rob." She rolled her eyes and went over to

217

give him a kiss, one hand clutching the trousers and the other around his neck. "I think I'm pregnant."

***

They changed their plans. In the intimacy of their kitchen, they ate a take-away, laughed, held hands, and could hardly believe what was happening to them.

"I don't know why it didn't dawn on me before." Janie shook her head as Rob offered a refill. She'd already had two glasses of wine, and she made a little moue. "It's unfortunate that I've only gone off coffee and not wine."

Rob pointed to her empty plate. "I can't say I've noticed you going off food. I thought all pregnant women got morning sickness."

"So did I." She reached across the table and took both his hands in hers. "Once it's confirmed, we'll tell Dan and Barbara, and she'll help me, but please don't let on tomorrow, will you? Just in case."

"I won't." His eyes filled with tears as they both contemplated the same thing: the sorrow of one life ebbing away just as a new one was coming into being. Janie instinctively placed a hand on her belly.

Standing up to clear away the plates and empty cartons, Janie said, "I'll get a test kit tomorrow while you're in Brighton, and we'll do it together when you get back. Then we won't have to wait till I see the doctor on Monday."

Rob ran a hand through his hair and wiped his face before pouring the remaining wine into his glass. "I'd better finish this. We're going to save a fortune on wine these next few months…" and laughed as he caught the wet dishcloth and shot out of his chair to pay her back.

"You wouldn't hurt a pregnant woman now, would you?" She dashed round the other side of the table but he was too quick for her. Tossing the soggy cloth aside, he picked her up, carried her into the snug and dropped her on the sofa.

"When was it then, do you think? March sometime?"

Janie pretended to look serious. "I don't know. Let me think now, there have been so many times recently."

"Yes, alright. Very funny. I can't help it if I've been working hard, and I'm not as young as I used to be."

"Neither am I." She gave him a little punch on the arm. "I think it might have been March, but my periods are still irregular and I don't keep track of them like I used to. I can remember feeling exhausted at the Book Fair in April, but I didn't think anything of it at the time. The Book Fair's always exhausting. I couldn't shake it off, though, and I made this appointment to see the doctor on Monday thinking I had a virus or something."

"Let's hope it's the 'something'. Did you feel this tired before?" It was the first time either of them had referred to the miscarriage.

"Yes, I think so. Apparently it lasts for the first three months and then I'll be up ladders, painting and decorating and drilling walls. I'll be so full of energy, there'll be no stopping me."

"Mmm, we'll see about that." Rob reached over and gently stroked her stomach. "Promise me you'll be careful. This may be our last chance."

Suddenly, everything had got a bit serious.

~ 40 ~
Late May 1986

Impending fatherhood had given Rob a different perspective on things.

He found he could now face looming deadlines without suffering anxiety filled, sleepless nights, and he was reconciled to the fact that nothing more could be done for his mother now that they'd found a good care home for her.

All his focus was now on Janie and the baby. Without knowing how much he'd wanted this, they were about to become a complete family, and suddenly, the idea of buying a large house in the country didn't seem so ridiculous. That is, if everything went well.

The doctor who'd confirmed Janie's pregnancy had taken over Dr. Kelly's old practice. He'd been told about her earlier miscarriage and their failure to conceive afterwards. He was not concerned. Apparently, early miscarriages are more common than people imagine and, quite often, go unnoticed. The main thing to remember, he told her, is that there's usually a good reason for it. Rob smiled to recall her indignation at being called a 'geriatric primigravida' (older first-time mother) and how smug she had become when the doctor told her she was perfectly fit and healthy with an enviably low blood pressure. He warned against working too hard, but foresaw no problems for her, and insisted she see him immediately if she was worried about anything at all.

That was all good. What was not so good, was seeing Janie

tossing and turning at night as she wrestled with a spate of nightmares. He blamed Alice and the diary. It seemed every time a new batch of transcripts came through, there was another dead baby.

Janie was having a day off today and, as he left her to go to the studio, they both heard the rattle of the fax machine upstairs.

****

Hi Janie,

Sorry to be so late with this. What did you think of the last lot I sent you? Interesting, eh?

On balance, it appears you're right – William's using Alice – although, if one were to be charitable, William's disappointments, coupled with his apparent drink problem, may be responsible for his aberrant behaviour. (I think I can hear you saying 'rubbish').

Alice's woes continue with only her friendship with Elisabeth to sustain her. Incidentally, my research has turned up nothing on Elisabeth Turner. I'll keep trying.

After the last entry I sent you, I was beginning to think that the diary was descending into one long account of how to run a farm. In short, there was nothing interesting, to me at least, and I didn't waste time transcribing these. I hope you'll forgive me. On the plus side, they are fairly easy to read and I think you'll be able to do it yourself if you feel so inclined.

However, there were two important exceptions to the above; one dated October 1668, and one dated March 1669, and these I'm sending now. Not much, I know, but the next batch all cover the same month, July 1669, so I'll send those together.

I must admit that only Aphra concerned me at the start of this exercise but, like you, I find myself eager to know how the Oakwood Grange saga plays out...

Affectionately,

Dick

PS. I enjoyed our lunch enormously.

***

Alice's Diary

October 1668

He came to me last night for the first time in months; unsteady on his feet and with sour breath.

I refused him – the only time I have ever done so. It made no difference.

The act was violent and hateful and I was left in no doubt as to the extent of his resentment and bitterness, which he spewed into my ear with every thrust.

I cannot bear to face him today. He will pretend that everything is normal and, indeed, he may not even remember what he did. But I will remember.

March 1669

I have a reply from Elisabeth!

It seems that Ann's troubles are over (I still do not know what they were, but perhaps I shall find out now), she is well set up in London and has no further need of a travelling companion. Elisabeth still sees her regularly but spends most of her time with some French friends who have started a business in London and need help with the language.

But she has accepted my invitation! She is to stay until my baby is born and I am so looking forward to having my friend here once more. William may not be as pleased as I, but I care not, and he will no doubt spend even more time with his new drinking and hunting companions.

***

"The bastard." Janie spoke this out loud, although only Cat was present to acknowledge the sentiment.

Her first thought was to rush over to the studio and tell Rob, but she hesitated, aware that he'd rather lost interest in what happened to Alice and William lately. She might mention it in passing.

Cutting through the walled garden, Janie stopped to give Hedges his mid-morning coffee. "How's Mrs. Hedges getting on with her new hip, is she up and about yet?"

"Oh, aye, thanks for asking. There'll be no stopping her now, you know." He seemed resigned rather than pleased. No more needed to be said. Cat had followed Janie and was now stretched out in amongst the herbs. "She's a rare one, that cat. I thought she were after catmint, but there's none in there. I think she just likes the smells."

Janie laughed, "There's nothing normal about Cat, apart from her love of the warmth, but we love her, and she follows me around like a dog." She clicked her tongue and, together, she and Cat went to look through the studio window. Rob had his back to her, working at the easel. Feeling it was unwise to disturb him, mistress and cat made their way back to the house.

Picking up the latest postings from Dick, she read them again.

A third pregnancy for Alice, possibly the result of a drunken rape, and Elisabeth's return the only light on the horizon. Janie made a little silent prayer that Elisabeth would stay this time – as if that could change what happened 300-odd years ago.

Dick's assurance aside, Janie knew that her empathy with Alice was bordering on an obsession. She couldn't explain it to anyone, but it felt as if something was driving her on, to what, she didn't know.

~ 41 ~
Oakwood Grange, April 1669

*M*artha knew what he wanted. He was no different from the village boys despite his age and position.

At first he'd found some excuse to talk to her in the dairy. "How are you finding the work, Martha?" "Can I get you some help, Martha?" "When do the milkers come in, Martha?" She was only 15 years old, but she was wise beyond her years and wasn't about to jeopardise her position by making any rash move.

On the last few occasions, he'd made no effort to converse at all but had just watched her going about her business. She brushed past him to and from the workbench, teasing as she sensed the longing in him. In the end, abandoning her own counsel, Martha tentatively took his hand. He pulled away. "Perhaps one day you'll change your mind, sir." She nearly bobbed a curtsey but thought better of it and turned back to her work. They both waited in silence for a long minute before he finally left.

That day came a week later. It was unseasonably hot for April, there was a heavy workload and Martha had removed her head covering and jacket. She was working in just her bodice with a scarf around her neck. William entered through the dairy door and immediately shot the bolt. He leaned against the door, barely able to look at her, silent and swaying slightly, waiting for Martha to stop what she was doing. Bolting the door was her cue – she knew this. She removed the scarf, wiped the sweat from her neck and chest, took his hand which, this time, offered no resistance, and drew him into the stalls, closing and bolting the milking parlour door on the way.

She led him to the last stall and he sat down heavily in the corner where the straw was deepest. Despite Edmund's efforts to protect his daughter, it was obvious that at least one village swain had breached his defences and Martha knew exactly what to do. She swiftly unlaced his breeches and was pleased to see that, although he'd taken some drink, it had had no effect on his capabilities. Just as quickly, she hoisted her skirts and straddled him, sliding him inside her with ease.

Martha's body had changed from a child's to a woman's so quickly that her old bodice was no longer adequate and, with very little encouragement, she spilled out of its confines and, for the first time in daylight, William saw full, creamy-white breasts, delicately traced with violet veins and with rosy pink nipples standing out like coat pegs. They bounced before him as she rode him hard and leaning forward he buried his face in the soft young flesh and held her tight as he exploded inside her.

The sound of footsteps outside made them draw away from each other. The parlour door rattled. "Martha, are you there?" Then more footsteps followed by banging on the dairy door.

Martha rolled off him, hoisted her bodice up over her breasts and smoothed her skirts. William groaned and sank further into the corner of the stall. She unbolted the dairy door and bobbed a curtsey to Elisabeth who was waiting, jug in hand.

"Is everything all right, Martha? Why were the doors bolted?

"I'd finished my work, Miss, and I was so tired I thought I'd have a little nap, but please don't let on or my father'll whip my hide."

It was a plausible lie, but there'd been no time for Martha to replace her kerchief and Elisabeth's experienced eye had already taken in the telltale red flush spreading across her chest and the unmistakable smell of sex clinging to her. Given the over-ripe body this child had developed in the last year, Elisabeth feared it was always going to be a struggle for Edmund to keep his eldest daughter chaste. But Elisabeth did not judge; she had been that girl herself not so long ago. "Oh, I understand, Martha, I do," and she smiled as she patted her arm. "Don't worry, your secret's safe with me," and she swept past her into the dairy. "Now, Mrs. Lynd needs some more milk. Shall I take it from this churn here?"

***

Leaving the dairy, Elisabeth hurried back across the yard into the kitchen, plonked the jug on the table and ran up the back stairs to her room. There, she opened her casement and leaned out slightly to get a view of the parlour and dairy doors. She was intrigued to find out which likely lad had dared to take Martha practically under her father's nose. A brave one or a stupid one; she couldn't decide. Amused though she was by the whole incident and despite her promise, Elisabeth wondered whether she should tell Alice, who would know how to handle it.

She didn't have long to wait. She saw him leave by the dairy door, leap over the fence into the field, circle behind the outbuildings and enter the kitchen garden under her window. Shocked, she pulled back from view but she still had the stay in her hand and the window creaked as it moved.

Elisabeth was in a panic. He must have heard her conversation with Martha. Had it been obvious that she knew someone was there? Did he suspect she'd seen him leaving the dairy? Surely he hadn't seen her behind the window. Perhaps he thought it was Jennet or one of the maids cleaning her room.

Or perhaps he knew.

Elisabeth lay down on her bed, waiting for her heartbeat to return to normal and wondered if she would be able to act normally when she saw William next. If she couldn't convince him that all was as normal, she feared what would happen. She had seen the change in him; he had become irascible and argumentative since her last visit and was obviously still drinking despite Alice's efforts to curtail his consumption. It was clear that Alice needed Elisabeth now, more than ever, and she mustn't give him any reason to send her away. And Alice must never know about Martha. No one must know.

~ 42 ~
June 1986

"Janie! Long time, no hear. How are you?" The voice at the other end of the phone was so loud, Janie held the receiver away from her ear.

"I'm really good, Min. How are you?"

"Good too, although heaven knows how with three children in the house."

"Last I heard you only had two…ah, Max, just got it. You don't know when you're well off; he's a gem." There was never much preamble with Min, it was like slipping into a comfy cardigan. "I'm hoping he is, anyway. Do you fancy coming down for a girly weekend? No husbands, no kids?"

"Do I? What do you think? Although, if Tash's gonna be there, I might not. She makes me feel so insignificant and ugly, I wanna fade away like the Cheshire Cat." Janie knew she wasn't joking. Tash had that effect on most women.

"No, just you and me, honey; Rob's in Germany for the weekend, being wined and dined by his new clients. I could have gone with him but I didn't fancy it. What I did fancy, was spending some quality time with my old mate, a bit of shopping, going to the theatre in Chichester on Saturday, and a meal or two out. How does that sound?"

"When you want me?"

"Friday night, if you can manage it. I'll pick you up from the station. Why don't you clear it with Max first, and ring me back?"

"You're on. I ring you back wi' train times."

***

Min got out of the car and sniffed the air. "What's that smell? London never smells like this."

"Come with me." Janie took her hand and led her through the gate into the walled garden where the roses were doing what roses do best; and it had been a good year for the roses. Ramblers, climbers, shrub roses and ground cover roses crowded together artlessly, with no hint of the underlying planning and Hedges' hard work. For once, Min was speechless. Then she sneezed.

Once Janie had settled her in the best guest room and forced an anti-histamine tablet on her, Min was keen to see how far they'd got with the renovation. They started with the new bathroom and dressing room in the master suite.

"It's huge, Janie. This bathroom bigger than our bedroom. I could swim in that bath. Don't tell me, that's the one Guy and Tash sent?"

"Mmm - you've got to admit though, this room needs a bath like that. I'll fill it up for you tomorrow morning, and I swear you'll be a convert." Janie led her back to the landing. "There's not much else to see up here, we're still deciding what to do with these smaller rooms at the back of the house, but my office is looking a bit more lived in now. Come and see. I expect Cat is in there, anyway."

"Cat, this is Min. Min, meet Cat." Janie waited. It could be tricky; there was no knowing who Cat would get on with. Lying regally in the centre of the little sofa, she blinked lazily as Min fell to her knees and they met each other's gaze.

"You are one beautiful cat." Cat blinked once more, and showed her appreciation by stretching up to meet Min's hand.

"Oh, good," said Janie, "I thought you two would get on, cats being a Chinese good luck symbol and all."

Min stopped stroking Cat and jumped to her feet. "Aah, that reminds me, I gotta get something outta my bag," and she scurried back to her bedroom. "This," she said, on her return, "is a present from my parents, who still think you walk on water and that I'm the worst daughter in the world."

Janie laughed and took the box. "That's not true, and you know it."

Min shrugged. "Second bit is true. They wanna come live with me and Max, and I say 'no'. Anyway, open it; let's see what tacky stuff they give you. If it's a beckoning cat, then I take it away."

It wasn't a beckoning cat. Wrapped in shantung, lay two Chinese knots with long, lustrous tassles, beautifully crafted from red silk; good luck symbols that Janie had last seen at Min and Max's wedding.

"That one is a 'true love knot," said Min, picking up the other one and straightening the tassles, "and this one is a 'double happiness knot'. You are, therefore, doubly blessed, and there's no chance that evil will befall you." She handed the knot to Janie.

"I love them. They're going to stay in here, and I shall put them either side of the fireplace. I'll write, anyway, but please thank your Mum…" Janie was cut short by the sound of the phone and the fax springing into life. She watched as the pages rattled out of the machine, then stacked and placed them on her desk.

"I hope you're not gonna be working this weekend, Miss Mallory."

"No, this is something much more interesting. Let's go back downstairs, I'll get you a drink and then I'll tell you all about it while I'm preparing supper."

Hours later, the remains of the meal still on the table and with Cat firmly in place on Min's lap, they were still discussing the diary. Janie had given her the full story so far, and they'd dissected all the characters, pondered on their actions, and speculated about their futures. Min was so hard on William that Janie found herself in the unusual position of defending him. "Of course, we only see these events through Alice's eyes. If we had William's side of the story, we might find it's six of one and half a dozen of the other."

"I'd like to bet it isn't. Any man who imposes his puritanical values on his wife yet indulges himself in every other way, is a hypocrite. It wouldn't surprise me if he went whoring, as well."

"Min! Where did that come from?" Janie looked a little taken aback. That had never crossed her mind.

"He's the type, isn't he? Sexually repressed and religious? It's classic." She lifted Cat up and spoke to her. "Pity his poor wife, eh Cat?" and received an affectionate head bump under her chin.

Janie shook her head. There were no grey areas with Min. "Well…if you're in the mood, we could see what Dick's sent us. It might throw more light on William's character."

Min was cuddling Cat like a child and tickling her tummy, which appeared to put her into a stupor. "Okay, but I swear you said you like to read it on your own."

"Not tonight. Tonight, I want to read it with you. I'll go and get it."

Cat was reluctant to move, so Janie made some hot chocolate and then started to read out loud.

Alice's Diary

July 1669

It was too hot to go out today – I am too big and too uncomfortable. Elisabeth and I played chess inside.

Jennet is very distressed. She and Edmund have discovered that Martha is expecting a baby and she refuses to name the father for fear of what Edmund might do. I am more than happy for her to stay on the farm but Edmund will not have it. He has already arranged for her to go to his widowed sister who has a young family and will be grateful for the help.

Martha has always been the apple of Edmund's eye and he is feeling this very deeply.

15th July 1669

So much has happened during these last few days and my memory, although sharp when recalling some details, is a little hazy in respect of others.

I do remember the birthing pains. Hour upon hour of unproductive labour; I thought I was going to die. The pain was so awful, I wanted to die and, catching the glances between Jennet and Elisabeth, I was convinced I would die.

Jennet tells me that Elisabeth saved my life. She wouldn't give up and eventually succeeded in turning the baby. Shortly afterwards, she was born. A beautiful baby girl, perfect in every way save for the cord around her neck.

I was inconsolable.

I am inconsolable.

Jennet washed her, wrapped her in a shawl and placed her in my arms. Elisabeth, exhausted and emotional, kissed us both before leaving us. I was barely aware of William coming in but I don't think he stayed long. When I awoke, baby Elisabeth was still in my arms and for one tiny moment I experienced such joy until the realisation of her death washed over me, as it will do again and again, I know. Jennet was still by my bed, watching over me, and it took all my strength to pass my baby over to her.

***

She couldn't get to the end of the page. The tears were

coursing down her cheeks and she thrust the paper over to Min. "You finish it."

Min read the last few lines, even though her own throat was thick with unshed tears. They sat in silence until the ticking of the clock became too loud, then Min went to sit next to Janie. "When were you going to tell me?"

Janie screwed up her face and clamped a hand over her mouth. After one big heave, she dashed away the tears and managed a little smile. "Is it so obvious?"

Min handed her some tissues. "I'm no Sherlock, Janie, but your boobs have shot up a cup size at least. Then there's the real give-away, you're not drinking." She reached for her friend's hands. "It's wonderful news. You must both be thrilled. I will, of course, make a wonderful godmother."

Laughter quickly replaced the tears. "We've got a scan next week, and then we'll tell everyone, but, until then, well… you know." She gave a little shrug.

"Janie, look at me." Min adopted her Tiger Mother persona. "Nothing bad is gonna happen. You've been so wrapped up in what happened to this Alice, 300 years ago, you're worrying yourself silly. This is the twentieth century, and you will be fine."

Janie's eyes welled up again. "But I'm a geriatric primigravida."

"Congratulations. Not everyone can say that."

Soon they were both crying with laughter. "I don't know about you, Min, but I can't take any more emotion tonight." Janie started clearing away the plates. "Let's read the rest tomorrow, shall we?"

***

As the bath was double-ended, they bathed together in the morning, reducing the time it took to fill the tub. Min grudgingly accepted it was a brilliant way to start the day.

They shopped in Petworth, where Min bought a first edition Ian Fleming for Max's birthday, and then moved on to Chichester. Janie allowed herself a half of shandy at lunchtime and the rest of the afternoon was spent trying to stop Min dragging her into baby shops. They had a brilliant time. Finally exhausted, they made their way to the cathedral for a rest and a sit down.

"He had something to do with this cathedral – William." Janie mused. "I think he knew Christopher Wren. He was responsible for rebuilding the spire; Christopher Wren that is, not William."

Min raised her eyebrows. "See, a hypocrite." She waved the guide in front of Janie. "According to this, the Parliamentarians desecrated it in the Civil War."

The subject was dropped and they finished the tour, sauntered around the Bishop's Palace Gardens and then went for an early supper before picking up the car and driving to the theatre.

"I so enjoyed that. It was brilliant. Really atmospheric." Driving back home on a beautiful summer's night, they were full of the play. "Rob would have hated it."

"Max, too. Sitting through 'Jane Eyre' would be his idea of hell. I loved it though, and I thought Jenny Seagrove was amazing. This is such fun, we should do it more often."

Back in the kitchen at the Grange, they both silently acknowledged the presence of the fax, still lying on the table. "I'm up for it, if you are." Janie checked the clock. "The night is still young, and I think I've developed a yearning for hot chocolate."

Alice's Diary

16th July

Reverend Fawcett came to see me today.

My faith is shattered and I no longer believe in God's will. If I believe in anything, it might be God's punishment.

But the Reverend was very kind. He stayed for a long time, listening without offering platitudes, and his calm and largely silent presence was a great comfort. He left before William returned for supper and, not for the first time, I sense that a distance has opened up between the two of them recently.

Our baby girl's burial is to take place tomorrow but I am not well enough to attend. She is to be interred next to her grandfather. Only William, Jennet & Edmund, Henry & Mrs. Lynd will attend. Elisabeth has insisted on staying behind with me and we shall conduct our own service for her namesake.

17th July

Elisabeth has gone!

There has been no explanation and no word of goodbye. I saw Edmund loading her belongings onto the coach this afternoon and I fear she will not be returning.

William must have sent her away. I can think of no other explanation. I have never seen him so overcome with emotion as he was at our baby's death and I suspect he blames Elisabeth, being unable, of course, to blame his God.

I feel desolate and abandoned.

18th July 1669

I have a note from Elisabeth. Jennet brought it to me after William had left the house this morning.

She begs my forgiveness and promises that we shall meet again someday in happier circumstances. She says she knows this to be true.

She offers no explanations for her disappearance but says the Reverend Fawcett would be willing to speak to me – alone. It is signed 'Your most affectionate and loyal friend, Elisabeth'.

I feel such loss, and this bedchamber, with the echoes of all my failures, is compounding my sadness. Fit or not, I am determined to get dressed and go downstairs. Jennet will help me. I must talk to William and if he won't come to me, then I shall go to him.

~ 43 ~
Oakwood Grange, 19th July 1669

*J*ennet was helping Alice into her day clothes as she was perched on the side of the bed. She knelt to fit one shoe onto an icy cold foot and then sat back on her heels. "My love," she pleaded, "you're stone cold and white as a sheet. Please don't do this. It's too soon. Let me put you back to bed and get you a nice warm drink."

"I'll be fine." Alice smiled and wiped away a solitary tear from the other woman's cheek. "Don't fret so." With a loud sigh, Jennet fitted the other shoe and helped her mistress to her feet.

They hadn't quite reached the door when Alice doubled over, biting her lip as a rush of warm blood left her body. With one hand on the wall and the other clutching Jennet's arm, she took several deep breaths before straightening up. Their eyes met and Alice nodded in silent appreciation for the amount of padding she had earlier insisted was unnecessary.

Progress down the stairs was slow and painful. The damage to her body had not had time to heal and she was still very weak. Her head, though, was clearing with every breath of fresh air that wafted up from the open hall door and her resolve was strengthening with every step. Jennet settled Alice in her father's chair - now William's, but still referred to as Thomas's - and drew up his old gout stool. "There, pop your feet up on this and I'll fetch you a nice drink."

Alice did as she was told. "Is there any of Elisabeth's brew left, do you know?"

"Oh, Miss Alice," Jennet looked away and nervously straightened the front of her apron, "I think it's all gone. I'll just go and check with Mrs. Lynd," and she scurried out of the room. She knew there was no more brew. William had stormed into the kitchen just as Cook was preparing his breakfast that morning, swept all the herbs from the table into the fire and threw the pan with the brew out of the kitchen door. He'd pointed at both Cook and Jennet. "There'll be none of that in this house from now on".

Jennet had always thought of William as a temperate man, in his manner if not in other ways recently, but just then, with his hair unkempt, his eyes narrowed in anger and his mouth a hard, cruel line, she'd seen a different man. She'd hoped that all this business with Elisabeth was but a temporary madness brought on by grief, but now feared that she might be wrong. She was frightened for Alice and ran to warn Edmund to be on hand should she need him once the master returned. Little explanation was needed.

Alice sipped the hot milk and brandy and as the warmth spread throughout her body she was grateful that, on this occasion, there was none of the herbal infusion left. She waited patiently for three hours, taking the odd nibble of bread and cheese to sustain her, before she heard William returning from his ride.

The front door slammed shut behind him and she heard him fling down his hat, gloves and belt. He wandered into the room and stopped short, startled to find Alice sitting there.

"Alice, what are you doing here? Shouldn't you be in bed? Are you feeling better?"

She had thought that she would be fearful of confronting William, but, instead, she found herself to be quite calm, in control and determined to speak her mind. "Well, now that you ask – no, I'm not, but if you'd been in to see me these last two days, you would have known that." Visibly taken aback by her tone, William opened his mouth to speak but Alice continued, "It matters not. Where is Elisabeth?"

William shut the door to the hall, took a little time pouring himself a brandy and prepared himself for the fray. "She's gone. I don't know where she is." He drained his glass, poured another drink and turned to face her.

"Why did she go?" Alice continued to look him in the eye and registered how unsettled he'd become by her calm, defiant demeanour.

"Dear wife," At this point William affected a nonchalant smile and leant back against the table, spreading his arms wide, "surely Jennet or Durling or any one of the other tittle-tattlers has told you by now?"

"Unfortunately not. There appears to be a conspiracy of silence around the subject. Perhaps you will tell me why she went?"

"Alice," William tried a more conciliatory tone, "I know you think that woman was your friend, but she was not. Admit it, you know very little about her; where she came from or anything about her family, and the fact that she is a friend of Mrs. Bean's says something about her morality."

"It is true that it's preferable to know something of a person's background before allowing them into your house, but then I've always thought that a person's character is defined by how they treat others and how they conduct their affairs." Satisfied the barb had hit home, Alice carried on, "Also, your prejudice against Mrs. Bean, for being nothing worse than an independent woman, should not be held against Elisabeth who, as far as I'm aware, has shown modesty in all things."

"What I see with my own eyes is not prejudice." William wagged a finger in Alice's direction. "She never once accompanied

us to church – is that not strange? And why, Alice, do you think that is?" He didn't wait for an answer. "It's because she worships something else, that's why."

"Yes, she's Catholic."

"Oh, no, no, no…I've seen her mixing noxious brews in our kitchen and I've seen her performing strange rituals, laying her hands on your body and summoning spirits. That's not Catholicism. What on earth were you thinking of?"

Despite herself, Alice found she was blushing but refused to be cowed. "That is ridiculous, William. The brews of which you speak are old herbal recipes – few people still have the knowledge to produce them – and they are proven remedies for many ailments. As for summoning spirits, since when has singing become a heathen practice?"

William pushed himself away from the table and paced up and down the room. He came to a halt in front of her chair. "Why did you not allow the surgeon to bleed you when you were with child?"

Alice tilted her chin and looked him squarely in the eye. "Because I could see no good reason for it. I have little enough blood as it is."

"Really? And not because your Miss Turner advised against it?"

"We were both against it."

William shook his head and resumed pacing. Eventually, he faced her again and held up a hand to prevent her from speaking. "I did not want to spell this out to you, Alice, but I fear I must. That woman took against me. I could see it in the way she looked at me and she, oh so subtly, turned you against me, too."

"That is not true, William." Alice was so angry, she struck the arms of the chair with her fists. "You know full well that any disagreements between you and I have had nothing whatsoever to do with Elisabeth."

William came closer and pointed a finger at her. "You have been duped, dear wife," and now he was shouting, "and you cannot see that your so-called friend was responsible for killing our babies."

Alice sank back heavily in the chair, open-mouthed and with eyes wide. "Surely, you can't believe that. And why on earth would she want to? Do you think she hates you so much that she'd kill the one thing we both want – a family?"

"That's exactly what I think."

"It's madness, William. I suppose you think she killed our first baby too; before we even knew her?"

"Once is an accident, but three dead babies, Alice – three! That's no accident."

Alice's head was throbbing and she supported it with her hand. "You don't know what went on in that chamber, William. Elisabeth worked tirelessly for hours to save my life…"

"…at the expense of our child. I'm well aware of that, Alice."

Alice closed her eyes and remained silent, hoping for a retraction that never came. As far as she was concerned, there was nothing more to say. But William hadn't finished. He came to rest his hands on the arms of her chair and leaned forward till his face was close to hers. "And, just in case you are still in any doubt, your Miss Turner had a few last words for me." His voice was shaking. "A curse. Apparently, neither I, nor any of my blood will live long enough to find peace in this house. Or should I say, your house. Does that make you happy?"

He turned and left the room. Edmund moved away from his post outside the window and went back to the stables. Jennet, listening from the morning room, returned to the hall and waited for Alice to summon her.

~ 44 ~
End June 1986

"That's baby's heart beating away. Can you see?" The sonographer was gliding the probe over the gel on Janie's stomach and stopped once she'd got a good picture. She never got tired of seeing the joy on the faces of prospective parents, especially the ones who'd been trying for so long.

"Is he alright? I mean, can you see anything wrong?" Rob hadn't taken his eyes off the monitor.

"Well, first off, we can't see the sex, although we may be able to at the next scan, if you want to know, and secondly, everything looks okay at the moment. I can see two arms and two legs. The next scan will tell us more."

"We don't want to know the sex, anyway, do we Rob?" He shook his head without looking away from the image.

"This scan is really to assess the age of the baby and to try to give you a due date. I think you said, Mrs. Whittaker, that you're unsure about the date of your last period, but I reckon this little one is about thirteen weeks."

Janie grinned, remembering the make-up sex they'd had after the 'Dick thing'. "Yes, that fits with what we were thinking." Rob shot her a sideways glance and gave her hand a squeeze.

"So," the sonographer consulted a calendar, "your little parcel of joy could arrive anytime between Christmas and New Year."

***

"When Barb was pregnant with Amy, it was 1978, just before we met in fact. I remember Dan ringing me up and going on about the scan, they were fairly new in those days, and I couldn't understand what he was getting so worked up about." Rob shook his head at the memory. He was driving them back from the hospital at a good ten mph. slower than his normal speed.

Janie had her arms folded over the slight bulge in her stomach. "I know, it is pretty amazing, but that's only the first hurdle, there's a long way to go yet. I don't think we should get carried away until after the next scan."

"Agreed, but I don't think we can go ahead with our original plan for the back bedrooms. The more I think about it, the more I think we should make it a proper children's wing, and," he added quickly before Janie could interrupt, "that's really got nothing to do with our situation. We already have two good-sized guest rooms for adults, but their kids will be much better off in smaller bedrooms. And, if we ever sell our place, then I think it needs to look like a proper family house."

Having pulled into the drive, he turned to see her reaction.

"Not that we are ever going to sell, but I guess you're right. John's plan was going to be wonderful; in fact, that suite would have been better than ours, but totally unnecessary." Janie gathered up her bag, "I think you should call him now, and we should go have another look at the plans."

John Hobden was secretly pleased with the decision. He had his suspicions about the change of heart, but was never convinced, anyway, of the wisdom of getting rid of the smaller rooms. He told them he'd be back on Monday and they'd go over the new plans then.

In the event, it was remarkably easy to create a possible playroom and two bedrooms with small bathrooms, from the current rooms. There was only one structural wall, which didn't need to be touched, and all the other walls were partitions.

Satisfied with the plan, Janie rolled it up and put it to one side. "I haven't told you about the latest goings-on with Alice and William yet."

Rob flicked some cat hairs from his trousers. "Is it more doom and gloom?"

"'Fraid so. Do you want me to tell you, or not?" Her voice was a little clipped.

Rob caught her hand and pulled her onto his knee. "Give me the short version."

Janie straddled him, pushed away the dark curls and took his face in both her hands. "The baby was stillborn with the cord round her neck."

"Oh, bloody hell, Janie. Is it a good idea to keep reading this thing? It's too depressing for words, especially now."

"I know, I know. Don't give me a lecture. I've already had that from Min. Alice has been and gone, and if I've been identifying with her or imagining, somehow, that history will repeat itself, it's ridiculous." She gave him a tender little kiss. "But honestly Rob, I don't think I've been thinking that. I just feel her heartache. I think it's as simple as that."

Rob enfolded her into his arms and they stayed like that, heads on each other's shoulder, until Cat jumped up and forced her way into the gap between them.

"Jealous cat." Rob picked her up and put her over his shoulder. "Either you can't bear to be left out, or you're hungry." Being mute had its limitations.

Janie got off his lap. "Okay, you feed her and I'll put the kettle on." She was standing with her back to the range when he came back. "Anyway, I doubt there'll be many more upsets or surprises in the diary. Apparently, William has sent Elisabeth away, Ann/ Aphra has already gone, and, although the diary continues for another eighteen months or so, Dick says there are fewer entries and many damaged pages."

"Good. Let's hope there's a happy ending."

Janie reached for a couple of mugs and turned to take the kettle off the hob. "Min thinks it highly unlikely. She's tagged

William as a drunk and a pious hypocrite, who's sexually repressed and probably goes out whoring on the quiet."

Rob snorted with laughter "I bet she's right, too!"

***

At the very time Janie was convincing Rob that the diary would throw up nothing else of interest, Dick was discovering the opposite, and not just because Ann, Elisabeth and Thomas made another appearance.

Alice's Diary

20th July 1669

William has sent Elisabeth away because he believes her to be a witch who has killed our babies in the womb. All this to spite him because she does not like him. How is it possible for an intelligent man to believe such a thing? He will not listen to reason and further believes that he has been cursed.

22nd July 1669

I asked for Reverend Fawcett to pay me a visit today as William left for Chichester this morning.

I am shocked by what he has told me.

The night Elisabeth disappeared, at about 3am, Henry heard a cart approaching his cottage. He clearly saw William driving and two men in the back struggling with a woman in a nightshift. He thought I was the woman and, panic stricken, rode to The Rectory to rouse the Reverend who took Henry's horse and eventually found William and the others by the river. My blood ran cold at the mention of the river. I pressed the Reverend for more but he would not be drawn.

He assured me that, although distressed, Elisabeth had not sustained any lasting injuries and he had taken her back to The Rectory. It was he who had passed Elisabeth's note to Jennet and he who had arranged to pick up her belongings.

Ann sent a carriage for her this morning and she is now on her way to London.

I confided to the Reverend that William has convinced himself that Elisabeth is a witch. He just nodded. I asked him if he had heard Elisabeth curse William which, as far as I could remember, was something like "neither you nor any of your blood will live long enough to find peace in that house." He shook his head. Elisabeth did mumble something to William but the Reverend was too far away to hear.

As he was leaving, he took my hands and kissed my forehead.

I miss my father.

I cried tonight: full of self-pity. I cried for my babies, for my friend, for my loveless marriage and a long, long, unhappy future.

1st August 1669

Yesterday, I received a letter from Ann Bean, and today, I have one from Thomas Culpepper – both handed to me by Jennet.

They are outraged by Elisabeth's ordeal.

I am not surprised that Ann is urging me to leave William, for I suspect she has always despised him, but I am shocked that Thomas, too, is so concerned for my safety. I fear that the Reverend has been withholding much more than he admitted he knew. There is no point in confronting him again – I know he will not tell me more. And I cannot bear to resurrect the subject with William who, at any rate, has been largely absent for the last for'night.

Ann says that her home is my home and she would welcome me as a sister and Thomas, dear Thomas, is willing to physically escort me safely away. I am grateful for their concern.

They are assuming, of course, that this house, chattels and farm now all belong to William and that I find myself in an impossible position. Thankfully, they are wrong.

This is my home, my farm, my life. I am not leaving.

September 1669

William knows that I have been corresponding with Ann Bean and Thomas and must assume that I know all the details of what happened to Elisabeth.

He was in a particularly foul mood at dinner and harangued me on what he 'knows to be my plans', although I have no plans that concern him.

I suspect that he fears they will persuade me to seek dissolution of my marriage and force him out of this house. This would leave him in dire straits.

I have done my best to reassure him that, despite anything he has done, we remain man and wife and this is our home.

I do not think he believes me. I would not be surprised if he attempts to contest the marriage settlement

October 1669

I am relieved.

Mr. Pinkerton has assured me that it is extremely unlikely that the marriage settlement will be changed. William's lawyers may advise him to go to Chancery but it will be very expensive, William does not have the means and the chance of succeeding is very slim.

I fear what this latest failure will do to him, although I cannot imagine how he could be even more bitter and resentful than he already is.

~ 45 ~
Early July 1986

"**C**ongratulations, Mr. W., and I have to say that the missus is looking even bonnier than ever. I'm very pleased for you both." John shook Rob's hand and Kevin gave a thumbs-up and a silly grin.

"We'd stopped hoping, really." Rob couldn't keep the smile off his face. If it were up to him, he'd be telling everyone. "Makes you wonder, doesn't it?"

"That's true. Moving into a new house as well; I've heard of it happening to other folks, too, when they've moved. No rhyme or reason to it, but there you are."

John and Kevin were sitting on the floor with their mugs of tea, taking a break from knocking down the partitions. Rob joined them.

"You know I told you about the diary Janie found? Well something interesting's come up. The short story is, that a guy who lived here, soon after it was built, appeared to have some sort of breakdown after losing a third child, and accused his wife's friend of being a witch." Rob pointed a finger and let it sink in.

"So, mystery solved, then." John nudged Kevin, spilling hot tea over his jeans.

"Cheers, Dad."

John threw him a rag. "Great soft thing," he muttered, and turned to Rob, "Bets are then, it were him as made those marks, eh? Probably put the other stuff up there as well. I don't suppose you've told Mrs. W…."

Rob stood up and shook the dust off his jeans. "Ooo no, no, no.. and it's too late now. So, Kevin, remember, no slip-ups, eh?"

"Yes," John nudged him again, "don't you let on. There's no telling how a pregnant woman will react to being kept in the dark over summat like that."

***

Janie had a niggling little ache in her lower back, and was lying on the floor of her office, with a pillow under her knees and another under her head. It was strangely comfortable. She closed her eyes and tried to think of nothing.

It was not possible. Thoughts of Alice kept bubbling to the surface and she relived the disbelief, sorrow and then anger she'd experienced when she first read the latest entries. Had William really tried to 'duck' Elisabeth? Alice obviously didn't know for sure, but something drastic had happened judging by Ann and Thomas's reactions. Dick had written, in his covering note, how pleased he was to see Thomas named as Thomas Culpepper, even though he felt there had been no doubt. He remarked also on Ann's response to the incident. Many contemporaries reported that Aphra Behn was a true and loyal friend, and her offer to Alice, 'my home is your home', was typical of her character.

Janie reminded herself that Alice was not yet 26 yrs old. She had witnessed the death of both parents, been disappointed in marriage, and lost three babies. It seemed that the only light in her life, apart from her love of the farm, was discovering a true friend and equal in Elisabeth. Now that had been taken from her as well, immediately after the loss of her last child. It spoke volumes about her strength of character that, when offered a way out of a horrible situation, Alice dug in her heels, refused to relinquish her inheritance, and decided to make the best of her marriage.

Janie sincerely hoped that William had been cursed.

With that last thought, and a fleeting image of witches' marks, she melted into the floor as her muscles relaxed and drifted away accompanied by the now familiar smell of rosemary.

***

She woke to the sound of the phone ringing on her desk.

Rolling on to her side, she came face to face with Cat. "Have you been guarding me, Cat? You should have been a dog," and she rose slowly to avoid a head rush, and just managed to pick up in time.

"Janie, are you all right?" Since hearing of the pregnancy, Joyce Hunter had appointed herself responsible for her boss's welfare. "You sound a bit groggy."

"No, I'm fine, Joyce. I've just woken from a little nap, that's all. I'll be in tomorrow, Wednesday and Thursday, all being well."

They chatted at length about work and Joyce wanted to know if she could fax over some information on computers. Janie agreed, on the understanding that she wasn't about to make any rash promises to buy yet more expensive equipment at present.

No sooner had she replaced the receiver, than it rang again. This time, it was Min telling her that she had a pile of baby clothes and other stuff that Janie was welcome to. Having recently had the same conversation with Barbara, Janie could see that they were going to be overrun with kind donations, but thanked her anyway and agreed to take them. By the time Min had run out of news and stories about her boys, Janie was smiling and feeling so much better. They were just about to ring off when Min said, "Oh, by the way, I was telling Max about your diary – poor Alice and her horrible husband, William – and we both reckon that he's the father of the milkmaid's baby."

"Min!" Janie couldn't help laughing. "That's such a cliché, and there's no basis for thinking that. Certainly, Alice doesn't even hint at it."

"She most likely doesn't suspect. And, anyway, I do think there's evidence for thinking that. Illegitimate children were commonplace in those days and I think Alice writes that she was happy for whatshername to stay on the farm."

"Martha."

"Martha, then. So, ask yourself this. Why was she sent away?"

"Because Edmund was embarrassed and ashamed?"

"No, she was apparently the apple of his eye. It was because he suspected William was the father, and this was the best way of avoiding trouble all round."

Janie shook her head. "You have a vivid imagination, Min, I'll give you that. But it's academic, anyway, because we'll never know, will we?"

She sat holding the phone for a little while, even after Min had rung off, then carefully replaced it in the cradle and reached for the diary.

***

"Did you tell her about Elisabeth and the curse and William's attempt to overturn the settlement?" Rob was in the studio, washing his brushes at the sink when Janie popped in to spend some time with him.

"No, it didn't seem fair to give her even more ammunition. I find myself trying to defend him; she's so vitriolic about him."

"Ah, ha! You see…" Rob turned round and pointed, accidentally flicking water from the brush in his hand, and gave her a self satisfied little smile.

"Well I still can't feel sorry for him." She walked over to the sink and hugged him from behind, laying her head on his back. "What do you think of Min's theory?"

"Ah, well," Rob finished wiping his hands and turned round, "while it fits neatly with her idea that he's sexually repressed, I suspect it probably has more to do with her memories from Chinese folktales." He took her face in both hands and kissed her. "Right now, I'm much more concerned with you and our baby. Come on, let's go back to the house and see how they're getting on with the children's wing."

"Back bedrooms."

***

"It's a job to say." John was scratching his head. "It depends on the plumber really. Once he's been up in this loft over here, we'll have a better idea of how long it's going to take ,but, problems aside, it shouldn't be more than a few weeks. You'd best start thinking about what sort of fittings you want in here. It's best to be ahead of the game, eh?"

Bathroom fitments, tiles and lighting occupied them for the rest of the evening.

Janie didn't give the diary another thought until she came home on Thursday night.

***

Dear Janie,

Well, here we are at last: the end of the diary.

For me, the initial pull was to find any new material about Aphra, but like you, I have found myself increasingly interested in the life of the Harryman household and the rather enigmatic Elisabeth Turner, who remains, I'm afraid, stubbornly untraceable.

The later entries have suffered the most damage, but of the parts I was able to read, Alice was occupied mainly with Henry and the farm. I'm sending all the entries I could find where William was mentioned, and a couple of others that were decipherable and which I think you may find interesting.

I shall say no more, except that I know Alice's life, after the diary, is catalogued in the House Book and I should dearly love to know what happens to her.

You'll be wanting the diary back now. Shall I post it, or do you want to come and collect? Please say you'll collect…

Looking forward to seeing you soon,
Affectionately,
Dick

***

Alice's Diary

February 1670

I attended the christening of Martha's baby today, along with Jennet and Edmund, who now seems reconciled with his daughter.

Martha and her baby, Celestine, were a picture, both bonny and blooming. And Jennet tells me that Martha has a new swain, who was not at the christening, and that a wedding will not be too far off. That will please Edmund.

It was a happy day.

It did not seem appropriate to visit my baby's grave. I shall return tomorrow.

March 1670

William has not touched spirits for months and now only takes the occasional ale. Alas, this has not improved his mood and he finds fault with everyone and everything.

Nothing pleases him, he no longer cares for the company of his hunting companions and he mopes around the house all day.

He still does not accompany me to church although I know this is not due to a lack of faith. Jennet tells me that he has fashioned a corner of his bedchamber into some sort of shrine and, last night, I heard him praying well into the night.

March 1670

A beautiful day.

Henry and I are in good spirits. The animals have been turned out having all survived the winter. We had just enough fodder and the young calves and lambs are doing well. Our experiment seems to have worked. We take delivery of our new Dutch bull this summer so next year will be even more exciting.

It was hard work in the milking shed and dairy in the cold months and Jennet had to help out the new girls who, as yet, do not have the skills of the Sandford women! But we were all grateful to have a plentiful supply of milk and butter over the winter.

Ploughing is nearly finished and Seth has proved so good at this that Henry wants him to enter the Petworth Ploughing Contest.

Sowing starts next week unless we get some hard frosts.

Late December 1670

The cold weather continues and we are all suffering.

Henry struggles to feed and water the animals even though all hands and their children are helping as best they can. Edmund spends all his free time replenishing the woodpile, which is nearly exhausted, and we're not yet halfway through winter. Jennet is back working all day in the dairy. Several workers are too ill to help out.

I feel I shall never be warm again. Despite all my layers of clothing I am cold through and through, as if the very bones of me are frozen.

William sits in the inglenook, so close to the fire that I fear for his boots, and even the dogs, who do not normally leave his side, are forced to back off for a while. His cough is much worse and he has no appetite. Gambrill has been several times to let his blood but he is no better and there is no point in my advising against this.

8ᵗʰ January 1671

Christmas and New Year were bleak and it proved impossible to get out to go to church.

William is much worse. He doesn't leave his bedchamber where we keep a fire burning day and night. Reverend Fawcett managed to reach us today but William turned away and refused his blessing. He soon went.

I sat with William all afternoon, bathing his forehead, feeding the fire and listening to his mutterings, but I could make no sense of his words until, during one brief lucid moment, he opened his eyes and said, "I was right," quite clearly.

He is asleep now.

~ 46 ~
July 1986

"What's up? You okay?" Rob was aware of Janie getting out of bed and glanced at the bedside clock. 2:16am.

"Go back to sleep." She walked round to his side of the bed and pulled the cover over his shoulder. "I'm fine, just a touch of indigestion, I'm going to sit in the snug till it goes away."

Sitting on the sofa in front of the dying moments of the fire, Janie pulled up her knees and hugged them to her, rocking gently. It probably would have helped the indigestion, if there'd been any. However, it wasn't doing much to dampen down her rising anxiety.

Celestine. Celestine Palmer, who may or may not be Janie's ancestor, must surely be related to Martha's baby – possibly a great-granddaughter - a descendant of servants who became mistress of Oakwood. Such social mobility in the seventeenth and eighteenth centuries, Janie suspected, was surely not the norm. The thought had niggled away at her all evening.

Lying in bed, unable to sleep, she made the connection. Min could be right. If Martha's Celestine was William's child and, as it turned out, his only child, he might have been minded to provide for her. It always seemed to Janie that William's desire for a child took precedence over everything else.

Until recently, such a connection would have seen her itching to get back to St. Mary's in Petworth to delve further back into her family tree.

Now, she wasn't sure she wanted to know.

She'd checked back to find the exact words that Alice had quoted. 'Neither you, nor any of your blood, will ever find peace in that house'. Her rational mind told her it was stupid to worry about an allusion to a supposed curse, some 300-odd years ago. And yet, and yet…Miles Lyckfold had married Celestine Palmer and they had moved into Oakwood Grange in 1812. The loss of a child in the Napoleonic Wars was not unusual, but the fire that killed several of their children and forced them to leave their home, most definitely was.

Tears ran unchecked down Janie's face. The witches' marks dancing across the bressummer seemed to mock her and she buried her face in a cushion. What she couldn't understand was, if she and her baby were related to William, why did she feel so happy and comfortable in this house? Indeed, it was more than that: she knew she belonged, somehow.

The fire had died completely. She was a little chill, but there was no point in going back to bed. She'd only wake Rob again. Taking all the cushions off the chairs, she lay down on the sofa, wedging them all around her body and tried to decide on what to do next. If she told Rob, he'd think she was either crazy or over emotional. She was pregnant, right? Either way, he would worry about her. If she didn't tell him, would he pick up there was something wrong?

She dozed. The door was slightly ajar and it creaked as it opened a fraction more. Janie was instantly awake, with her heart leaping in her chest and her eyes unable to see in the dark. Before she could reach for the switch on the table lamp, the cushions moved. Janie thought she was going to die of fright.

"Cat! Oh, my God. What are you doing in here?" Cat rarely entered the snug of her own volition. Nevertheless, Janie was grateful for the company, especially when Cat slipped onto a cushion behind her. The vibrations from the silent purring soothed them both to sleep.

***

Things always appear clearer in the morning. Janie was bustling about the kitchen when Rob came down. She'd adopted a breezy, 'I'm fine', manner, which didn't exactly chime with her mood, but she had a plan and that made her feel much more in command of the situation.

"I can't believe you slept on the sofa. Why didn't you come back to bed?"

"I got really comfortable, and anyway, I didn't want to disturb Cat." She gave him a silly little grin. Rob rolled his eyes.

"So, what are you doing on your day off, then?"

"I'm going to do some shopping in Petworth, I think. And I might even pop down to Chichester, I'm in desperate need of bigger trousers." She stuck out her belly, rubbing her hands over the bump. It was all true, but not the whole truth.

***

"Mrs. Whittaker," the young vicar of St. John's found her in the graveyard looking at the tomb of George and Grace Parsons, "it's quite a piece of work, isn't it?"

"Very impressive," Janie agreed. "These two were responsible for repairing our house, the Grange. There'd been a fire, in 1815 I think, and they took it on and rebuilt the front of the house. I don't think they were short of money."

"Obviously not."

Janie was glad to see that he was much more relaxed than he had been at Tom Kelly's memorial service. She wasn't a churchgoer, but Lorraine told her that he was well liked and very hands-on. "Actually, I wonder if you could help me?"

"I'll do my best."

"I'm researching the families who lived and worked in our house, and there's a mystery about the parentage of one them. It's a long time ago, 1670, do you still have records going back that far? This would be a baptismal record and I know the exact date."

"Yes we do. Your place is older than it looks, then. And

you know the exact date from so long ago? That's amazing."
He really did have a lovely smile. "Most folks come with only
a vague idea of names and dates, and finding what they want
takes ages, but this should be much quicker. We could go and
look right now, if you want."

The very old parish registers were big, heavy tomes, even larger
than the ones she'd seen in Petworth, and they were kept in an
old trunk. There was a distinct smell of mildew when the lid was
lifted. The look on Janie's face didn't go unnoticed.

"I'm afraid these conditions aren't ideal for storing old
documents, but I don't know what else to do with them." The
vicar knelt down and studied the dates on the spines, "I think
the one we want may be right at the bottom."

Once they'd hefted it out onto the floor, it took no time at
all to find the entry.

'Celestine, daughter of Martha Sandford. Spinster.' "That
doesn't get you any further, does it? I'm sorry."

" I'm not surprised," Janie gave a rueful look, "But I had to
check."

The vicar waited a moment before asking, "Is it important to
find the father? I mean, don't tell me if you don't want to, but…"

Janie put a hand on his arm. "It's only important if the father
turns out to be who I think it is; if that makes sense." Leaving
aside any reference to the curse, she explained her reasons for
suspecting William. "But it doesn't look like I'll be able to prove
it now."

"I'm not so sure." The vicar replaced the register in the trunk,
closed the lid, and sat on it. "My mother's into all this genealogy
stuff. Every time I go home, she has another connection she's
made to another branch of the family. One of these was through,
what my mother calls, a 'natural son'. She only found out about
him because she ordered a copy of the father's will for some other
reason, I forget what that was, and there was a bequest for this
boy, 'my son', and his mother."

Janie perked up. "I was wondering about the possibility of a will, but I've no idea how you go about finding one."

"I can help you there. You need to go the Public Records Office. Mum went to the one in Brighton, but then she was researching families in East Sussex. I guess there's one for West Sussex, it might be in Chichester, it'll be in the phone book, anyway."

Janie ran over to him and gave him a hug. "You have been such a help, thank you. I was on my way to Chichester now, anyway. I'll find it."

The vicar stood up and beamed. "Well, I'm glad I could be of some use. Good luck. Let me know how you get on."

Janie was half way to the door when she turned to say, "By the way, if you happen to see my husband, don't mention this, will you? I'll tell him if I find anything."

He laid a finger on the side of his nose, "Mum's the word."

"Very funny."

***

The clerk in the Public Records Office was a fussy, little man with sparse strands of hair slicked down over a shiny pate. He pulled himself up to his full 5' 4", peered at Janie over his half moon glasses, and resisted any urge to respond to her smile. "You may know the name and year, madam, but we can't just drop everything and look for it now. The proper procedure is to fill in this form, which will then go in a queue, and we will post a copy of the will when, and if, we find it."

"Fine. Thank you. I don't suppose you know how long it will take?"

"We're very busy." His mouth stretched at the corners in nothing like a smile.

Her gaze shifted slightly as two young clerks took the mickey out of him behind his back, for her benefit, she suspected. She had to bite her lip and turn away quickly to avoid laughing.

A quick look at her watch told her there was just enough time to get the trousers she needed, but the trip to St Mary's in Petworth would have to wait.

~ 47 ~
A Few Days Later

Rob was sitting at the kitchen table, reading the last few entries of Alice's diary. "It's not looking good for poor old William, is it? Have you looked in the House Book yet?"

"No, but it's been a struggle; I want us to do it together." Janie put Harriet's copy of the House Book on the table in front of them. "What do you reckon?"

"I think he kicks the bucket."

"Obviously…but when? She opened the book and started to read from the marriage entry:

<u>Alice Crayford</u> married William Harryman on 15th October 1665

- <s>Hannah</s> Harryman, born and died on 13th July 1669
   Elisabeth

<u>William Harryman</u> died, aged 40 yrs, on 10th January 1671

Janie flicked back to the diary. "He died two days after the last entry."

"Christ, he was only 40, two years older than me. That must have been considered young, even in the seventeenth century, don't you think?"

"Certainly in the landowning classes, I guess." Janie was concentrating on the baby's entry. "What do you make of this?"

"They changed their mind about what to call her?" Rob suggested.

"I don't think so. Alice wanted to call her baby Elisabeth but, by that time, William had got it in for Elisabeth, and remember, neither Alice nor Elisabeth attended the burial. I think he called her Hannah, probably after his mother, and when we look in the original House Book, I bet the 'Hannah' entry is in a different hand from the 'Elisabeth' entry."

"You missed your vocation. Turn the page, let's see what happened to Alice once she was free of William."

The next page detailed the estate workers, their families, where they lived and their duties, as well as a tally of all the farm livestock, acreage under crops and the total fodder and grain in store. There were cross-references to the farm account books. Alice was proud of her business. Janie skipped to the following page.

<u>Alice Harryman</u> married Joseph Rawlinson, 3rd May 1675

- <u>Anne Elisabeth Rawlinson</u>, born 29th March 1676, daughter to Alice and Joseph

- <u>Astrea Elisabeth Rawlinson,</u> born 15th January 1678, daughter to Alice and Joseph

<u>Jennet Sandford</u>, faithful servant & friend, died aged 69 yrs, on 5th February 1689

<u>Anne Rawlinson</u> married Samuel Lyckfold, 2nd June 1697

- Tobias Joseph Lyckfold, born 7th August 1698

- Charles Edward Lyckfold, born 17th November 1699

<u>Astrea Rawlinson</u> married Sir Henry Griffin, 10th April 1700

Joseph Rawlinson, beloved husband, father & grandfather, died aged
63 yrs, on 26th July 1701

- Alice Elisabeth Lyckfold, born 21st December 1701

Alice Rawlinson, beloved mother & grandmother, died aged 65 yrs, on
13th July 1708

Janie stopped reading. "Well, that's good news. It seems that Alice found herself a good man and had a family."

Rob put an arm round her and pulled her close. "Happy now?"

"Relieved. I so wanted her to have what we have. I think we should celebrate." She gave Rob her most winning smile. "Do you think I could have a very weak G&T? Please?"

"Only if you don't make a habit of it for the next few months." He pushed his seat back and went to the larder. By the time he'd prepared the drinks and found some olives –another of Janie's cravings, along with hot chocolate - she'd quickly read through the remaining entries.

"Alice's eldest daughter, Anne, named after her mother I suspect, not Ann Bean, married a Samuel Lyckfold. Her eldest son, Tobias, inherits and then it appears to be a straightforward succession through Henry to Edward Lyckfold. Unfortunately, Edward is unmarried and childless, and the house then passes to Edward's nephew Miles Lyckfold."

"Why 'unfortunately'."

"Because, Miles marries Celestine Palmer, the house catches fire and several children lose their lives."

Rob laughed. "You said that as if the fire was a result of Miles marrying Celestine!"

Janie, head down, pretended to be consulting the House Book again. "As you know, they didn't return to the house, and it passed to Miles's sister, Grace. She married a military man called George Parsons, and the house then passed down through a series of Parsons, all military men, until Harriet was the only one left. Incidentally, I was wandering round the churchyard the other day, have you seen George and Grace's tomb? It's enormous."

"Is it? No, I'll go and have a look. What were you doing in the churchyard, anyway?"

Janie hesitated. "Oh, nothing really. I just stepped in to pass some time with the vicar, he's such a nice chap, we ought to have him round. I don't suppose he knows too many young people round here." She saw the look of surprise on his face. "It's all relative, we're young in comparison with his congregation." She closed the book and pointed to the dish of olives.

"Celestine's an odd name, isn't it?" Rob pushed the dish towards her. Do you think that Miles's wife was related to Martha's daughter?"

"Maybe. Now, what shall we have for supper?"

~ 48 ~
Early August 1986

There was panic at Mallory's. Joyce Hunter was in hospital undergoing an emergency operation.

Under normal circumstances, Joyce's absences were planned and, thanks to her careful preparation, the office got by without her, but this had really thrown a spanner in the works. Visiting her in hospital, Janie found her sitting up in bed, making 'to do' lists and worrying about the office. Snatching the list from her, but stowing it safely in her bag, she brushed aside her concerns. "Just forget about us, will you? We're managing. Chris has your diary and we're spreading out the work between us. We'll be fine until you come back."

"I'm so sorry, Janie. It couldn't have come at a worse time. Just when you need to be winding down, you're back doing five days a week."

"Don't be silly, I'm full of energy. And actually, it could have come at a worse time. I'll be 7 months pregnant for the Frankfurt Book Fair in October and I'll definitely need you then." She took the pad and pen from Joyce and laid them on the bedside cupboard. "Just do as you're told and get better soon."

Leaving the hospital, Janie flagged down a cab and made her way to The Savoy. Emerging from the revolving doors, she nodded to the front desk, and walked over to the man who was rising from his chair with glass in hand and a surprised look on his face.

"Well, this is unexpected." Dick looked down at her swollen belly. "I don't know what to say. Congratulations!"

Janie reached up to give him a peck on the cheek. "That'll do. We are, of course, delighted."

Dick was beaming, "Me, too. You look ready to drop. Did you know when I last saw you?"

Janie flopped into the chair opposite him. "Actually, I was pregnant then but I didn't realise it and, I know I look huge, but I'm only five months gone. Heaven knows how big I'll be come Christmas when it's due." She caught a waiter's eye and ordered a tonic water. "Anyway, thanks for coming to London. It means I can treat you to a great lunch by way of a thank you for all your work on the diary and I don't have to spend a day away from the office; we're all working flat out at the moment." No chance of bumping into Margery either.

Dick reached into his bag and handed her the diary in a large brown envelope. "In case I forget later, after what I hope will be a very boozy lunch."

Janie laughed. "Well, I wouldn't have forgotten, and I'm off all alcohol but don't let that stop you. I am, however, drinking large quantities of drinking chocolate, which may have something to do with my weight."

It seemed a pity to lunch at The Savoy and not order what they do best, so they gave in and enjoyed the smoked salmon, then the roast from the trolley, followed by their amazing mille feuilles. Dick was feeling very mellow over his coffee and cigar. "I could get used to this, Janie, thank you."

Over lunch, he'd read Janie's note of Alice's life, post-William, and he was now pointing to the daughters' names. "Do you know the relevance of these names?"

"Elisabeth as their middle names, that's obvious, isn't it? In her mind, her dead baby was called Elisabeth, so neither of the girls could have that as a first name. Anne, I think was named for Alice's mother, clearly shown in the House Book with an 'e', whereas Ann/Aphra was always written without."

Dick looked up from his food and pointed his knife at her. "That's a good point, I didn't know that. I just assumed she was named after Ann/Aphra. Although, I'm inclined to think that Alice and Ann/Aphra did maintain their friendship after the diary, because of Astrea."

Janie held up both hands. "It's possible that's wrong. That's what it looks like in Harriet's copy of the House Book, but she's put a question mark after it. I haven't checked it in the real House Book."

"Oh no, I think that's right. Aphra used many aliases for one reason or another, and Astrea was one of them." Dick gave a little chuckle. "Ironic when you consider that Astrea in Greek mythology was the virgin goddess of innocence and purity. That's probably why she chose it!"

Janie dabbed at her mouth with the napkin and leaned back in the chair, hands on stomach. "I'm glad about that. I didn't want to think that the friendship had broken down completely after Elisabeth's ordeal, it seemed so important to Alice."

***

Back in the office, Janie briefed Chris and the two girls, left them with Joyce's to-do list, and decided to go home early. She'd been too busy recently to spend time chasing Celeste and Celestine, but the anxiety hadn't gone away and there was no news from the Public Records Office. But she could still investigate her relatives back to the eighteenth century to see if there was ever a Celestine. This had been her plan before Joyce went off sick, but then she'd had to cancel an appointment with the lovely vicar from St. Mary's in Petworth. Luckily, the curate had gone back from whence he came.

"Vicar, it's Janie Whittaker. I'm sorry I had to cancel last week, but I was wondering if I could come over late this afternoon? I could be with you about 4pm."

He didn't mind.

***

"If I'm not being presumptuous, I think congratulations are in order, Mrs. Whittaker?" He settled her at the table and attempted to smooth down his long grey hair, before turning to the bookcase and selecting one of the registers. "This'll be the one, I think. I'll leave you to it. Call me if you want me, I'm just next door."

Janie's search for her great-grandmother Lily's baptismal record in Fittleworth had shown her father to be Frederick Remmant, but there was no other record of any kind bearing his name. She was back in Petworth now to see if their records could produce something. And they did. She found the marriage entry but no baptismal records for either of them, so she was no further forward.

Janie tapped lightly on the adjoining door and the vicar poked his head round. "That's good then, eh? Another link in the chain?"

"Yes, thank you. I was looking for the next generation further back to see if there was a Celeste Boxall or a Celeste Remmant, but no joy, I'm afraid. I might have to start looking at other church's records when I've got a bit more time."

The vicar laughed, "You'd better start soon then. In another few months, by my reckoning, you won't have any time to yourself at all."

Janie patted her bump. "You're probably right."

It was a beautiful drive home. With the sun roof fully open and all the windows down to create a through draught, she turned off the radio and just enjoyed driving through the English countryside on a perfect summer's late afternoon. The small frown lines on her brow disappeared and a little smile remained in place all the way home.

It didn't last.

***

Rob was in the kitchen preparing to roast a chicken, still the only thing he could cook. "I hear you've been sloping off work and secretly meeting your favourite vicar, Janie Whittaker." He waved a spoon in her direction. "Confess now, are you carrying his love child?"

"What can I say? I've been meaning to tell you…" She hugged him from behind. "Mmmm, stuffing as well, you are coming on." Cat vacated the chair by the range for her and then immediately leapt back onto her knee. "How did you know, anyway?"

"He's just phoned." Rob slid a piece of paper towards her with one finger. The phone number was barely visible through the greasy fingermarks. "He caught me in the middle of stuffing the bird."

"What did he say?"

"He said he'd found something of interest in the churchyard. He thinks it might be something you were looking for? Anyway, he'll be on this number until 7pm if you want to speak to him today." Rob put the chicken in the oven. "This won't be ready until about 8pm so you've got plenty of time to ring him and have a bath, if you want."

Janie went up to her office to ring him.

The vicar was in a hurry and a little breathless. "Oh, Mrs. Whittaker, after you left I had a vague recollection of a gravestone in our churchyard, and when I eventually found it, I was pleased my memory wasn't playing tricks. I rang straight away because my brain is full of stuff at the moment and I was afraid I might forget to phone you otherwise." There was a little pause and a rustling of paper. "I've written down here exactly what it says:

Celeste Remmant b.1815, d.1881

Widow of Ernest

Beloved Mother and Grandmother

Now Resting in Peace

"Is that what you were looking for, do you think? I couldn't remember if the date fits."

Janie closed her eyes and tried to keep her voice light. "That's definitely it, the date fits with Celeste being Fred Remmant's mother. Thank you so much for ringing, you're very kind. Yes, that's one more generation for the family tree. And if you don't mind my coming back again, I really need to find Celeste's maiden name and her mother."

"That's good, I'll look forward to seeing you. You know my numbers…I must dash now. Goodbye."

Janie sat with her elbows on the desk, chin resting on her interlocked fingers. Lily was most likely named for her paternal grandmother then, and now her family had a Celeste only a generation away from Celestine Palmer.

~ 49 ~
August 1986

"I was just ringing to make sure you're okay and not down the pub making merry with the local lads."

Janie grinned, tucked the phone under her chin and stretched out on the bed. "I thought about it but Cat and I decided to watch Dallas instead. How's Berlin?"

Rob sounded weary. "It's been a long hot day, it's pouring down now and I miss you."

Cat crept onto Janie's belly and spread out. "Well, we miss you too but it's only one night. It's been glorious here today by the way – you've missed a wonderful sunset. I took a photo for you."

"Great. Look…you've never slept in the house on your own before and I just want to make sure you…"

"Oh, for heaven's sake, Rob, I'm 34 years old – not a child."

"Yes, alright. Just do me a favour and make sure all the doors and windows are locked."

"I will. Now go get some sleep, it's late where you are. See you tomorrow. Love you."

"You, too. Sleep tight."

With the ground floor all checked and secure, Janie climbed the back stairs slowly, wondering how on earth she'd feel at the end of the pregnancy. It was probably time to cut out the hot chocolate every night. She did a double take as she passed her study, knowing she was sometimes guilty of leaving her window wide open and Rob's voice was still echoing in her ears. It wasn't exactly wide open but nevertheless she went to close it, reaching over the desk as best she could until - that was odd. Alice's diary was open. When Dick had returned it, she distinctly remembered putting it at the edge of her desk, closed. True, she was a little forgetful recently, but she knew deep down she hadn't moved it and Rob certainly wouldn't have.

This had happened before. A few months back she definitely recalled asking Rob if he'd been reading the diary and then shooing Cat off the open book. Her stomach gave a little flip as she stared at the date at the top of the page; 17th July 1669 and Alice's first line read 'Elisabeth has gone!'

***

The dream was in monochrome and silent, although nothing like an old movie. At first difficult to make out, the image of someone lying in a foetal position eventually became clearer. It was a woman, dressed in white, bound and gagged. Straight away, Janie felt fear; her heart rate was quickening and her scalp tingled. A distinct smell of sweat made her recoil and there was something else she couldn't identify but which reminded her of rotten vegetables. It made her want to gag.

Tossing and turning, she kicked off the bedclothes willing herself to wake up, but there was no such luck. A little jolt startled her, the sort that usually rouses someone from a bad dream, but not this time. The scene moved on. Janie sensed fresh water and earthiness and could see the woman now lying on open ground, her long black hair covering her face. A feeling of utter hopelessness overwhelmed her, compounding the fear. She wanted to cry out and her throat clenched with unshed tears.

Then all was confusion. Everything came at Janie in a rush and from all sides; the scent of horses, lamp oil and burning wood but more worrying, the stink of unclean bodies and foetid breath heavy with spirit. She could visualise the scene even though all she saw was the woman.

Elisabeth; of course it was Elisabeth, she knew it from the start and sensed there was worse to come. Humiliation, shame and intense anger; Janie felt all these emotions as rough hands stripped Elisabeth, poking filthy fingers into her body and rolling her over in the dirt. Janie's body reacted strongly, arms flailing uselessly.

The river would be next. She knew it and was completely helpless to stop it.

Elisabeth's face was very clear now, her brown eyes huge and her mouth wide in a silent scream. Janie shuddered as the blow came out of the blue, knocking Elisabeth sideways and then they were both fighting for breath, choking, fading…

Gasping, clutching her throat, Janie woke with a start and propped herself up on one hand, head bowed, waiting for the hammering of her heart to slow. She knew she wasn't still dreaming. She also knew she wasn't alone. There was the now familiar scent of herbs and the temperature in the room had suddenly dropped. Slowly, she raised her head, knowing there was nothing to fear. Despite the dark, she had no trouble making out the figure of Elisabeth, standing at the foot of her bed, clutching a cloak with two hands, her hair wild and her lip oozing blood.

They held each other's gaze for some time, Janie unwilling to let Elisabeth go, for instinctively, she knew she wouldn't see her again. For some reason it was important to Elisabeth's restless spirit that Janie should know what had happened to her, and Janie considered it a privilege. A nod was all it took from Janie, and Elisabeth faded away into the gloom.

The tears came then, hot and fast. Cat appeared from nowhere, head-bumping her arm, and Janie relaxed into the pillow, exhausted.

***

She woke late, arms wrapped around Rob's pillow. It was a glorious summer morning. Sunlight streamed through the curtains, the air was alive with birdsong and Cat was curled up beside her. So far, so normal. She swung her legs over the side of the bed and took a little time to clear her head. A quick glance round confirmed her memory of the night before; the duvet was half on the floor and one of her pillows down near the foot of the bed. How on earth had she managed to fall into such a deep sleep after that awful dream?

The dream – was it all a dream?

Logic told her that last night was easily explained away. Either the whole thing had been a dream or, in some semi-conscious state, she had imagined Elisabeth standing in her bedroom. Weren't scientists always telling us how little we know about the brain?

Even if she'd wanted to though, Janie couldn't rationalise it away. On the contrary, Elisabeth's appearance had made everything fall into place. From her impulsive decision to buy the house, to discovering Alice's diary and so many other weird little happenings, Janie just knew that none of that was by accident or a coincidence. A quote came to mind: 'There are more things in heaven and earth, Horatio, than are dreamt of in your philosophy.' Too true, she thought, I'm with you on that Shakespeare.

***

The phone rang as Janie was on her second cup of tea and half way through reading the newspaper.

"Janie, are you alright? I rang you at work but Joyce said you weren't too well today."

"Morning, darling. No, sorry to worry you, I'm fine. I guess I just found it hard to get to sleep in a big empty bed without you, that's all. I woke up really late, so I made an excuse to treat myself to a day off."

~ 50 ~
Mid August 1986

"Here's one for you." Rob tossed the brown envelope down the table. "Looks official?"

A swift glance and her heart began to thump as she peeped inside. "No, it's nothing, just a flyer from Chichester Theatre." Having just seen the postmark, she was surprised at how quickly the lie had come and it made her blush. "Gosh, I think I'm having a hot flush. It's too hot in here for me." Fanning her face with the envelope, she left up the back stairs.

***

"Oh, bloody hell. Bloody, bloody hell!" Janie picked up the copy of the will and read it again:

In the name of God, Amen. I, William Harryman, of Oakwood Grange, Upburton, in the county of Sussex, being weak in body but of good and perfect memory, do make this my last Will and Testament in the manner following:

To my Sisters, Abigail Foster & Sarah Beddows

– I leave my clothes and jewellery and all inherited possessions from our Father, except my gold signet ring, seal and silver tankard, to be

divided equally between them or their heirs should either one of them predecease me.

To my Daughter, Celestine, by Martha Pullen (nee Sandford)

- I leave my freehold property in Chichester and all rents from the leasing of said property which are held in trust for my daughter until she reaches one and twenty years or marries, whichever is the sooner, whereupon she will be able to draw from the Trust according to the provisions laid out. If my daughter dies before producing offspring, everything in the Trust to be shared equally between my sisters or their heirs.

The management of the property and the Trust are in the hands of Messrs. Blagden & Emmett, Chichester

To Martha Pullen

- The Trust to pay her 6 pounds per annum to house, clothe and provide a sound religious education for Celestine, in addition to teaching her housewifely skills, until she reaches one and twenty years or marries, whichever is the sooner.

To My Wife, Alice, who I thank for her understanding and forbearance

- I leave all the rest of my Goods and Chattles unbequeathed. I do make my Wife, Alice, the sole executrix of this, my last Will & Testament, my debts being paid and funeral charges discharged.

I commit my soul unto Almighty God, my Creator, and to His only Son, Jesus Christ, my Lord Saviour and Redeemer, by and through

whose death and passion I do trust to have Salvation and Forgiveness
of all my offences and to be received into His everlasting Kingdom.

I wish my body to be buried in the Churchyard of Chichester
Cathedral, next to my father.

In witness whereof I have set my hand and seal, this 28th day of
December 1670

William Harryman   (His Seal)

Witnesses: Gabriel Loyd

Bertha Lynd

Henry Durling

Janie sat, head in hands, until she heard shouting and Rob's voice on the landing outside her door.

"What's going on?" poking her head round the door.

John Hobden, standing next to Rob, pointed up the stairs to the attic. They were both giggling like schoolgirls.

"Get that bloody cat out of my way." Mick, the plumber, a hard man by anyone's standards, was seemingly trapped round the bend of the stairs. His disembodied voice held a note of real fear and Janie pushed her husband aside to see what was going on. Cat was positioned at the turn of the stairs, legs straight as ramrods, back arched and fur standing out like a lavatory brush. Mick took a step back as Cat advanced, spitting and hissing.

Janie leapt up the stairs, sweeping up Cat on the way. "Mick, I'm so sorry, I don't know what's come over her. You can come down now, I'll lock her in my office."

Embarrassed, Mick made it to the landing where John and Rob were making no effort to spare his blushes. "It's not that funny, summat must've spooked that cat. I get on all right wi' all animals, I do."

"Ignore them, Mick." Janie put a soothing hand on his arm. "She's not a normal cat and you're not the first she's taken against. I'll make sure she's not roaming around while you're working here."

***

Rob rolled over to find the other side of the bed empty. Recently, this wasn't unusual, but some sixth sense prevented him from drifting back to sleep. He went looking for her and found her in her office, nursing Cat and a mug of hot chocolate. With a weak little smile, she put down the mug and moved some paper from the sofa next to her.

He sat down and pulled her close. "Are you going to tell me what's eating away at you?" Silence. "We'll manage, you know. Look at me," he gave her shoulder a squeeze, "I know it's scary, having this baby, and things will change but it won't all be down to you, sweetheart. We're a team, me and you, and we'll just…"

"I'm not worried about that." Janie did look at him then. "I know we'll cope. It's this," and she handed him the piece of paper.

He read the will twice, and then looked at her questioningly. "So William fathered a bastard, we're not surprised, are we? Even Min guessed. What does it matter?"

Janie rubbed a hand across her face before turning to face him. "I know, that as soon as I put my fears into words, they'll sound ridiculous and you'll think I'm crazy."

"Try me."

She tried. He didn't exactly say she was crazy, but he didn't need to.

"Are you telling me that you now believe in witches and curses?"

"I don't know." The bottom lip was wobbly and Rob swallowed his next remark. Janie carried on. "The thing is, I don't believe in coincidences either. You said the other day, it sounded like I was blaming the fire on Celestine Palmer. Well, perhaps. I'm sure research will show that she's a descendant of William. And then, there's William himself, dead at 40 years of age." The tears came now and her voice rose. "It's easy to dismiss all this as eyewash and, honestly, I think it wouldn't bother me at all if I weren't pregnant – but I am, Rob – and I can't bear to think that I might be responsible for…."

Rob held her tight until the sobs subsided. When Cat pushed her way between them, Janie broke away to reach for a tissue. "You think I'm bonkers."

"I don't think you're bonkers, but I do think you're getting worked up over nothing." He took the tissue from her and wiped some snot from the end of her nose. "There's no such thing as curses and, even if there were, the chances of you being related to William are slim, at best."

"Hopefully. Do you think all pregnant women become a little paranoid?" She balled up the tissue and threw it in the bin.

"According to Max, they do. But then, Min's no barometer, is she?" He removed Cat from her lap and took her hand. "Come on, let's go back to bed, and promise me you'll ring your nice vicar first thing. I'm coming with you this time, and we'll keep searching until we prove that Celeste Remmant had nothing to do with Celestine Palmer."

Just before she fell asleep, Janie whispered, "Rob, did you notice something about the will? The bit about thanking Alice for her 'understanding and forbearance'? I think she already knew about Martha and the baby."

"Mmm, perhaps he told her. Confession's good for the soul when you're scared of dying."

~ 51 ~
September 1986

Joyce Hunter was back at work, only part-time, but it meant that Janie could now take some days off.

Everything was good in Janie's world at the moment. A two hour long search of church records had produced irrefutable proof that Celestine Palmer had nothing to do with any branch of her family. The relief that had brought changed everything. She regained her sense of fun, she slept better and felt able to make plans for the baby, especially now another scan had just confirmed the presence of only one foetus and not two, as her doctor half expected. She suspected that, of the two of them, Rob was the more relieved.

To celebrate, they'd driven to West Wittering to sit on the beach and eat ice cream. "The next time we come here, we'll be a family." Rob shook his head, "I still can't really believe it." Janie linked his arm and rested her head on his shoulder as they people-watched. The children were back at school but there were a few babies in slings and several dog walkers.

"How do you feel about getting a dog?" Janie was watching a terrier tirelessly retrieving a ball from the surf.

"I've never thought about it. We never had one."

"Nor us, but I loved the dogs at Grandma's. There's something special about the bond between children and dogs and, if we do get one it seems sensible, don't you think, to get the puppy stage and baby stage all over and done with at the same time?"

Rob shot her a sideways look. "If you say so. I'm not sure how Cat would react though, eh?

***

Back home, Janie spent some time with Hedges, picking flowers for the house and making plans for next season's fruit and vegetable crop, whilst Rob headed inside to see what the builders were up to.

Just as she placed the vase on the table, there was a loud thump from upstairs. "Rob?" She called up the back stairs, "What's going on, are you all right?"

"Yeah, fine." He appeared at the head of the stairs, grinning and clearly holding something out of sight. "Don't come up just yet. I'll call you in a bit."

There was more thumping. Janie took the newspaper and a cup of tea into the snug where she could put her feet up, and with impeccable timing, Rob found her just as she'd completed the crossword. "I've got something to show you," he said and, still grinning, grabbed her hand and hauled her to her feet.

Pushing open the door to the room, which had now been designated as the nursery, he watched her face carefully to see her reaction. "What do you think?"

Both hands flew to her mouth. "Oh, it's gorgeous. When did you get that?" She went over to the cot, running her hands over the rails.

"I didn't. Mick was doing something with the water tank and this was stacked behind it, in kit form. Langridge must have missed it when they sent stuff to the auction."

"I'm glad he did. I love it. Is it mahogany?"

"According to Mick, who seems to know about these things, it's Cuban mahogany and it's bloody heavy. Victorian, obviously. Anyway, it still had all the bolts and bits and pieces in a little bag, so it didn't take long to put it together."

It was actually a cot-bed, suitable for a child up to about two years of age, with solid mahogany head and tail boards and mahogany framed wicker panels on the side, which could be removed when the child was older. Janie was sliding the panels up and down. "Wow, look at that, it works beautifully. I'll see about getting a mattress made for it next week."

Rob pointed out a bracket on the outside of the headboard. "Mick thinks there would have been some sort of metal arm that slotted in here, but it's not in the attic, we've searched."

"Oh, I see what he means. Yes, probably, to support a drape, I guess. Well, we can easily get one made." She was hugging him when she noticed an old biscuit tin on the window sill. "Is that what the bits were in?"

"No, we found that next to the cot. It's full of old photos. I had a quick look and recognised some of Doctor Kelly when he was young. I thought you'd like to see them.

***

"Are you sure you don't mind me going?" Rob had been co-opted into John and Mick's darts team at their local pub, standing in for Kevin who had backed out in favour of his new girlfriend. "Why don't you come with me, Janie?"

"No, I don't want to be in a pub when I can't drink." She was stacking the dishwasher and turned to nod in the direction of the tin box. "I'll be fine, and anyway, I shall have a fun evening looking through the photos."

They turned out to be more revealing than she imagined.

~ 52 ~
Lydia's, September 1986

Lydia was in her front garden when she saw Janie walking down the road. She leaned on the gatepost and waited for her. "Look at you, all blooming and the picture of health. I hope you've come to see me. I've just finished weeding and I'm ready for a drink."

"As it happens, I have." Janie leaned over and gave her a quick kiss on the cheek. "If you're sure I'm not stopping you."

"Nay lass. I'm only weeding 'cos I've got nowt else to do," and she laughed her deep, throaty laugh. "Come in."

They sat out in Lydia's back garden, sipping home made lemonade and stretching out under the late summer sun, chatting about this and that until Lydia pointed to the tin. "Don't tell me you've brought me some fifty year old biscuits?"

"No…I think you'll find this much more interesting." Janie lifted the lid and removed the first few photos. "Rob found these in the attic," and she slid them across the garden table.

Finding her glasses from down the front of her blouse, Lydia perched them on her nose and squinted at the photos. "This one's Harriet and Tom, not long before she died." She turned the photo over. "That's right, 1979," and then stared at it in silence for some time.

"She was a handsome woman." Janie broke the silence.

"Aye, she were that. Not pretty, but always well groomed and elegant. She was proud of her hair, even though it had turned white it still looked good. She'd lost quite a bit of weight when this was taken." Lydia put the photo to one side and picked up the others. "I recognise this one. This was their wedding photo; there were one on the piano in the Grange. Look at how young she seemed here, 1952, although she were nearly thirty."

Janie smiled. "Tom looks quite young to me, too, even though he was a good deal older than her." She pointed to the other wedding pictures. "I'm thinking that must be Harriet's mother and father? And who's that next to Tom?"

"I don't know, some relative. His parents were too elderly to make the trip and I think they'd fallen out over the divorce any road. So…yes, that's the Brig, with all his medals, and that's Lily."

"Harriet looks nothing like her mother." The photo showed Lily to be a pretty, feminine little woman, completely dwarfed by her giant of a husband.

Lydia laughed, "I think there was a bit of jealousy there when Harriet was growing up. The genes on the Brig's side proved to be by far the stronger; all three children took after him, tall and big-boned." She watched as Janie reached into the tin. "I wonder why all these were in that tin? They had albums wi' all these in, I know, and a drawer full of duplicates and negatives."

"Mmm…it seems odd. Have a look at these." She laid out the next batch showing teenagers in 1930's sepia, playing tennis and croquet in the garden; young, innocent and carefree in a pre-war idyll.

"I haven't seen these before. Harriet and her brothers are there and I suppose the rest are friends. It was probably a birthday party." She flipped it over to see the date. "There, 1936, it might have been Charles's eighteenth."

"Is this Charles?" She pulled out a studio portrait of a young man in uniform.

"Yes. That were in the Brig's study. To be honest, I think it makes him look a bit spivvy, wi' that 'tash, but they were all trying to look so grown up then." She seized on another snap, showing Harriet standing between two tall young men, each one leaning on Harriet's shoulder. "I haven't seen this one either, but that'll be Charles on the left and Roger on the right; they look similar but I know Roger wore glasses." She drew the snap closer for a better look. "He was much more handsome wi'out the 'tash, wasn't he?"

There were other family snaps going back in time to when the three Parsons children were small, and then a formal, hand coloured portrait on card of the Brig, in a Captain's uniform, and his very young and beautiful bride, in what was obviously a well-to-do wedding. The date was 1917.

"There's just one more thing." Janie held up a tiny bracelet and handed it to Lydia.

"What's this?"

Janie shrugged her shoulders without answering.

"It looks like a baby's bracelet, the sort they put on newborns. What's it say? I can't read what's on it." She handed it back to Janie.

Janie didn't need to read it. "It says, 'Baby Parsons, DOB 21:2:48, Sex: Boy.

"Nay, lass, that can't be right. Lily would have been in her fifties, and anyway, I'd have known. Are you sure it doesn't say 1918?"

Janie shook her head. "I remember you telling me that Harriet went away for a while. Can you recall if that was late 1947?"

A few seconds of silence and then, "Oh, my word." Eyes opened wide as the realisation dawned on her. "It could have been." She thought for a little while. "Yes, the more I think about it now, the surer I am. She definitely missed one Christmas at the Grange, and I remember thinking how strange that was." She slumped back in her chair, trying to remember how Harriet had been when she finally came home. "Could there be some other explanation, do you think? She never let on, and she always said she couldn't have children."

"I can't think of another explanation. The boys were dead by then and anyway, only a mother would keep a baby's ID bracelet." Janie had kept one photo back and she put it on the table next to the bracelet. "Tell me who you think this picture reminds you of."

It was an informal close-up of Charles, taken as he was laughing at the person behind the camera, one hand carelessly pushing his dark wavy hair back from a prominent widow's peak. It was the first photo to show his dimples.

Lydia didn't know what to say. The likeness was unmistakable. "February 21st 1948 is Rob's birthday."

"And Rob found these? What does he say about it all?"

"He doesn't. He didn't bother to look beyond the first couple of snaps. And before you ask; if he's adopted, he doesn't know it."

~ 53 ~
Langridge's Office, September 1986

After laying out the evidence on Gilbert Langridge's desk, Janie repeated Lydia's recollection of Harriet's absence in late 1947 and early 1948. Then, sensing his reluctance to comment, she continued. "My reason for approaching you, Mr. Langridge, is because of your close family friendship with the Parsons and, as their solicitor, I feel sure that you would have been party to information others might not. I can assure you that anything you tell me will go no further, my only interest being whether or not this involves my husband. The date on that bracelet is his birth date." Janie leaned forward, elbows on his desk, willing him to speak.

"And all these were in this biscuit tin, you say, in the attic?" Langridge examined the tin, leaning back in his chair.

"Yes, and that's another thing. Is this a secret little memory box overlooked during the clearance of the attic, or something else?"

Langridge replaced the tin and looked her in the eye for the first time. "Tom was right. He had you down as intelligent, inquisitive and perceptive, and I have no doubt that this tin was left to point you in the right direction. Harriet did have a child, in a private nursing home in Brighton, where her baby was adopted."

Janie felt it like a body blow. She had expected Langridge to hedge and hide behind client confidentiality, and this had taken the wind right out of her sails.

The solicitor pressed the intercom. "Hold all my calls for the rest of the morning, will you, Mrs. Watkins, and we'll have some tea, please." He then moved his chair to the front of his desk and placed a hand on Janie's shoulder. "Do you want to call your husband, so that I can explain everything to the two of you?"

Janie shook her head. "It's more complicated than you think. He doesn't know he's adopted."

"Ah, I see. That does make things tricky."

"Do you know who the father is? Did Harriet ever say?"

"Oh, I'm sorry, my dear, I should have said. It was Tom, of course." Janie's mouth fell open in astonishment.

Langridge carried on, "I'd better start at the beginning. Tom Kelly joined the local surgery in 1937, young and attractive with a soft Irish accent, and immediately became the target for many single women, and some not so single, if you take my meaning. Being in a reserved occupation during the war only made him more attractive; there were very few young men around at that time. Anyway, there was talk, with far too many women turning up for examinations, and it all became a bit too much for old Dr. Ferguson, who more or less told Tom that it was time he settled down – or else. Why he settled on Mary Fletcher is a mystery. Don't get me wrong, she probably was the prettiest girl in the village, but she'd been engaged to Stuart Burrows, whose parents owned the pub, for some time."

Janie interrupted him. "I remember you telling us that, when he was less than friendly when we went in there once."

"That's right, I did. Mary's version, of course, was that they might have had an 'understanding' at one time, but they were never engaged. So, Tom married Mary in 1942, they had two children in short order, and it wasn't too long before he realised they had nothing in common. Harriet started working as secretary at the practice after the war and they fell in love. It was an impossible situation, made even worse when Harriet fell pregnant."

There was a knock on the door and Langridge went to receive the tea tray, which he placed on the desk and checked inside the teapot before pouring.

"Did her parents know?" Janie was wondering how all this would have played out back in the 1940's.

He handed her a cup and saucer, having remembered how she took her tea. "For me, that was the most remarkable thing. Lily, with a mother's instinct I guess, confronted Harriet and I understand there was a terrible scene, but her father was restrained and far from censorious. Tom was called to the Brig's study for a man-to-man talk, Lily was kept out of the way, and the decision was made to send Harriet away and to have the baby adopted. She was spared the plight of many young women in her situation, who were treated very badly in 'homes for unmarried mothers'."

"Gosh, what a mess." Janie instinctively placed a hand on her tummy. "Did Mary know about Harriet?"

"No, and I don't think she would have cared, anyway. Tom reckoned she was already having an affair with a chap in the next village. They divorced a few years later and that's when Mary took the kids off to Australia and Tom never saw them again. I admit I haven't tried very hard to trace them as Tom wanted the remainder of the estate to go to Rob if and when he discovered the truth."

He offered a refill and Janie held out her cup. "Was the plan always for Tom and Harriet to get married eventually?"

"I wasn't privy to that conversation, but my guess is that you're right. Harriet was very much her father's daughter, strong willed and determined; she may have agreed to the adoption but she wasn't about to give up on Tom. Once Dr. Ferguson retired and Tom became the senior partner of the practice, he was able to divorce without losing his job, and they were married shortly afterwards with the blessing of both her parents. In fact, they all got on remarkably well."

Janie looked a little puzzled. "Forgive me, I know this is none of my business, but why didn't they have any more children?"

"That was a terrible sadness. I believe there were complications after the birth, I don't know the details, but Tom always said that was the reason."

Janie blinked away tears, conscious that this wouldn't be the first time she'd cried in Langridge's office. More to herself than to the solicitor, she said, "They gave away their only child."

"But Tom found him again. You have no idea how happy that made him."

"How did he know, though? Not just by the way Rob looks, surely?"

"Well, that's what drew him in the first place. He knew Charles Parsons as a friend, before he ever became involved with Harriet, and so the resemblance struck him right away. Then, of course, he found out Rob's background and his age and he had to discover the truth, although he'd already decided you were going to buy his house by this time and dropped the price to something you could afford." He gave Janie a knowing little smile.

"But how did he discover the truth? The adoption rules are particularly strict, I think."

"They are, so he didn't go down that route. He did something that would give him absolute proof. He took some hairs from Rob's coat and a cup used by Rob, just for good measure, and sent them off, along with his own DNA, for a paternity test. He was a doctor, remember, he could still pull a few strings."

"So there's no doubt?"

"No doubt whatsoever. Tom and Harriet were your husband's natural parents."

Janie couldn't speak. It was all too much to take in and she was just beginning to think about Elsie and Dan. "How could Rob not know he was adopted?"

Langridge took her cup from her and replaced it on the tray. "I was wondering that myself. The birth certificate of an adopted child clearly shows the adoption details. Have you seen Rob's birth certificate? Did he produce it when you were married?"

"He did, but it was a funny little thing, nothing like my certificate, and I was told that we needed either his full certificate or his passport. So we used his passport; he said he'd never been given a full certificate."

Langridge nodded. "What he had was a Short Certificate, it gives no mention of the adoption. It looks to me like his parents were determined he should never know of the adoption and, by applying for a passport for him, hoped that he wouldn't ever need to apply for the full certificate. Tell me, was he happy at home?"

"Extremely happy. His father is dead but he's devoted to his mother, who's suffering from dementia now, and he has a close bond with his brother. That makes everything so much more difficult."

"I don't envy you, my dear. I have fulfilled my promise to Tom that, should either you or Rob ask the right questions, then I would tell you the whole story, but he didn't realise that it might cause problems."

~ 54 ~
Mid September 1986

Never again would she keep a secret from Rob. That's what she'd promised herself after the 'Dick thing', but then she hadn't envisioned anything like this.

Dan was sitting opposite and he reached across the table to take her hands. "Janie, you've got to tell him."

No reply. He shook her hands gently but she refused to make eye contact and dropped her head even further. He waited. A tear dropped onto the table and she pulled her hands away to wipe her face. Only then did she look at him.

"I can't."

"You must. It's too big a deal to be kept from him, even for a short while. It'll eat away at you, and you can't afford to be stressed right now."

She gestured with both hands, angry now, her voice high and shaky and with fresh tears about to fall. "Well, you see, here's my problem. If I don't tell him, it'll feel like a betrayal and, if I do tell him, it risks destroying everything he's ever known – including his relationship with you." She sat back in the chair with her arms folded, miserable.

"Then I'll tell him." Dan also sat back and waited for the explosion.

"No, I can't let you. Not now. You've had plenty of chances to tell him over the years."

"You know that's not true. It was never my secret to tell, that was down to our parents, and to be fair, it would never have been an issue if you hadn't bought this house."

Janie thumped the table, anger flaring up again. "Every adopted child should be told the truth!"

"You're right, of course they should." They were getting nowhere. Dan carried on, "I think you're wrong though, about the damage it will do. No biological brothers could have a stronger bond than the one Rob and I have. I loved him from the moment I set eyes on him when I was just four. It was only later on at school, when I saw my friend's pregnant mother that I suspected he'd come from somewhere else."

"And you never asked the question?"

"No. Instinctively I knew never to mention the subject and, anyway, it was of no matter to me. By then, Rob and I were a team, opposite but complementary. Even when the four year age gap should have been a problem in my late teens, Rob was such a big, confident lad with a huge personality that my swotty friends and I were only too glad to have him around - especially as girls couldn't leave him alone. I might still have been a virgin in my twenties if it hadn't been for Rob."

She couldn't help a rueful smile. "And you're prepared to risk all that?"

"That's my point. I don't think anything is going to change all that."

"What about your mother?"

"Mum doesn't even recognise us half the time and what she doesn't know isn't going to hurt her. Who's going to tell her anyway? Do you think Rob would? 'Cos I'm pretty sure he wouldn't. He always adored her; their shared love of sport and all things arty created such a special bond." He said it without a flicker of jealousy.

"I know all that, Dan, I know. I've told myself the same thing over and over, but I've read up about this and adoptive children who find out late in life can become very depressed and resentful." Her face screwed up in an attempt to stop the tears. "I couldn't bear to be responsible for that."

"I'm sure some do feel that, perhaps the ones who've had an unhappy upbringing, or never fitted in, or feel terrible rejection or resentment. But how does that relate to Rob? It doesn't. He had a wonderful childhood with a loving family and, once he knows about his real parents, there is nothing there for him to resent. For Christ's sake, Janie, he's met his father and he doesn't even know it. His parents' ashes are scattered in that garden. This house and all its history is his birthright, his heritage, how can you deny him all that?"

Janie snatched at the kitchen roll and tore off a couple of strips to mop up the tears, which were now falling fast. "Oh, fuck it – I don't know," she wailed.

Dan was undeterred. "And what about this child? It's his or her history, too. You've been determined to discover the secrets of this house and its inhabitants; you felt sure there was a connection with you and Rob. And you were right, unexpectedly as it happens, but right all the same. So, what now? You keep all that to yourself?"

"No." She wailed again and dropped her head to her folded arms on the table. "I feel like Pandora."

Dan got up and went to stand behind her. He wrapped his arms around hers, kissed her head and whispered in her ear. "And what was left in the bottom of the box?"

She lifted her head and smiled wanly. "Hope. Not bad for a scientist, Whittaker."

He slipped into the seat next to hers. "There's something else I haven't told you. I was talking to this nurse at Mum's home the other day and we were discussing the memory box we made for her. She told me that they're invaluable for keeping dementia patients talking, but said that, sometimes, they stir up all sorts of memories from the past and quite often there's a tendency to confess guilty secrets. Just in case, I think it would be better if he already knew, don't you?"

"I know you're right." Janie hugged her brother-in-law tight.

"I love you Daniel Whittaker. I'm not brave enough to do this on my own. Promise me you'll do it with me."

They both looked up as they heard a car in the drive.

"There's no time like the present."

~ 55 ~
August 1991

Concentrating hard, she gently tugged at each ruby red fruit to release it from the creamy hull, and placed it carefully in the punnet with the others. Now that she was nearly five, she was allowed to do this unsupervised, but it was proving to be a bit tricky. Over-ripe fruit looked perfect but fell to the ground at the slightest touch, and other berries, which looked tempting, could be under-ripe and put up too much resistance. She was getting frustrated.

"Stumpy, stop it! Daddy, Stumpy's eating all the raspberries."

Rob looked up from the border he was working on. "He can't be eating them all, he's only a foot from the ground. Anyway, he shouldn't be in there."

He struck his spade in the ground and went to join her in the fruit cage. Hearing his name, the Jack Russell had reversed out of the raspberry canes and was awaiting instructions. Rob picked him up so that they were face to face. Stumpy licked his nose.

"You can't get round me like that, Stumpy old chap. Lizzie says you've been a naughty boy, so sit over there and behave," and he threw him on to the grass.

"Daddy. You'll hurt him."

"No, I won't. Look, he's fine. He's tougher than he looks. Anyway, missy, let's see how you're doing."

Lizzie held out the punnet. "Do you think there's enough for Mummy?"

Rob looked at the few berries barely covering the bottom of the punnet, and said, "Well, a few more won't hurt, just to make sure. Come on, I'll help." A few minutes later, with a full punnet, Rob closed the fruit cage and tossed a raspberry to the chastened Stumpy.

"Daddy, don't. He'll have the squits and Mummy'll be cross with him."

"He's not going to get the squits from a few raspberries. It's when the plums fall that we have problems," and he tossed another one. "Right then, I think you can take these in now, and could you ask Mummy if she could get me a drink, please? Stumpy, you stay here with me."

Rob went back to the border, decided he'd had enough of spade work, and picked up his secateurs to tackle the roses which needed deadheading and tying in. Looking through the gateway, he could see Lizzie's small figure, walking very slowly and deliberately, eyes glued to the glass she was carrying.

"Mummy was busy with Thomas, so I brought it instead. I've only spilled a little bit of it," and she licked the spillage from her fingers. "Ooo – that's horrid."

"That's because it's beer and you're not old enough to appreciate it yet." He sat down on the grass and thought how lucky he was; a beautiful day with time to tend his garden, a glass of beer, and the company of his daughter and his dog. Life didn't get much better.

Lizzie sat as close as possible and linked his arm. "What's that?" She pointed to the wall where he'd pruned the roses.

"It's a plaque."

"What's that?"

"It's something that reminds people about other people who have died."

"What does it say?"

"It says… 'In Memory of Harriet and Tom Kelly, who loved this place. November 1985.'"

"Were they brothers?"

"Not Harry; Harriet, a lady. They were married and they lived here before Mummy and I did. When they died, their ashes were scattered in this garden."

"Yuk"

"No, it's not yuk. It's a good thing, it means that a little part of them is here forever." He stopped then, thinking he probably shouldn't have talked about dying. "One day, when you're older, I'll tell you a story about Harriet and Tom."

"Is it a love story?"

"It is. It's also a detective story."

"What's a 'tective story?"

"You know. Like, when there's a mystery and someone has to solve it."

"Is it a ghost story?"

Rob frowned and turned to look at his daughter. "What made you think that?"

"Like Ghostbusters, on TV?"

Smiling, and hugging her close, he said, "No, nothing like Ghostbusters, but it's an interesting story."

She put on a wheedling voice. "Can't you tell me now?"

"No. You need to be – ooh – probably as tall as Mummy before you'll be able to understand it."

"What were they like?"

"Well, I didn't know Harriet but I did meet Tom a few times. He was a doctor, a very kind man by all accounts. I think you would have liked him and I know he would have liked you."

"Was he as nice as you?"

"Much nicer."

"Was he as nice as Uncle Dan?"

"Don't be silly. No one's as nice as Uncle Dan."

Lizzie giggled and stretched up to whisper in his ear. "Well, I think you're nicer than anyone."

"That's 'cos you're my daughter," and he stood up and handed her his glass. "We'd better get a move on, Lizzie Whittaker. Uncle Dan and Auntie Barbara, Amy and Ollie, will be here in a few hours, so we'd better go in and see if we can help Mummy, I think."

"I'm going to ask Mummy about Harriet and Tom."

"She'll tell you what I told you."

"I don't want to wait till I'm big."

"Tough."

EPILOGUE
Oakwood Grange, December 1701

lisabeth pushed the door open quietly, crept across the floor and carefully drew aside the bed hangings. "Ah, you're awake, good. I've brought you a drink and a few sweetmeats." She put them on a small table and leaned over to kiss Alice. "Did you sleep well?"

"Thank you. Yes, I did. That is, until I heard Anne pacing up and down in the corridor. I fear she's well over her time now and cannot sleep."

Elisabeth helped her friend sit up in bed and handed her the cup. "I'll go and see what I can do for her once I've got you up and moving about, for today's the day that we see how well your leg has mended."

"Excellent. I'm so sick and tired of lying in bed doing nothing." Noticing a letter tucked into Elisabeth's cuff, Alice said, "Have you had word from Jean-Michel?

Elisabeth removed the letter. "Yes. He's moving back to France at the end of the month. His parents are too old to continue in the business and Jean-Michel doesn't want to let it go."

Alice's heart sank. "And?"

"I've decided that I can't go with him. Our daughter was born in England and both she and I do not want to live in France." Elisabeth opened the letter. "He's a good man, Alice. He says here that, should

we want to stay, he has made arrangements with his partner for us to remain in the rooms which we currently occupy and for us to draw a weekly allowance from the business." She folded the letter again and tucked it back in her cuff.

Alice reached over and took her hand. "I'm so sorry, Elisabeth. This must be hard for you."

"It's sad, but it's for the best. We have grown apart these last few years and I think I always knew he would want to go home."

They were both silent for a while and then Alice made a decision. "Why go back to London? There's nothing for you there anymore. Stay here and make your old friend, and lonely widow woman, happy."

Elisabeth smiled. "You're very kind, but this is your house and now Anne and her husband live here – it wouldn't be right."

"Nonsense. You are already part of this family. You brought my daughters into this world, you are their sponsor, and you will no doubt deliver Anne's baby very soon indeed. We have been friends for over thirty years and there is no one I would rather live out my final days with."

Elisabeth couldn't speak. She closed her eyes to stop the tears and squeezed Alice's hand hard.

Alice pressed her advantage. "And there's another reason you should stay. I understand that a certain young gentleman from Petworth is determined that your lovely daughter shall not return to London."

Elisabeth smiled as she dashed away the tears. "I think you're right. I expect Celeste will be married before the year is out."

***

Entry in the House Book

Madame E. La Montagne

Sponsor to Anne and Astrea and loyal family friend, departed this life on 12th October 1725, in her 83rd year.

Author's Note

This is a work of fiction.

With the exceptions of Aphra Behn and Thomas Culpepper, all other characters in this book are entirely fictitious and any resemblance to persons alive or dead is a coincidence.

Similarly, Oakwood Grange and and the villages of Upburton and Thatchling are a product of the writer's imagination.

A little license has been used when describing St. Mary's, Petworth and its graveyard.

If you have enjoyed reading this book, please consider leaving a review on amazon.co.uk. Search 'The House Book by Susan Greenwood'.

Thank you.

***

Bonus Content

To read the backstories of Janie Mallory and Rob Whittaker, click on www.susan-greenwood.co.uk

Acknowledgements

My thanks go to Neil Cobbet at The National Archives for providing information on the holding of Wills in a pre-digital age.

On the tricky subject of death occurring between Exchange and Completion of a property sale, I must thank Patrick MacQueen, a lawyer, who gave sound advice via a now-defunct site.

Valuable information on birth certificates was given by Adoption UK and HM Passport Office.

***

Reference

'Samuel Pepys: The Unequalled Self' by Claire Tomalin, Penguin Paperback 2003

'A Visual History of Costume: The Seventeenth Century' by Valerie Cumming, Hardback 1984

'Women and Property in Early Modern England' by Dr. Amy Erickson, Paperback 1995

'A Memoir of Mrs. Behn' by Montague Summers, A University of Adelaide e-publication, updated December 2014

'The Archaeology of Folk Magic' article by Brian Hoggard 1999